I0523493

38 CRASH

This book is produced by Fruit Salad Publishing.

Copyright © Eilidh Direen 2023

The moral right of the author has been asserted in accordance with the Copyright Amendment (Moral Rights) Act 2000. All rights reserved. Except as permitted under the Australian Copyright Act 1968 (for example, fair dealing for the purposes of study, research, criticism or review) no part of this publication may be reproduced, stored in a retrieval system, or transmitted in any form or by any means, electronic, mechanical, photocopying, recording or otherwise, without the written permission of the publisher.

Title: Thirty-Eight Crash

Author: Direen, Eilidh

ISBNs: 978-0-6457705-2-0 (print)
                 978-0-6457705-3-7 (epub)
                 978-0-6457705-4-4 (Kindle)

Subjects: FICTION / Romance / Humorous / Fantasy

This story is entirely a work of fiction. No character in this story is taken from real life. Any resemblance to any person or persons living or dead is accidental and unintentional. The author, their agents and publishers cannot be held responsible for any claim otherwise and take no responsibility for any such coincidence.

IG: @eilidh.direen
Website: eilidhdireen.com

Cover design and layout by Jacob Everest (Grapesoda Studio).

Dedication

To Laura V.D.L.,
You are 'the gilder of every pleasure, the soother of every sorrow,'
You have loved Henry longer than anyone else,
And without you, his story might never have been finished.

38 CRASH

Or, I'm A 38-Year-Old Single Man And My Family Keeps Nagging Me To Get Married And Have Children But I Just Want To Be Left Alone To Do My Research

Eilidh Direen

Chapter One – Henry

Dr Henry Biddlesnoot-Bloomington closed his eighty-seventh and final tab, let out a sigh of relief, leaned back in his chair, and stretched. He'd been up all night, skimming journal articles for his literature review. The sun had risen around the closing of the seventy-first tab, and muffled noises below him indicated that the Social Sciences building was coming slowly to life: the early commuters had arrived, heralding the beginning of another working day.

Presently there was a knock at the door, followed by Dr Robert Jones sticking his head through the opening. "Henry, how's the paper coming along?"

"Slowly," his colleague replied, but with a tired smile which indicated that the quality of work hitherto achieved more than compensated for the quantity. "There's a lot of literature out there on cryptocurrency and the meme market, but nothing specifically about Gold Yamre, and one can only go so broad in one's overview of godstonks. But I did find an article by T. H. Jenkins which bridged the gap considerably."

"Fantastic!" said Robert, who, his bailiwick being PolSci, knew very little of technocultural futurism, but who recognised a breakthrough when he saw it. "Well done. As a matter of fact, I just came to let you know that Felicity from Comms is handing out cupcakes downstairs for her birthday. Apple cinnamon. Come join us?"

Henry looked at his watch with a pained expression. "Thanks, but I'm running late for my uncle's funeral. Tell her I said happy birthday." And with that, he heaved himself out of his chair, gathered his things, and departed.

∴

There weren't many at the funeral. Uncle Bertram had generally preferred the companionship of plants over people, and as such, had made few friendships over the course of his lifetime. He had never married, nor had he any living relatives besides Henry. (The Biddlesnoot-Bloomingtons were a small, rather accident-prone family, and most of them had died well before fifty.) So it was just Henry at the funeral, and a couple of neighbours, and the lady from the nursery who had always sold Uncle Bertram the nicest plants for his collection. Nonetheless, it was a touching ceremony. Henry gave the eulogy; he was not nervous, as he had written it years ago in preparation for this moment. But he did, somewhat to his surprise, feel a tear begin to well up in his eye as he stood before the gathered crowd and spoke.

"My Uncle Bertram was greatly beloved by his family. He has been a dear friend to me for many years, particularly since the deaths of my parents almost twenty years ago, when I was still just a bright-eyed undergraduate. For the longest time we have shared the joys and sorrows of life together at Biddlesnoot-Bloomington Manor. Naïve as I was, I thought I was doing him a kindness by keeping him company during his middle years. I now see, however, that the kindness was all his. He would have been perfectly happy keeping to himself and his plants, but out of love for me, he gave me a home and a family in place of what I'd lost. And for that, I will be forever grateful."

Henry cleared his throat and blinked. It was unusual for him to feel this strongly about anything save his research. "I don't believe in categorising people as 'good' or 'bad,' as though goodness were something you could measure with a litmus test or an exam. But if I did, I would say that Uncle Bertram was indeed a good man: as good as they come. And I think you would all agree with me, else you would not have come here today. And for that, I give you my heartfelt thanks. It means a lot to me, and I can assure you it means a lot to him too." And with that, Henry wiped his eyes and sat down to a very small but enthusiastic scattering of applause.

∴

There was no wake, of course. At least not in any traditional sense. Henry went straight back to work from the funeral, and then at eight o'clock he left his office and went to the bottle shop. He purchased a top-shelf single malt scotch and went home to Biddlesnoot-Bloomington Manor, a large colonial-style building that, like its sole living occupant, was growing shabby on the outside, but was warm and welcoming on the inside.

Uncle Bertram met him on the veranda. "Henry, my boy! Good funeral?"

"Delightful, Uncle. An intimate turn-out, and the music was excellent. You would have been proud to see it. How's the afterlife treating you?"

"Fine, fine." The ghost ran a translucent hand ruefully through his hair. "I rather fancy I look better now than I ever did in my living years. Still, swings and roundabouts and all that. Hard to enjoy a drop like that one when you're dead." He nodded meaningfully at the bottle Henry was carrying. "Have one for me, would you, lad?"

"Of course, Uncle. And now," Henry rummaged through his pockets for the front door key, "let's celebrate." He threw open the heavy oak door and stepped into the polished marble entrance hall. A thousand pale translucent faces greeted him with a cheer: the Biddlesnoot-Bloomington family line (deceased).

"The prodigal returns!" roared the ghost of his father, Samson Biddlesnoot-Bloomington, a short round man with jolly red cheeks (at least, they *had* been red while he was yet living, but for all their current lack of colour they were no less jolly). "What kept you so long, Henry? It's well past close of business. We've been waiting for you to start the party, and the funeral was *hours* ago!"

Henry nodded deferentially. "I'm sorry, Dad, I couldn't leave the office until I'd finished drafting my literature review."

"Literature-shmiterature," scoffed the ghost of his triple-great grandmother, Doreen Biddlesnoot-Bloomington, a tall, angular lady with a wicked twinkle in her eye. "How does it feel to be the only living Biddlesnoot-Bloomington left?"

Henry shrugged. "It'll be easier to cook for one, I suppose."

"For shame!" a number of ghosts cried.

"Henry, why must you tease us like this?" implored his mother, Adelaide Biddlesnoot-Bloomington, a melancholy woman whose chief claim to beauty had been a perfectly-shaped nose, until she'd broken it whilst mountain-climbing in New Zealand back in '77. "You *know* your duty, and you aren't getting any younger. Isn't it time you settled down, found a nice girl, and gave us a child to carry on the family name?"

Several dozen ghostly relatives chimed in their agreement, and the entrance hall was drowned beneath the clamour of a hundred haunting voices telling Henry what he already knew: that it was up to him to save the Biddlesnoot-Bloomingtons from extinction, and if he failed in this endeavour, he would be shunned by his ancestors for all eternity. The party forgotten, each of the ghosts said their piece, and, when it became clear their dutiful heir had no reply for them, faded from the room, until only Uncle Bertram was left, watching closely as his nephew let out a deep sigh and unstoppered the bottle of scotch. He had been the only one of Henry's relatives who had remained silent during the brouhaha.

"Cheer up, old sport," he now said, as Henry took a generous swig. "They're only trying to save you from repeating their own mistakes."

"What mistakes?" Henry said bitterly. "I like my life the way it is, Uncle. I have my studies, and that is enough for me. If I died tomorrow, I would die happy."

"I know, Henry," Uncle Bertram said gently. "I know. I felt the same. But you can't blame them for wanting to protect the family name——"

"Hang the family name!" Henry cried in frustration. "I don't give a damn about it! It's a ridiculous name, anyway. Who in their right mind would care about carrying on a name like *Biddlesnoot-Bloomington*? I tell you what, Uncle, if I could be bothered with all the bureaucratic wank, I would've changed it myself years ago."

Uncle Bertram, of course, disagreed, but knew better than to say so at present. So he simply patted his nephew on the shoulder – a gesture that was appreciated, if not materially felt – and faded, leaving Henry with only the scotch for company.

∴

The next day, Henry woke up at 4:45AM, put on a fresh shirt and linen pants, threw on a jacket, slipped into his boots, brushed his teeth, filled his pockets with muesli bars and headed out the door. This had been his morning routine every day, six days a week (on the Lord's Day he rested), for the past twenty years.

It did not actually take him that long to reach the university – only fifteen minutes by car or thirty by bus – but he had always felt far more at ease on campus, alone with his studies, than bumming around Biddlesnoot-Bloomington Manor with all his dead relatives constantly haranguing him to get a real job and find a good woman who would bear him a tidy number of little Biddlesnoot-Bloomingtons to ensure the continuation of the family line. So, six days a week, he left the manor as early as humanly possible and spent the day at the university, studying the intersections between current trends in technology, society, and media, calculating how they might evolve in the near future, and how best to take advantage of those intersections as they appeared (which all sounds very impressive until you get into the nitty-gritty of his field of research, which generally involved trying to predict which memes would be popular on the internet some days from now, and how they might affect the technocultural landscape in years to come) – until finally he would return home anywhere between 7:00PM and 11:00PM, eat a light supper, and sleep, to repeat the entire process the next morning (unless the next morning was Sunday, in which case, as previously remarked, he would spend the day in rest and devotion to the Lord who had blessed him with such a fruitful and fulfilling life).

Today was no different from any other, save that Sarah Banks was waiting for him outside his office when he arrived. "Morning, Dr B.," she said cheerfully, offering him a firm handshake as he approached. "How's the project going?"

Henry liked Sarah Banks. She was intelligent, friendly, and the only digital news reporter left in the country who still preferred to meet with 'talents' face-to-face. On top of which, she took a keen interest in technocultural futurism, and, like Henry, was singularly devoted to her work. She had interviewed him about several of his projects over the years, and they had built up a jovial rapport. But it was all talk, and nothing more.

Henry smiled. "Fine, thank you, Sarah. I finished drafting the literature review yesterday, as a matter of fact. It'll take ages to finish the whole thing, of course, but I could give you a couple of grabs, if you wanted…?"

"Actually, if you don't mind, I was hoping to do a joint interview with you and your partner…" Sarah said hopefully, darting a glance over his shoulder.

The good doctor was confused, and looked behind him to see nothing but the empty hallway. "Partner?"

Now Sarah looked confused. "Your research partner, Dr Honeysett. I heard she just got assigned to your project yester…" She trailed off, seeing the look of horror and bewilderment upon his face. "You mean – you didn't know?"

Before poor Henry could even begin to find the words he needed to reply, he heard a slight noise, and turned again to see a small strawberry-blonde woman some years his junior standing right behind him.

She beamed at him and held out a hand. "Dr Henry B.? It's so good to finally meet you! I'm Louisa Honeysett, your new research partner."

Chapter Two – Louisa

"I won't stand for this."

"Nonsense, Henry."

"It's outrageous."

"Everybody collaborates from time to time."

"It's unfair."

The dean sighed. "Henry, you know as well as I do that faculty are expected to be open-minded and inclusive. Your field in particular is riddled with interdisciplinary rabbit holes that will prove to be your downfall if you don't start working with some other specialists. Dr Honeysett is a highly accomplished media studies researcher, and I think she will be an excellent fit for your project."

"But it's *my* project!" Henry said exasperatedly. "You can't just up and *decide* to put someone else on my project, let alone someone I've never even met! That's not how these things work."

"Not usually, no. But since you haven't chosen to collaborate of your own accord for over a decade, I decided it was time I stepped in and gave you a push in the right direction. Your blatant isolationism is throwing a poor light upon the entire College of Arts, and the student body is starting to write some very nasty things about us in the campus newsletter. I would be remiss in my duties if I let you carry on like this and drag the rest of us down with you. Do you understand?"

Henry glared at her, understanding perfectly but unwilling to say so. Something in his face must have unsettled the dean, however, because after a moment she ducked her head, almost in embarrassment, and continued. "Just give her a chance, Henry. One month. If Dr Honeysett really can't grasp the vision of your project, then maybe I'll reconsider. But I think you'll be pleasantly surprised at how much a second opinion will help you with your research."

I already have a second opinion on every other part of my life, Henry thought bitterly, remembering the ruckus of the night before. And a third, and a fourth, and a thousand more besides. What difference could one more critic make?

"Very well," he said aloud. "One month. But if there is any indication during that period that our collaboration will inhibit my research, then I insist you either take her off my project, or take me off your payroll." And with the dramatic instinct born of countless years spent in the company of wailing ghouls and vengeful spirits, he swept out of the room.

∴

Louisa Honeysett was waiting for him in his office when he returned some minutes later. She was sitting right where he'd left her, thumbing through a battered copy of *Nicomachean Ethics*. Sarah Banks, however, had perhaps sensed that now was not the time to be conducting interviews, and had left.

At the sound of the office door creaking open, Louisa looked up at Henry and smiled. "How'd your meeting go, Dr B.?"

Henry regarded her gravely before replying. He had nothing against her personally, nor yet any reason to believe that she lacked competence. Moreover, as a consequence of being routinely henpecked to within an inch of his life by his meddling ancestors, he cherished a deep respect for the dignity of the human person, and was loath to treat anyone discourteously if he could possibly help it. So, despite his growing feeling of concern for his research, he returned her smile and took a seat beside her. "Please, no need for formalities; call me Henry." He gestured to the book she was holding. "Is that for work, or for play?"

"I don't believe in the distinction myself," Louisa said brightly. "But speaking strictly, it's for work. I unearthed an old meme page a couple of weeks ago dedicated to the writings of St Thomas Aquinas, and I was thinking of doing a yarn about it for the winter edition of /REL/. But of course, true appreciation of any commentary on Aquinas requires a phat stack of background reading."

Henry resisted the overwhelming urge to raise an eyebrow. Submissions for /REL/ closed in a week. It would take a supernatural grace to get an entire article drafted and sent in by then, especially if she hadn't even moved on from Aristotle yet. He fought down another wave of resentment towards the dean. It was this kind of loose-unit maverick attitude that he'd specifically wanted to avoid when he'd insisted against collaboration. But there was no point in letting Louisa know that, since they were stuck with each other regardless.

So he nodded graciously. "Of course. Er, can I get you a tea? Coffee? Muesli bar?" He took one from his pocket for demonstration.

"Oh," said Louisa, taken aback by the plethora of choices. "I'm not really, er… Well," (wavering), "are the muesli bars oat-based or nut-based?"

"Nut-based."

She beamed. "Perfection, in bar form."

Henry found himself beginning to relax. "The finest confection *bar* none, if you will."

"I will," she chuckled.

He tossed her one of the lauded victuals and she bowed her thanks. He cracked open a bar of his own and there was a minute's silence, punctuated only by meditative chewing. He contemplated not for the first or last time in his life the ineffable communion of souls brought about by the breaking of bread.

When they had finished, Louisa said, "Tell me about your project, Henry."

Henry felt his misery returning as his mind was wrenched from the transcendent back to the ugly temporal. He swallowed and did his best to ignore it. "How familiar are you with the interaction between crypto- and memetic economies?"

"You mean the stonk market?"

His heart sank a few inches further. "That was the prevailing, ah, theory some time ago, but the current discourse is more around what we classically term 'godstonks'."

She nodded. "Right, I'm with you."

Henry cleared his throat. "Right. Well, the hierarchy of godstonks is somewhat disputed, but most communities would agree that Gold Yamre is the emergent front-runner. This intrigues me, because Gold Yamre entered the markets less than a month ago, and I have yet to find an explanation for its popularity. It has none of the memetic or cultural indicators shared by other leading godstonks, or even older cryptocurrencies like Bitcoin or Dogecoin, and I cannot find any discourse on any forum or any existing literature that can offer an alternative explanation. So, I decided to investigate this phenomenon myself. The project is in its infancy, however; I'm still drafting my literature review, and have yet to find any significant leads."

"Riiight," Louisa said, nodding slowly. "So what you're saying is, you want me, a media studies scholar, to help you solve an economics problem."

Henry felt as though he'd been plunged suddenly into a pool of icy water. "Yes," he said reluctantly, "I suppose I am."

∴

Henry returned home that night in a dark mood. He was not usually given to violent fantasies or notions of revenge, but as he shoved open the front door and stalked inside, his thoughts towards the dean were neither pleasant nor kind.

His first impulse was to go directly to his sitting room cupboard where he had left the remainder of the scotch the night before. But he was a conscientious man, and despised the idea of using a twenty-year-old whiskey as an emotional crutch. Music, then, was the means by which he would soothe his rumpled soul.

He walked slowly but purposefully into the lounge room, where the gramophone was kept. Leafing through his family's ancient collection of records, he selected *Takeo Ischi's Greatest Hits*, removed it reverently from its sleeve, and set it onto the machine. He exhaled deeply as the music played, feeling the tension slowly leave his body.

"Rough day at work, Henry?" his great-aunt Rosalind asked, materialising out of a nearby sofa.

"You could say that," her nephew grumbled, thrusting his hands into his pockets and scowling at the floor.

She clucked sympathetically and gave him an incorporeal pat on the hand. "Why dontcha you tell me all about it, sugarpie?" She had spent the majority of her afterlife watching indie soap operas set in the Deep South, and had taken on the accent without ever realising it.

Henry sighed. "I don't suppose it would make any sense to you, Auntie."

"Try me, honey."

Although Henry despaired of ever being understood by his undying relations (save perhaps Uncle Bertram on select occasions), he had a soft spot for Aunt Rosalind, and did not wish to upset her by his own petulance. So he sat down on the sofa beside her and said, "Well, you see, the dean assigned another researcher to my project without consulting me, and I fear it will be the ruin of everything I've been working towards."

"You think so?" Aunt Rosalind said. "Why, what's this person like?"

"Like?" cried Henry, his voice cracking slightly as the anxiety rose up in him again like floodwater. "She's perfect! Perfect in every way – charming, intelligent, professional, exceptional taste in muesli bars, and I dare say she feels very passionate about her work… It's only that *she knows absolutely nothing about my field of research!* That's it, her one and only flaw. Perfect in all other aspects. But that doesn't help me, because what I need is someone who *understands* what I'm trying to do!"

"Oh sweetpea," Aunt Rosalind murmured, stroking ineffectually at his hair, "it can't be as bad as all that."

"She used the term 'stonk market' unironically," her nephew groaned, flinging himself back against the sofa cushions in a paroxysm of grief.

Seeing that he was in no fit state to listen to the distilled wisdom of the ancients, Aunt Rosalind wisely said no more.

∴

The following morning, Henry marched resolutely into his office, having lain awake most of the night deliberating about how to resolve his predicament. He'd tossed and turned for hours, drifting in and out of nightmares in which he delivered countless inane presentations cobbled out of negligible findings and platitudinous conclusions at a myriad of futurist conferences until at last he became the laughing-stock of the academic world.

Upon waking from a particularly vivid dream in which his own Ph.D. students mocked him for the gross banality of his results, he determined to inform Dr Honeysett that, while he appreciated her enthusiasm and had most certainly enjoyed her company, he did not think she would be a good fit for his project, and perhaps it would be best to persuade the dean to assign her to another post where her expertise would be made better use of.

Imagine his surprise, therefore, when he found her waiting for him at his desk, her hair rumpled and her shirt stained with coffee, but her spirits untrammelled by whatever experiences the night had brought her.

"Morning, Henry!" she chirruped. "Guess what I found?"

"Did you…have you been here all night?" Henry asked, staring at her in shock and awe.

"I know, I probably look terrible, but believe me, it was worth it. Come and see!" And she shifted her chair to the side and motioned him over to look at her laptop screen.

Henry scanned the page slowly, feeling dazed to the point of illiteracy. "'YamreAU Beta Fan Forum'…What is this?"

"It's kind of hard to tell, because the site is encrypted, but I'm pretty sure the OP on this thread had a hand in the creation of Gold Yamre, or at least knows someone who did. Isn't that so cool? It's like uncovering a new piece of history!"

"I don't understand," he mumbled. "How did you find this?"

She turned suddenly and gave him the cheekiest smile he'd ever seen. "Let's just say I know my way around the deep web, my g."

Henry gazed at her in awe. There was no doubt about it, she was a loose-unit maverick. But maybe, despite that or *because* of that, she was also the kind of person who could actually get away with writing an entire research article from start to finish in the week before submissions closed.

"Louisa, I——" He swallowed hard, remembering the bitterness he'd felt the previous evening, and fought back a hot surge of shame. "I don't know how to thank you. This could be the breakthrough I've been waiting for." He took her hand and shook it fervently. "I am indebted to you."

Louisa flushed with pleasure and embarrassment. "Don't thank me yet; the decryption is going to be the *really* tricky part. But then again," (regaining her composure), "I've always been a sucker for a good brainteaser."

Despite himself, Henry smiled. "Me too."

∴

"So tell me, Dr B.," said Sarah Banks, checking that her recorder was switched on, "what exactly is at the heart of your project?"

"Well, Sarah," Henry said sagely, "I think perhaps it would be better for my colleague to answer that question. Louisa?"

Louisa grinned. "We're on a quest to uncover the hidden mysteries of Gold Yamre, King of the Godstonks."

"Couldn't have said it better myself," Henry agreed, as Sarah burst into startled laughter. "And I have full confidence in our ability to complete such a noble quest. In fact, I think we'll have some preliminary findings within a fortnight."

"I should hope so," Sarah said, once she'd taken a moment to adjust to the new dynamic unfolding before her. "Considering the reputation of your competition, I imagine that speed will be a deciding factor in your project's success."

Henry stiffened. "Competition?"

Sarah seemed puzzled. "You hadn't heard? Dr Mackenzie from Macquarie University is doing a yarn on Gold Yamre as well."

"*Mackenzie?*" said Henry. "I thought she was on long service leave!"

Sarah shrugged. "I guess she had a stroke of inspiration while she was away. I'm surprised you hadn't heard anything about it, to be honest. It's been public knowledge for a while now."

There was a heavy pause as Henry frowned into the empty space before him.

"You alright, Henry?" Louisa asked softly.

Henry stared at her, uncomprehending.

Then a wild gleam entered his eye, and he grinned broadly.

"Oh yes," he said. "I've missed this."

Chapter Three – Trish

February, 1986

"Hey, kid!"

Henry turned and stared, unsure if it was him being addressed. A short, stocky girl with messy black hair and thick-rimmed red glasses stood glaring at him from the other end of the playground. He dimly recognised her as being from Class 1C.

"What d'you want?" Henry asked.

She marched forward until they were standing a metre apart. Despite being the shortest in his class, he was easily a head taller than her. "Do you have two dollars?" she demanded.

Nonplussed, Henry dug around in his pocket. "Sure." He found a coin and handed it to her.

"Thanks, kid!" She slapped him on the back. "You're my friend now. What's your name?"

"Henry. What's yours?"

"Trish." She gave his hand a hearty shake. "Nice to meet ya!"

∴

February, 1996

Henry was roused from a pleasant daydream in which he'd just been made the newest member of the Power Rangers when he turned a corner and collided head-on with another student. Before he knew it, he was sprawled on the ground amidst a war zone of books, papers, and other debris, blinking in confusion and conscious of a pain in his left shoulder.

"Hey, watch where you're——" The student broke off, eyes alight with recognition behind thick red glasses frames. "*Henry?*"

"Trish!" He allowed her to take him by the hand and pull him up. She was a lot taller now; they were nearly the same height. "I didn't know you were back!"

"Yeah, we moved at the end of December." They stared at each other in amazement and delight. "I forgot you lived around here," Trish admitted. "Imagine us going to the same college!"

"Do you have a problem with that?" Henry joked, to cover a sudden burst of insecurity. She'd forgotten him?

Trish smiled. "Not at all."

∴

June, 1998

"Well, that was a colossal waste of time," Trish grumbled as they rode the wave of students out of the examination room.

"Tell me about it," said Henry. "I can't believe they tortured us for two years at college over the stupid TCE, and now we're actually *in* uni and the exams are literal child's play."

"Mm. So…pub?"

"Pub."

They made a beeline for the bus stop, continuing to debrief the exam – then stopped as they were met at the campus edge by Uncle Bertram.

"Uncle?" said Henry, staring in bewilderment at the tall, wispy-haired figure before him. He hadn't seen Uncle Bertram outside of his greenhouse in about ten years. "What are you doing here?"

Uncle Bertram looked at him with kindly eyes, but there was an unmistakeable sadness in his voice. "Henry, my boy, come with me for a moment. I have something to tell you."

Henry scowled, wary of his family's machinations. "Anything you have to say to me, you can say in front of Trish."

Uncle Bertram shrugged. "Very well. I received word this morning that your parents crashed their car on the highway. I'm afraid…they didn't make it. I'm so sorry."

The world around Henry seemed to blur out of focus. "My parents…?" He felt his knees begin to shake, and took hold of Trish's shoulder to steady himself. It was so bright outside, almost too bright to see…

"Henry," said Trish, her voice sounding very far away. "Henry?"

His eyes were wet. His face was wet. He couldn't see, couldn't breathe…

Together, Trish and Uncle Bertram held him while he wept.

It was a long time before they let go.

∴

December, 1999

"New Year's Eve party tomorrow," said Henry.

Trish grunted, not looking up from her computer. "Can't go, I gotta finish this damn paper. As if a whole new millennium is about to start and I'm still sitting here like an *idiot*, doing my fricking undergrad."

"Well that's what you *get* for taking a summer unit, ning-nong."

"It was worth it," she said, with a feigned sob. "While you're out partying with hot babes, I'll be in here, growing wise and learned in the ways of otaku trucker rallies, and *then* you'll be sorry you didn't sign up with me when you had the chance."

Henry chuckled. "I'll save you a glass of champagne."

She winked at him. "How 'bout you save me a spot under the mistletoe instead?"

"Uhm." He stared at his shoes, unsure how to respond. She went back to her typing, unfazed. After a moment he asked, "What d'you think you'll do after we graduate?"

"That's a whole 'nother year away, Henry. Why would I be thinking about that?"

Henry shrugged, and there came a pause. Then for the first time, Trish turned away from her work and gave him her full attention.

In the fading light coming in from the library window, he looked much older, somehow. "Why…what are *you* going to do?" she asked.

∴

April, 2005

"Congratulations, Trish and Henry!"

The office erupted with applause as the Head of Media held the journal aloft, brandishing it left and right before the entire department's gaze. "First article published! And a cracking read it is, too. Excellent work, the both of you."

Various colleagues crowded around the dynamic duo, shaking hands and slapping backs and proffering sundry little compliments and kind regards. But the world of academia keeps on moving, and before too long, everyone had gone back to their work, leaving only Henry and Trish sitting dazed in the staff room.

"That was fun," Henry said eventually. "I never thought my first publication would be a collab, but I'm glad we did it that way."

Trish smiled. "Me too, my thesis made so much more sense after I read your abstract." Her smile broadened. "Bet you I'll be first to publish a solo piece, though."

Henry chuckled. "You're on," he said, and they shook hands, knowing they would never collaborate again.

∴

March, 2006

Henry sank back into his chair, head spinning. He could feel his heart rate spike as he reread the email, just to be sure he wasn't going mad. Surely it was too good to be true. And yet…and yet it *was* true! His article had been accepted for the next edition of *TeCH*! In all his years of undergrad, he'd never dreamed… A journal this prestigious, with *his* name in it…! It really was too good to be true.

His blood pounded in his ears as he leapt up from his desk and charged out the door, racing for the office at the end of the hall. He had to tell Trish right *now*.

"Guess what?" he cried, bursting across her threshold without bothering to knock. "I have some incredible news!"

Trish looked up at him from her desk, face flushed. "Me too!"

Despite himself, his heart sank a fraction of an inch. Was she also about to be published? Had he lost the bet? He gritted his teeth and rebuked himself for his lack of humility. "Oh…you go first."

"No, no, you go first, I can see you're excited."

He didn't argue. "My article's coming out in the next edition of *TeCH*!"

Trish's jaw dropped. "*TeCH*!" She launched herself from her chair and threw her arms around him. "Congratulations! You deserve it, you've been working so hard." As she drew back, however, a familiar twinkle entered her eye. "You'd better *keep* working though, because I won't lose next time."

Henry chuckled. "I won't lose to *you*, either." He took a moment to steady himself. "What about you? What was your news?"

"Oh, that." She lit up again. "I've just accepted a job at Macquarie University."

His heart dropped the entire distance this time. "Macquarie?"

"Yes."

"In *Sydney*?"

"Yes!"

"*You're moving to Sydney?*"

"I'm moving to Sydney!" She laughed and hugged him again. "Can you believe it, Henry? It's almost too good to be true!"

Yes, Henry thought numbly, tightening his grip on her as though unable to let go. Yes it is. Almost too good to be true.

∴

September, 2008

The corner of Henry's elbow caught against the desk, and the spring edition of *Forward* slid off the top of a precarious pile of journals and papers onto the floor. He did not bother to pick it up. He'd read it cover to cover twice already, but the only article he'd read through both times without skimming was 'The Dark Knight and Sustainable Energy' by T. C. Mackenzie from Macquarie University. It was brilliant.

Massaging his elbow absently, Henry looked down again at his phone screen, a rueful smile playing about his lips as he read her text a third time: *your move, loser!*

It was a victory well worth gloating over. *Forward* was the only technocultural journal bigger than *TeCH*. Henry and Trish had both been submitting to it for years, but this was the first time either of them had been accepted. Sighing, he composed his reply: *Congratulations. I'll beat you next time.*

∴

Present Day

"You've missed what?" Louisa asked, as Henry continued to stare blankly at the wall.

"Her," said Henry. "Competing with her."

"Dr Mackenzie, you mean?"

He nodded. "It's been a while since we had a good sparring match. She's been off exploring her own niche."

"Yeah, but before that, her record was 7-6 against you," Sarah Banks chimed in.

Henry just grinned. "I'll smash her this time." He turned to Louisa. "And *you're* going to help me."

Chapter Four – Mathilda;
or, Four Saturdays

On the first Saturday of June, Mathilda Smythe emerged from her tiny green cottage nestled between two cherry trees and walked ten minutes down the road to Corner Shop, her local café and favourite place in the world, which she had dubbed her 'secular cathedral'. It was a bright, crisp winter's day, and the sun was out doing its very best to warm the world below. (This is not to say that it was doing *well*, but we applaud its noble efforts nonetheless.)

The bell above the door tinkled as Mathilda entered the café. The only people inside were Mickey the Delinquent and Barista Frances. Mickey did not look up, but Barista Frances cast aside the newspaper she was reading and greeted Mathilda with a broad smile. "Hello! Triple-shot latte?"

Mathilda checked her watch; it was only ten-fifteen. "Could we make it four shots? Is that legal?"

Barista Frances chuckled. "Finishing an important chapter today, are we?"

"Hoping to," Mathilda said wryly, shrugging off her overcoat and fumbling about in its pockets for her wallet. Barista Frances always had a fire going at this time of year, and the café was like one of those grandmotherly cottages one reads about in twentieth-century children's novels: deliciously warm, and smelling of baked apples and cinnamon.

"What happens in it?" Barista Frances asked, raising her voice slightly over the hiss of the coffee machine.

Mathilda sighed. "Well, basically it's this big emotional scene where the main character is trying to confront his own hubris, but is thwarted by his lack of self-awareness. Like, he knows *something* inside him is off, and that's why he's having so much trouble reaching his potential – but he doesn't have the emotional language or the insight to pinpoint exactly *what*. And I'm just having so much trouble getting the tone right, because it's meant to be poignant, but also kind of funny. It's a hard thing to balance."

"Mm," said Frances. "Sounds tricky."

"Yeah." Mathilda threw her loyalty card onto the counter with an air of defeat. "But it wouldn't be worth it if it were easy."

Barista Frances nodded sympathetically and stamped Mathilda's card. "Take a seat, darl, and I'll bring your drink over in a sec."

"Thanks." Mathilda wandered over to her favourite seat by the window, set up her laptop and notepad on the table, and scowled into empty space for a few minutes, pondering how to begin.

Mathilda was thirty-five years old in October. She had published her first and only novel at twenty, and had spent the last fifteen years squandering her late father's fortune whilst working on the sequel. It was a bombastic splatstick space opera about an amnesiac war hero who'd become a pacifist in his old age and was running from his bloodied past. Although the time she'd spent working on it each week hadn't changed, her output had steadily diminished over the years as she grew continually more frustrated at her inability to make the words on the page match up to the vision in her head. And yet the vision kept ascending to ever loftier heights, burning within her, leaving her unable to abandon the work as her intention to express that vision passed the stage of simple desire and turned into desperate, clawing need, like the need for oxygen when one is underwater.

In between her bouts of artistic crisis, Mathilda liked to observe the people who patronised the café of a morning, not because they gave her any particular inspiration for her work, but more because they gave her a renewed appreciation and vigour for life in general. There was one man, for example, whom she had privately nicknamed 'Pineapple Pete,' who came in once every two or three weeks and always dressed completely in clothes that were patterned with pineapples: hats, shirts, shorts and socks. He carried himself with profound dignity and joy, and upon Mathilda's complimenting him on his outfit, had thanked her graciously and proclaimed, "I like pineapples!" Who could possibly feel disillusioned at the mediocrity of their creations after catching a glimpse of such a man?

Pineapple Pete was one of many different characters who drifted in and out of Corner Shop with startling regularity (Barista Frances being one of those venerable souls who won the hearts and purses of her customers from the first interaction). There was Mickey the Delinquent, who appeared underage and added a shot of Jameson to her coffees when she thought no one was looking; there was Simon the Mechanic, who called everyone 'kiddo' regardless of their age, but one didn't take offence because he was such a jolly and humble man; there was Carla the Weekend Newsreader, who presented on ABC News Friday through Sunday, and wore very nice scarves; and there were countless others, all of whom Mathilda loved with a deep and genuine affection despite knowing them very little. But her absolute favourite was Double-Park George, who came in every Saturday morning at eleven on the dot, ordered two piccolos concurrently, drank them one after the other with immovable serenity, and left exactly an hour later, tipping his hat to Barista Frances on the way out.

Mathilda knew nothing of Double-Park George, save that he was an avid reader of Dickens, and appeared to be some sort of crazed academic. George wasn't even his real name; she only called him that on account of a vague resemblance to George Clooney, and because it was a name that inspired her with fondness and warmth. She liked him because he was a man of contradictions. His actions were mechanical and consistent, giving off the impression of fastidious self-importance – which was then belied by a domesticity and gentleness in his manner of speaking. And although he was punctual, he never seemed impatient or hurried, but was totally relaxed throughout his visits. And yet, Mathilda sensed in him a deep sadness, or unrest, or...*something* to that effect. And she resonated with that. It was like they had both reached the point in their lives where everything should have been perfect, and yet there was something missing, and they were both racking their brains to figure out what – but were afraid to look *too* hard, for fear of actually finding the answer. This was the real source of Mathilda's love for George: she believed that he was a kindred spirit, that they were united by the same underlying despair.

On this, the first Saturday of June, at eleven o'clock, George entered the café with an unusual spring in his step, greeted Barista Frances with a cheery nod, and ordered *three* piccolos. How bizarre, thought Mathilda. She had never seen him break routine before. What could have happened? She promptly gave up her search for the exact perfect adverb to describe her hero's inner turmoil and tuned in to catch George's words to Frances as he turned towards his customary table.

"…marks a turning point in my career," he was saying. "I haven't collaborated professionally on anything in nearly fifteen years, but I think a fresh pair of eyes will do wonders for my research."

"That's so good to hear!" Barista Frances smiled.

"Thank you," he said, smiling back. "I'm very excited."

∴

On the second Saturday of June, the sky was grey and cold, and Mathilda put on an extra scarf before leaving the house. The café greeted her with its customary warmth and the smell of woodfire smoke and cloves. She ordered another quadruple-shot latte and took her seat by the window, dreading the moment when she'd have to open up her word document and see the glaring white blankness of the page before her, taunting her with its empty promises of artistic greatness if only she could muster up the discipline to darken it with words.

Double-Park George surprised her again this morning by arriving half an hour early, carrying a laptop under his arm and looking rather despondent. He ordered two piccolos (at least that was something normal) and seated himself by the fire, swapping the usual pleasantries with Frances but giving no indication as to the cause of his melancholy. Curious, Mathilda edged her seat out to one side so she could get a glimpse of his computer screen over his shoulder, but she could make out nothing save a page of densely spaced code in a language she didn't recognise.

Reluctantly, Mathilda returned to her work. But she was distracted for the rest of the morning by George's occasional sighs as he wrestled with his own occupational demons. It was poetic, she thought, how two separate computer screens could be so equally torturous to the eyes that beheld them – only one was full, and the other was empty.

∴

On the third Saturday of June, Mathilda had a breakthrough and was furiously typing when George came in at two minutes past eleven, on the phone to his mother.

"It isn't *like* that, Mum," he was saying, with the tone of long-held patience only just now beginning to fray at the edges. He did not speak loudly, but with a resonance and clarity which Mathilda had long ago become accustomed to tuning into. As if waking from a dream, she was pulled out of her flow state and into George's reality. "I told you, you're reading too much into it. Sorry, just a moment please – two piccolos, thank you, Frances." He hurried away to one of the corner tables, still on the phone.

"You have no *idea* the kind of results we're on the verge of finding, and *this* is what you want to talk about? I've told you time and again, I don't want… No, of course I'm not going anywhere. Mum, you aren't being fair about this. I'm trying to focus on my work, and you keep…"

Mathilda had little interest in domestic conflict; she was more inclined towards the intrapersonal and existential. With some effort, she pulled her focus away from George's conversation and settled back into her writing.

It was some moments before her attention was arrested again – this time by a joyful exclamation: "Oh! Mum, I'm sorry, I've got to go. My partner's just decrypted the YamreAU fan forum. This is what we've been waiting for! Okay, love you – love you – bye." And without waiting to finish his second piccolo, George gathered up his things and rushed out of the café, stopping only to thank Barista Frances before he left.

∴

On the fourth Saturday of June, Mathilda's entire perception of the world was shattered forever.

The day began harmlessly enough; the sun was once again shining, the café smelled of lavender and mulled wine and gingerbread, and Mathilda had finally thought of an ending for her troublesome pivotal chapter. Just as she was closing in on the exact phrasing she wanted for the penultimate line, however, the bell above the door tinkled, and in strode Double-Park George, accompanied by an unfamiliar woman!

Mathilda was flabbergasted. She had never known George to come to this café with anyone else before. He had always struck her as someone rather friendless, too much at home in his own mind to come out into the world and meet people there. And it couldn't be his mother – she was too young – nor his sister, for they looked nothing alike. So then…?

Smiling, George motioned to the woman to cross the threshold before him. "This is my favourite café," he said nonchalantly. "I come here every week."

"Oh, Henry…!" his companion gasped, looking around her at the large stone fireplace, the polished wooden tables, the glowing candles, dark leafy pot plants, and the hanging bunches of dried flowers and herbs that made the place feel more like an old country tavern than a café. "It's so lovely. How have I never heard of this place before?"

"Frances likes to keep it a bit secret," said George, whose name was apparently Henry, with a wink towards the counter. "Don't you, Frances?"

"Yeah, well," said Barista Frances, "it'd ruin the atmosphere if every man and his dog came in here. Now, how many piccies can I get you today? Three? Four?"

"Just the two, thanks," said Henry, as his companion burst into incredulous laughter. (She was very pretty, thought Mathilda, with neither admiration nor jealousy. She had a nice, wide, open smile.) "And Louisa, can I get you anything?"

"What?" said the woman. "No, don't be so old-fashioned, I can get it myself."

"No, I didn't mean – it's just, it's the least I can do to thank you for all your hard work," Henry said earnestly. "Believe me, if the Quartermaster's Arms were open right now, I'd be buying you a beer instead. Please, I insist."

"Oh, well in that case, I'll have a large cap, thanks." She smiled at Frances and led Henry towards a window seat he had never sat in before, and thereby out of Mathilda's field of vision.

With a sigh, Mathilda turned back to her keyboard, but the phrase she'd been looking for had escaped her. The sun beyond the window seemed all of a sudden to shine less brightly, and there was a sour feeling creeping into the pit of her stomach.

What was this she was experiencing? Disappointment? At what?

Was it just because his name was Henry, and not George? Was it because her romanticised image of him as the eccentric lone wolf had been debunked? Or was it something deeper than that?

No, she thought, feeling the sudden vicelike grip of despair at her own increasing certainty. Surely not… It's just hot in here, and I'm pinging off the four shots of coffee, and…and…

And surely *I'm not in love with Double-Park George!*

Chapter Five – Sarah;
or, Monday, End of June

5:01 AM

It was the extra minute of sleep that made all the difference.

Sarah Banks awoke, as she did every morning, to the sound of "Dare" by Stan Bush, and felt immediately refreshed.

She played the song on loop for the next hour as she leapt from her bed, wrenched open the curtains (even though it was dark outside), brushed her teeth, chugged a smoothie, and drove five minutes down the road to the gym. She had always found herself buoyed by Bush's lyrics, ever since her first encounter with them at the age of six, when her older brothers had introduced her to the 1986 classic animated *Transformers* film.

Today was chest and triceps. She spent the better part of an hour on the bench press, increased her max by two kilos, and finally moved on to another song, considering herself sufficiently empowered for one day.

∴

6:30 AM

Sarah was a self-help book addict. Every morning after she'd returned from the gym, showered, and dressed, she would sit for an hour and read a chapter or so of whichever andragogical tome had currently taken her fancy. At the moment it was a book called *Life After Tracksuit Pants*, by some nineteen-year-old from the UK who had purportedly discovered a correlation between casual wear and productivity.

This morning, she read 'Chapter 11: Coordinating Colours With The Seasons' and learned that she should always wear bright colours in winter to avoid seasonal depression. She then spent thirty minutes journalling, and made a note to buy that big red comfy-looking jumper she had seen in the Vinnies window last week.

∴

8:05 AM

It never took more than forty-five minutes to drive to work, even with heavy traffic, but Sarah always left the house at five past. She liked to be ten or fifteen minutes early, so that she could spend some time in the Japanese gardens outside the XYZnews office and clear her mind before heading in to begin her working day. Sometimes, if she listened hard, she could hear the wattlebirds chirping in the bushes nearby, and she would smile to herself.

∴

9:00 AM

There were never more than a couple of people present in the office at any one time. XYZnews only had a dozen employees on the payroll, most of whom preferred to work from home. Sarah, on the other hand, had read once in a book called *The New Holistic You* that one should keep one's workspace strictly separate from one's home space in order to maintain optimal work-life balance. She had interpreted this to mean that she ought to live and work in two separate buildings if she wanted to maximise her potential.

This morning, the only others in the newsroom were Kenneth and Crystal, who were nattering in the beanbag corner over a couple of turmeric lattes. They nodded at Sarah as she entered.

"Top of the morn!" she said cheerfully.

They mumbled standard workplace greetings by way of reply.

Sarah did not consider herself socially inept, but there was definitely a lack of connection between her and her colleagues. She thought perhaps it was because she was the only one who took the job seriously. Of course, she had never been anything but friendly to her fellow journos…but she could tell there was something about her that seemed to put them off. She didn't really mind – or at least, she told herself she didn't. In this line of work, there were plenty of opportunities to relate with people from all walks of life, so she was never in any danger of experiencing true loneliness. That was what she told herself, anyway.

She took a seat at her desk (everyone else hot-desked, but since Sarah was the only one who rocked up nine to five, she had been allowed to stake a claim to one tiny desk at the back of the newsroom), opened up her MacBook, and spent twenty minutes or so subbing a couple of stories that Brenda had cobbled together over the weekend. After filing those, she turned her attention to today's schedule. She had two interviews planned: one with an eight-year-old graphic designer, and one with a peg-legged war vet who had taught himself how to wind surf. Both yarns were to go up by five o'clock, which didn't leave a whole lot of time for subbing, particularly since the old man lived out on the east coast. But that was the thrill of the thing for Sarah. The ever-looming deadlines and the vicarious adventures she experienced through her interviews were the closest she ever came to an adrenaline rush, since she was too caught up in the potential consequences of her actions to ever be attracted to anything like sky-diving or bungee-jumping. With a smile, she grabbed her keys and handbag and headed back out the door.

∴

10:00 AM

"So, Madison," Sarah said, "tell me about your business."

Contrary to most pop-cultural depictions of unusually intelligent little girls named Madison that Sarah had seen, this particular eight-year-old was friendly, accommodating, and down-to-earth. It was a refreshing change after the last few child prodigies Sarah had interviewed, most of whom had been insufferable, pretentious, or just downright bizarre.

"It's nothing special," Madison said with a shrug – but also a smile which belied any false modesty. "I have an Insta profile where customers can send me ideas about the designs they want, and then I do a mock-up in MS Paint – but then I go over that in PaintShop Pro, so it comes out kind of cringe and retro, but also like kind of nice? It's hard to explain unless I show you." She pulled out a tablet and flicked through some of her portfolio.

"Yeah, I see what you mean," Sarah said with genuine admiration. "I really like that one——" (pointing to a whimsical depiction of a rat sitting atop a crescent moon), "——it's so…existential. But not, like, 2013 tumblr existential. Damn. I actually would wear that on a T-shirt."

Madison grinned. "The company that prints them mainly does socks. But I could probably talk to them for you and see if they can make you a T-shirt?"

Sarah chuckled. "That's very sweet. Let me have a think about it and get back to you."

The child looked up at her sagely. "You can think all you want, but in your heart, you already know the answer."

∴

11:45 AM

There was this one takeaway shop that Sarah patronised infrequently, on days when a lack of self-control coincided with a mighty hankering for kebabs. Her encounter with Madison had left her questioning whether she, at twenty-nine, had reached the same level of self-actualisation as this child seemed to have at less than a third of her age. Consequently, she was feeling rather fragile, and since she had done quite a strenuous workout that morning, she'd known that all hope was lost from the moment she'd got back into her car after the interview.

So here she now sat in her favourite corner booth, chomping away at the greasy mass of pita bread and shaved beef and garlic sauce, and loving every second of it. She had once read a book titled *Intentional Leisure*, which had argued that even the most depraved acts of self-indulgence will make a person happy if they are performed with the requisite deliberation. Sarah had her reservations about the universal applicability of such a proposition, but was more than willing to subscribe to it on occasions such as this.

She left the shop fatter and gladder than she had been on entering, and considered her time and money well spent.

∴

12:30 PM

The actual writing of the news stories was Sarah's least favourite part of the process. It was agonising to expose her thoughts and words to the public eye with so little time to polish and refine them beforehand. But she knew that this was the only way to tame her perfectionistic nature – and it was that same nature, that desire for excellence in all areas, which demanded that she continue to expose herself to the ravages of compromise and time-constraint, so that she could emerge from the ashes of imperfection and step forth into the glorious new realm of the acceptable minimum.

∴

2:40 PM

"So what inspired you to take up wind surfing?"

The old man looked at her blearily over a glass of Kriek lambic. "Watched a movie about it when I was a kid. This bloke, he was a champion wind surfer. Had the most *gorgeous* red-headed wife." He grinned shyly. "I was only fifteen when I saw it. I wanted to *be* him." He turned his head over his shoulder and spat. "Then I joined the air force instead, like a damned fool."

"You didn't enjoy your time in the military?" Sarah asked.

The old man shrugged. "You do anything long enough, you stop enjoying it." He kicked at his nearby surfboard with the end of his peg-leg. "Odds are I'll die first before I get sick of this, but if I'd started it when I was younger…" He trailed off and gave her a meaningful look. "How long've you been in *your* line of work?"

Sarah shifted uncomfortably in her seat. "A few years."

"Hmmph. You'll probably be alright then." He downed the last of his beer, then spat again. "Or not. I could be wrong. Been wrong about a lot of things before."

"Thank you for your time," said Sarah.

"Mind the step on your way out."

∴

4:37 PM

She stared at the blank page before her, willing herself to write. The old man's words raged and stormed within the walls of her brain, burning themselves deep into her psyche. But she just *couldn't* get them out onto the page in a way that made sense.

∴

4:59 PM

It was with a heavy heart that she hit 'submit'.

∴

5:05 PM

Sarah always knocked off at exactly five past.

Except today.

She glanced down as her phone buzzed, and debated whether or not she could be bothered checking it. After a minute, she sighed and opened the message.

It was from Dr B.: *We've made a breakthrough. Do you have time?*
She did not hesitate: *Always.*

∴

6:12 PM

"Thank you so much, Sarah," Dr B. said, giving her the usual firm handshake. "I hope the material will be of some use to you, if only a little."

She smiled warmly. "You could never disappoint. And Dr Honeysett, congratulations on spearheading the breakthrough! I look forward to hearing more about your future work."

Dr Honeysett nodded and threw her a gang sign. "Cool! I'm off to have a big fat sleep, I'll catch youse both later. Pax, paisanos!" And she swept her things together and swaggered out of the room.

Dr B. observed his partner's bombastic exit with befuddled amusement, then cleared his throat and turned back to Sarah. "Really, Sarah, I am so grateful for your interest in my work," he said, speaking more quietly now that his words bore the sudden weight of intimacy. "Not many would show the same level of investment as you do. Not that it bothers me," he hastened to add, "but it's nice to feel appreciated. Like what you're doing matters."

Sarah stared at him. In all their years of correspondence, he had never opened up to her like this. Their conversations had always been engaging, yes, and substantial…but they had always talked about the work itself, never the way he actually thought or felt about it.

"I know what you mean," she said at last. "Sometimes I think… Well, it doesn't matter what I think."

"Don't say that," he said, with a forcefulness that surprised her. Then, as if embarrassed, he paused before adding in his normal tone, "Well, I mean, to some extent, it doesn't matter what any of us thinks. But there's a difference between humility and selling yourself short. Don't ever let yourself be taken in by it."

She found herself rather moved, and had to force herself to meet his eye. "That's very true. Thanks, Dr B."

He smiled. "I'm never going to persuade you to call me Henry, am I?"

"Probably not," she said, and shouldered her bag, uncertain what had just passed between them. "Well, goodnight."

"Goodnight, Sarah. Take care."

∴

7:10 PM

Normally she ate at six-thirty, and would partake of some kind of home-cooked stir-fry or lentil dish. But nothing seemed to be moving according to plan tonight, and although part of her was distressed by the abandonment of routine, there was another, deeper part of her, which had lain dormant for quite some time, that relished this new freedom.

She made microwave macaroni and watched *The Castle* before bed. She hadn't laughed so much in ages.

∴

9:00 PM

She started to read another chapter of *Life After Tracksuit Pants*, then changed her mind, tossed it aside and went to sleep.

Chapter Six – Joey

Henry was wrested from the depths of his slumber by an unfamiliar alarm tone blaring in his ear. He had reset it the night before, something he did routinely as the cold weather intensified (and with it the difficulty of rising from his bed each morning). Fumbling for the switch on his bedside lamp, he felt a pang of regret as the last dregs of a very pleasant dream in which he'd led a long and fruitful life and made lots of wonderful friendships began to seep out of consciousness.

The venerable academic was halted in the act of pulling on his socks by his father Samson drifting in through his bedroom wall.

"What ho, my son!" quoth the patriarch.

Henry rolled his eyes. "Dad, you're not *that* old."

"Ah, Henry," Samson said, nodding sagely, "age is but a trifle in the afterlife. When once one has come to terms with one's incorporeal and eternal existence, one begins to realise that it has its perks – such as being able to indulge in sundry little archaisms in casual conversation whenever one wishes——"

"And why does *one* wish to be in my bedroom right now?" Henry grunted, struggling to knot his tie with cold-numbed fingers. "One did not even knock before one entered! That was very impolite of one, and I should think, what with all one's incorporeal and eternal wisdom, one might have learned otherwise by this point."

"Well you don't have to be so down about it," his father said peevishly. "I only wanted to ask you if it is true what your mother tells me about this woman you've been seeing——"

"I haven't been *seeing* anyone," snapped Henry, giving up on the tie and flinging it across the room in disgust. "If you're talking about my research partner – whose name, by the way, is Louisa and not '*this woman*' – then you and Mum are completely barking up the wrong tree."

"But are you keen on her?" his father persisted.

"What? No!" Henry all but screamed in frustration. "How many times do I have to tell you people this? I'm *not* interested in anyone, I'm *not* getting married, and I don't *care* if our stupid bloodline dies out! That is not my responsibility. I just want to do my research and be left alone. Is that *so* much to ask…?…!!"

For a moment, Henry and his father simply glared at each other. Then Henry thrust on his boots with an impatient snort and left the room.

∴

By the time he arrived at the university, Henry was still feeling pretty low. Arguments with his family were not uncommon, but he found it difficult to bounce back from emotional turmoil once he had succumbed to it.

Louisa, on the other hand, appeared like sunshine incarnate as he entered the office (which they were now sharing, because the whole of Social Sciences was being reshuffled to accommodate a new intake of interdisciplinary staff). "Hey homeslice!" she said, smiling as she looked up from her computer. "I'm shouting the first round of coffees today. Yours are over yonder." She nodded towards his desk, atop which stood two piccolos.

Henry could have shed a tear. "Truly, I am beholden to you."

"Dude, it's so chill, just get the next round. We're going to *need* it to get through all this frigging data." She leaned back in her seat and yawned. "I thought decrypting the forum was going to be the hard part, but there's like a billion threads on here!"

Henry shotgunned both his piccolos and came over to take a look at her screen. "Hmm." His brow furrowed. "Have you tried advanced search?"

She made a face at him. "That would be like trying to use a concordance to interpret the Bible. Like yeah, you could track down every passage that mentions Jesus, but that's not going to help you understand the narrative context of what you're dealing with."

"Don't tell me how to read my own holy book!" Henry laughed. "Just tell me how we're going to find the genesis of Gold Yamre, so I can finish my project and rub it in Trish Mackenzie's face."

Louisa scrolled to the bottom of the page, scowled at it, then scrolled back up again. "Honestly? I think we need some research assistants. No matter how you look at it, we're just going to have to read this entire forum from start to finish, and a couple of extra people would make a huge difference."

Henry sighed. "I suppose."

Louisa regarded him thoughtfully. "You really don't like working with other people, do you? What, are you some sort of misanthrope?"

Her words, though spoken in jest, struck a nerve, and Henry's temper flared up again at once. "I am *not* a misanthrope," he said curtly. "I just don't get a lot of time to myself at home, so I have to find solitude elsewhere. Is that alright with you, Louisa? Does that sit well with your spirit? Am I *allowed* to feel this way?"

There was a stunned silence. He could see hurt and confusion writ plainly on her face, and felt an immediate twinge of remorse. "I'm sorry," he said. "No one deserves to be spoken to like that, let alone someone who has shown me nothing but kindness. Will you forgive me?"

Louisa smiled. "Yeah man, water under the bridge. I'm sorry too, I didn't mean to upset you."

He waved a hand dismissively. "You didn't upset me; I was already upset, about other things. Anyway, it doesn't matter. If you really think we need an assistant, then I'm not opposed to it. My grant will only cover one person though, will that be enough?"

"One's a lot better than none! Do you know anyone who'd be good?"

"Do I *look* like I know people? You find someone."

"Fine, make me do all the work then, I don't care," she laughed. "Here – you take over reading these dumbass forum posts and I'll go hit up my contacts list and see who I can rope into helping us on this thing."

He smiled. "Sounds good."

∴

Three days later, Johanna Carter came stumbling in through the office door, breathless and panting and thirty minutes past the appointed time of arrival. Startled by her sudden entrance, Henry rose from his desk to get a better look at her. She was somewhere in her mid-twenties, but looked about twelve. She had short brown hair, long gangly limbs, and was wearing jeans, sneakers, and an oversized yellow woollen jumper.

"Hello," she gasped, staring wild-eyed into the pit of Henry's soul. "I'm so sorry I'm late – I've just witnessed a crime."

Henry stared back at her blankly. "A crime?"

"What crime?" Louisa chimed in. "Joey, are you alright?"

The girl had leant against the doorframe and started dry-retching. After about a minute, she recovered enough to speak again, although she remained very pale. "I was walking through the park on my way here, and I was on the phone to my sister, and then I saw this little dog come running up to me, and he was wearing one of those little vests, you know, with a lead attached to it – and I thought, where's his owner? And then I heard a weird noise, and I looked up, and there's this mulberry tree in the corner of the park, and there was an old woman beneath it with long grey hair and a turquoise cardigan, and – and she'd – *ugh* – she'd *pulled her pants down and was having explosive diarrhoea underneath the mulberry tree*!!"

"She *wasn't*!" said Henry, aghast, while behind him Louisa began laughing hysterically.

"Oh yes she was," groaned the youth. "I wish it weren't true – but oh!! There was *so much poo* everywhere! I took one look at it and I almost threw up – and my sister was still on the phone, and she started making fun of me – and then I had to report it to the police – and now I'm here, and I feel *so* sick!"

Henry sat down in astonishment.

Meanwhile, Louisa convulsed with helpless mirth. "'Underneath the mulberry tree'…!" she echoed faintly, wiping a tear from her eye.

It was an auspicious beginning to a long and beautiful alliance.

∴

Of all her housemates, Joey was the one who most hated mornings. Each day the sun rose, and one by one the other women would leave the house in varying states of disgruntlement, depending on whether they were bound for work or play. And Joey would sleep on, until she could sleep no further – at which point she would shake her fist at the cold, roll over, and fall into a stupor for some moments, until she became lucid enough to comprehend her phone screen. She would then spend an hour or so scrolling, until finally she was prompted by her bladder to slither forth from the subterranean wasteland that was her bedroom and venture out into the waking world.

Once awake, however, Joey was an unbridled mass of chaotic energy. She had a wide range of interests, from debating about art with strangers on the internet to singing harmonies with her friends, to exploring the urban wilderness in search of the perfect pub crawl route, to challenging stray cats to fistfights. Into these and other pursuits she threw herself wholeheartedly, believing that the only thing preventing her from becoming insufferable in her adulthood was a zeal for life beyond her professional sphere.

This zeal for life, however, coupled with her turbulent personality, seemed to cause Joey to be involved in all sorts of uncanny and bizarre incidents, of which an old woman publicly defecating beneath a mulberry tree is only a mundane example. In fact, it often gave Joey a sense of relief to come to the university and immerse herself in cerebral pursuits, as this helped her to slow down and relax for a time. Nonetheless, her relationship with her career thus far was conflicted. She had chosen lolcow studies as her primary field, writing her master's thesis on the emergence of Chris Chan cosplayers in regional Australia; and while the work was rewarding, enabling her to indulge her longstanding interest in subcultural anthropology, she had felt a yearning of late to contribute more practically to the 'real world,' as she continued to encounter that world in new and exciting ways.

It was this crisis of faith that had led Joey to consider undertaking a Ph.D. in technocultural futurism, thinking that it would be the perfect bridge between her more theoretical roots and her newfound desire for functional application. She had therefore jumped at the chance when Dr Honeysett, her master's supervisor, had got in contact and asked if she wanted to work with Dr Henry B., the university's leading technocultural futurist. And consequently, she had been mortified at the horrendous first impression she had made upon him yesterday, after her tumultuous encounter by the mulberry tree.

On this particular morning, then, Joey transcended her mortal limitations and woke up an hour early, intending to arrive at work well ahead of schedule, and in a much calmer frame of mind.

She decided, however, being as she was *so* early, to stop off at the local market and pick up a chilli on the way. It was her turn to cook that evening, and she was planning on making tacos. Her housemates often bullied her for not being able to handle spicy food, so she was going to use this occasion as an opportunity for personal growth. She entered the small shop, took a perfunctory glance at the specials shelf, then with a swiftly beating heart proceeded to the produce section.

It took perhaps ten minutes, but she managed to sift through the entire box of green chillies until she had found the very smallest one. Satisfied with her endeavours, she placed it into her basket loose, not wanting to put it in a bag and end up paying more for the weight of the plastic than the chilli itself. A few moments more and she'd arrived at the checkout – and it was here that tragedy struck. The cashier scanned the little green chilli, and found that it was so very tiny that its cost was calculated at only two cents. The cashier was unable to comprehend this. Much agitated, he scanned it again, with the same result.

"Sorry, just one sec," he said, frowning and turning on his radio. "Hey, can I get a price check at number two, please?"

The queue behind Joey lengthened, and the customers behind her began to grow irate. No one came to perform the price check. The cashier called three more times, with increasing confusion and dismay. The man behind Joey muttered something coarse under his breath. Joey broke into a sweat. This is the price I pay for evolution, she thought to herself.

Finally, the cashier gave up and handed her back the chilli. "Have a good one," he said, in a tone of utter defeat.

Unfortunately, by this point Joey was well out of time, and despite her best efforts, she was late for work again.

Dr Henry was, thankfully, just as understanding of her predicament as he had been yesterday. "That is a tragic happenstance," he mused, once she had finished explaining to him all about the chilli mishap. "But far be it from me to condemn a person for trying to expand their horizons," he added, smiling slightly. "I hope that your tacos tonight are a roaring success."

Joey nearly wept with gratitude. "Thank you so much, Dr B., I promise I won't let you down again."

The good doctor chuckled. "There there, nobody's letting anybody down. Now then, let's get back to it, shall we? These posts won't read themselves!"

∴

Louisa had come to think that she knew Joey Carter pretty well after supervising her for two years. They had talked of theorists and papers and memes, exchanged banterous viewpoints, shared coffees together, and made fun of the other media studies academics behind their backs. During that time, Joey had also related countless tales of triumph and woe, some more far-fetched than others, but all of them somehow believable, and all of them adding to the rich tapestry in Louisa's head of the way Joey lived.

But working with Joey on Henry's project was an entirely different matter. Now that they spent the larger portion of every weekday in the same office, Louisa could see that, while Joey came across somewhat manic and disorganised, there was another side to her that was ponderous and serene, which thrived in the quiet day-to-day plod of data-sifting. It was oddly comforting to have her around, to chat to if desired, but more often just to provide an extra presence, an added warmth – not to fill in what was missing, but to augment what was already there, and so take the edge off what might have been a very tedious couple of weeks.

As it was, the office had settled into a comfortable, almost lackadaisical languor by the time the breakthrough was made.

"Eureka!" cried Joey, springing up from behind her desk and cutting a caper.

"What is it?" Henry said urgently.

"I found it!" came the glee-tinged tautological reply. "Behold, Doctor – the origin of Gold Yamre!"

The three of them crowded around Joey's computer.

And then Henry let out a guttural howl of dismay: "*NO-O-O…!*"

As Joey turned to her distressed superior in confusion and shock, Louisa narrowed her eyes and carefully scanned the page. Bewilderment gave way to clarity, and her shoulders slumped. "Ahh," she said quietly. "She got you again."

Henry kicked moodily at the base of the desk. "She got me again."

For at the very bottom of the thread, beneath the revelatory spiels about currency and memeconomic theory, a certain T. Mackenzie had posted mere hours ago: *eat my DUST, henry!!*

Chapter Seven – Toni

Whenever Henry needed a break, he sought the company of his oldest friend, Toni Russo. She owned a small block of land up north by the river, about an hour's drive from Biddlesnoot-Bloomington Manor. He always visited her: never the other way around. That was the way it had always been, and it was the way he liked it.

On this particular Sunday afternoon, they were out fishing in Toni's little red dinghy. Much of the first two hours had been spent in silence, while Henry struggled to decompress after the trials and tribulations of his week. But the sun was out, and the green rosellas were calling to each other amidst the eucalypts, and the air was clear and cool. He took in a deep breath and let it out slowly, feeling the tension inside him release.

"Great spot you got here, Tone," he said presently.

Toni didn't answer, instead stooping to pick up a Wild Yak from the esky before throwing out another line. "She goes alright," she said at last, cracking open the beer and taking a contemplative sip.

Henry smiled. "She goes alright."

A few brown leaves trailed idly past the side of the boat, drawn by the current towards some distant paradise.

"WHAT AM I GOING TO DO?!" Henry cried out, startling a nearby flock of geese into expeditious retreat.

Toni blinked at him beneath the brim of her faded blue bucket hat. "Do about what?"

"My research," he moaned. "I've been working on this project for *months* now, and Trish-*fricking*-Mackenzie just comes *swanning* in and steals my findings right out from under my nose, like she always does. What's the point? I might as well pack it in altogether and be a goat farmer or something – I mean, I'm clearly not flourishing in academia as I ought to be if it really were my telos…"

Toni just snorted and handed him a beer. "The telos of man's got nothing to do with his career choices, ya nong. Here, have another Yak. Stop fretting over things you can't control, man, it's a waste of time and energy."

"And yet I seem to do little else," Henry said with a rueful chuckle. He took a swig of beer and continued, "You know, sometimes I worry that I might be too attached to my work…"

"You are."

"No, let me finish! Obviously, I think that it's good to be invested in what you're doing, because that's how you produce quality work. But if you're *too* invested, then you get all angry and depressed whenever the tiniest little thing goes awry – and then you have to sit down and ask yourself how it is that you are thirty-eight years old and chucking a tantrum because your browser didn't load correctly – though I give myself credit for *asking* at least, because you would not believe how many of my peers will get just as upset about *their* projects, and yet none of *them* ever seem to have a problem with that – I mean, here we are, sitting in our cosy little tax-funded offices, richer and healthier and safer than just about anybody else on the planet – and we break down over idiotic things like botched calculations and lizard blood samples and – and *memes* that people put on the internet! I mean, for crying out loud, are we even contributing *anything* to our civilisation that's worth getting this worked up over? Do you think al-Khwarizmi ever got this cranky when he was inventing algebra? Did Aquinas have a fit every time he misnumbered a bullet point in the *Summa*?!!"

"Probably did, knowing him," Toni said wryly.

"That's not the point," Henry sighed, gazing mournfully into the depths of his beer bottle as though hoping it were a crystal ball that foretold a brighter future.

"Well what *is* the point?" his friend asked, with the unceasing patience of Stoics and saints.

"The point, old chum, is that if I go to this extreme in my enthusiasm for my work, I succeed only in making myself miserable. But then if I don't do *that*, I go to the opposite extreme and can't even bring myself to get out of bed in the morning because the work doesn't matter, nothing matters, Freddie Mercury was right all along, nothing *really* matters, so I may as well just *die*."

Toni said nothing, but arched an eyebrow and waited for him to continue.

"I know what you're thinking," he began.

"Probably not."

"Shush, you. If you're thinking that the way forward lies between these two extremes, then you'd be right. But I know that as well as you do, but *knowing* it doesn't make it any easier to *do* it, and if anything, I just end up even more frustrated at myself than I would have been if I hadn't known it! So what's the point?!"

Toni shrugged. "You tell me, Hen." She adjusted her reel and downed the last of her beer, as unperturbed by her companion's silence as she had been by his outburst. "This is why I couldn't be stuffed with uni. All that study gets you thinking about yourself *way* too much. It's like…you delude yourself into believing that, y'know, you're contemplating Truth or something, but really, you're just indulging your own narcissism."

"I am *not* narcissistic," Henry said hotly.

"Yeah you are, you big goose. Why else do you come out here every other weekend and go on and on at me about your interior life? You're not in your twenties any more, you know, you've got no reason to be having this kind of existential crisis."

"What about a mid-life crisis?" he sulked.

"Nah, you don't get one of those."

Despite himself, Henry laughed. "Ripped off again." He wasn't really hurt by her polemic; they had been friends for long enough that he had learned not to take anything she said too personally. But he was irritated with his own feelings, because he knew that she was partly right.

"Just stop worrying about it, man," said Toni. "You're *always* worrying about something, asking all these questions and worrying about the answers. But what if you don't need the answers? The questions'll work themselves out eventually, whether you worry about 'em or not."

"You sound like a stoner," said Henry.

Toni chuckled. "Man, you have no idea. If drugs didn't have side effects, I'd do 'em all the time."

Henry just shook his head. "Degenerate."

They settled into amicable silence for a while longer.

The shadows lengthened.

Toni caught a fish.

Henry threw his rod down into the bottom of the boat in despair. "What am I going to *do* though?!"

Toni made an exasperated noise. "Just let it go, Henry! What's wrong with two different people working off the same data anyway? I thought everybody did that! Look, you and Trish, y'know, you're individuals, and you're both going to write completely different papers about your Golden Yamcha or whatever it was… Man, who *cares*? Fricken' Leibniz and Newton both came up with calculus at the same time, and no one cares about *either* of them now! Just write the damn thing and see what happens!"

Henry stared at her.

She reached into the esky and passed him another bottle. "Have a Yak. It'll make you feel better."

"Thanks," said Henry, somewhat dazed. "I think I will."

Chapter Eight – Eden

Today

Dawn 'comes early, with rosy fingers / When she appeared,' Henry arose from his blankets and decided – arbitrarily, to be sure, but with as much confidence as if it had been ordained by the Almighty – that today would be a good day.

He filled his pockets with choc-almond muesli bars, watered the geraniums on the window sill, and headed off to the university, where he spent a glorious few hours working alone in the office before Joey came in the door, wearing a psychedelic beanie that hurt his brain to look at. She had shadows under her eyes, and was carrying a large garden gnome under one arm. "Hi Dr B.!" she said. "How are you today, out of ten?"

Henry pondered this question. "Today," he said, with a grand sweeping gesture, "I choose to be a nine."

Her eyes widened. "That's so profound."

He gave a merry chuckle. "And how about you, Joey? How are *you* out of ten?"

"Well, I couldn't get to sleep last night, because I found a slug in my bed and I couldn't work out how it got there, so I kept thinking there must be some sort of breach in my bedroom walls that was letting all these slugs in, and the thought of it was just too horrible to contemplate! But I kept contemplating it anyway – and then I got out of bed this morning and I remembered it's my friend Katia's birthday on Saturday and I hadn't got her anything, and I never know what to get people for their birthdays because all *I* ever want is a subscription to the *New York Times* so I can do all their crossword puzzles, and no one ever gives me that because all my friends think that's a really lame present, so I can't exactly get that for someone else – so I went to Bunnings and bought her this nice garden gnome. She doesn't have a garden, but she does have a lot of pot plants on her dining table, so I thought she could put him there. So all in all, I would say I'm a solid seven and a half."

"That's the way!" said Henry.

"Although," she added sombrely, "I just remembered today's my last day helping out on your project, so that does put me back down to about a six."

Henry was stunned. He'd known, of course, that they would finish collating all the forum data today – but he'd forgotten that this marked the end of Joey's contract. How had the time gone by so quickly?

"Oh," he finally said. "We'd better have some cake or something then, hadn't we? I'm sorry – I should have thought – I mean——"

He was (mercifully) cut off as Louisa Honeysett materialised out of nowhere and made them both jump.

"Hey homies!" she said, handing them an iced latte and pair of piccolos respectively. "What are we talking about?"

"It's my last day today," Joey said, accepting the beverage with mournful gratitude.

Louisa's face fell. "Oh, true."

"I was just bewailing my lack of foresight in not providing a cake," said Henry.

"A cake?" Louisa repeated. "What are you, five? *This*, my friends, calls for a parmy and a pint! C'mon, who's keen?"

Henry looked at Joey, who grinned back.

"Alright," said Henry, smiling despite himself, "then we shall lament this season's passing over dinner at the Quartermaster's Arms – tonight!"

∴

Tonight

The Quartermaster's Arms was the smallest pub in the city; but as it was a Monday night, there were plenty of tables available. Henry et al. selected a corner booth near the upstairs window, which afforded a pleasant view of the empty street outside.

"I'll get the first round," said Henry, and he wended his way towards the bar, thoughts of farewells and godstonks and garden gnomes all melding together inside his head. He was still fumbling about in his laptop bag for his wallet (his pockets being reserved exclusively for muesli bars) when the bartender emerged from the back room.

"G'day, what can I get…*Henry?*"

Startled, Henry looked up and met the eye of a woman his own age, with wavy brown hair and a plaid shirt, who was staring at him in delighted disbelief.

His jaw dropped. "Eden!"

"It *is* you." Her eyes were dancing. "It's been such a long time. I haven't seen you since…"

"Since about 5:00AM on the first day of the new millennium," Henry said quietly.

"Wow," she said. "I can't believe it's been that long."

∴

About 5:00AM on the First Day of the New Millennium

"I can't do this any more."

Henry turned to look at her, as dawn's rosy fingers brushed the hilltop on which they lay together, clothes long since soaked with dew. In the early morning light, her face looked ancient and worn, like all the life had been drained from it.

Who had done this to her?

Had he?

He looked away.

"Yeah," he said. "Neither can I."

∴

Tonight

"You're looking well," Henry said, smiling.

She beamed at him. "Thanks, you too. Now, what can I get you?"

"Oh, er, yes, sorry. Three pints of the Seven Sheds, please." He fell into silence, watching her pour. Then he asked, "How long have you been working here?"

"I just started yesterday," she said brightly, wiping a dribble of foam from the outside of one of the glasses. "Before that, I was a manager at Kmart. But I found it rather uninspired work, and in the end, I decided to leave the K-way behind and seek my own way instead. That'll be thirty-three, thanks."

"Right," said he, still too dazed at seeing her again to articulate anything of consequence.

"What about you, what have you been up to?"

"Same old thing, really," he said. "Wrote a few papers on cultural priming, metymology, cryptonomics, that sort of stuff. I'm doing a project on godstonks at the moment."

"Nice," she said. "And what about Trish? Is she still around?"

He shook his head. "Would that it were so. She moved to Macquarie University a while back. We're still in the same field, though. Actually, we're pretty much doing the same project at the moment. She beat me to the findings, but my conclusion will *destroy* hers."

She smiled. "I bet it will."

Henry nodded, gathered up the three glasses with some difficulty, and turned to leave.

"Hey," Eden said, halting him in his tracks, "I'm having a birthday party this Saturday. Thirty-nine is a humble age, but I think it's still worth celebrating. I'd love it if you could come, and we could catch up properly."

Henry did not immediately reply. Some part of him had always wondered what this moment would be like when it came – if it came. He was surprised to find that, beyond the initial shock, he felt quite calm. There was no surge of euphoria, no anxiety, no anger. There was almost nothing at all. But then, it had been so long since everything had happened, none of it really seemed important any more. He smiled. "I'd like that."

He then returned to the corner booth, where Louisa and Joey were deep in conversation about ludonarrative dissonance. He set their beers down on the table and apologised for keeping them waiting.

"Who was that, Henry?" Louisa asked.

Henry kept his eyes on his drink. "Just a friend from years ago."

∴

Years Ago

"There's a new girl in my music tech class," Trish said. "She just moved here from Cairns."

Henry, halfway through eating his lunch, grunted by way of answer. It was unseasonably sunny, and the heat was making him sleepy.

"She's kind of weird," Trish went on. "But she seems alright. Never says anything, though."

"No one says anything in *any* of our classes," rejoined Henry.

"I guess so."

They were silent for a while. Then Trish continued, "She's weird, though. Like, she wears these long dresses and cardigans, like my grandma. But she doesn't seem like one of those typical Bohemian wannabes. She's weird. But she seems alright."

Henry pointed across the courtyard. "Is that her?"

"Yep."

The new girl was sitting by the fence, a little way away from the other students, reading a book.

"See what I mean?" said Trish. "She looks so edgy. But when you look at her up close, she doesn't seem that edgy. In music tech she's just sort of…there."

"Why do you care so much?" Henry asked.

"I don't, I'm just bored."

Henry stood up. "I'm going to go and talk to her."

"What?"

But he had already wandered over to where the new girl was sitting. She looked up as he approached, but said nothing.

"Hey," said Henry.

"Hello," she said with an easy smile, unperturbed by the interruption.

"Um." Henry put his hands into his pockets, unsure what it was that he had come to say to her. "How come you're sitting over here by yourself?"

She grinned sheepishly. "I prefer to dwell on the fringes of communion."

"The what?"

"You know, when you're part of the group, but you don't need to be in the middle of things to prove it." Her words might have sounded obnoxious coming from some other year twelve girl in a long dress, but she spoke with a levity that completely undermined any pretension.

Henry just stared at her.

After a moment, she chuckled. "My name's Eden. What's yours?"

"Henry," he said.

She smiled. "Nice to meet you."

∴

Later Tonight

Henry arrived home in a stupor, head swirling with meetings and partings and dark spiced ale. His mother Adelaide drifted past him as he crossed the threshold.

"Henry, my love, how are you?" she asked, brushing an immaterial hand against his cheek.

"You'll never guess who I bumped into tonight," her son replied, meeting her gaze with half-focussed eyes.

"Who, darling?"

"Eden."

His mother started. "Eden Thomas?"

"I don't know any other Edens, Mum."

"But you haven't seen her since you were doing your undergrad!"

"I know," Henry said patiently. "That's why I was surprised to see her tonight. She's a bartender at the Arms now."

Adelaide regarded her son with a mixture of curiosity and sadness. "Did she seem well?"

"I think so. And it was nice to see her again." He paused. "She invited me to a birthday party on Saturday. I might go, actually."

He could see her sadness win over curiosity, and found himself oddly touched. "Well, have fun," she said. "But Henry…"

"Yes, Mum?"

"Tread carefully with that one. You know how bad it was when it – ended."

The first time, Henry thought.

"Don't worry," he said aloud. "We've both grown up a lot since then."

His mother nodded and said nothing, but he could tell she wasn't convinced. And for once, he couldn't blame her.

∴

Tomorrow

"It's so quiet in here without Joey," said Henry.

"Why, am I not good enough company for you?" Louisa teased.

"Hey now, you were the one who wanted extra help in the first place, remember?"

"Yeah, because my back was aching from *carrying* this project. Do you even do *any* work around here?"

"Nah, I'm just here to look pretty, write the abstract, and take all the credit."

She laughed. "Yeah, alright. Come on, you mopey old thing, let's get this methods section written up."

"S'pose so."

∴

Years Ago

"Dude, you've been completely off the grid lately," said Trish. "What's keeping you so busy?"

Henry shrugged. "Nothing much."

"I tried calling you on Saturday, but you didn't pick up."

"Oh, sorry. I was hanging out with Eden."

"You're *always* hanging out with Eden. Did you get sick of me or something?"

"'Course not. I just like talking to her. Anyway, I'm here now, aren't I?"

"Only because she's on holiday in Cairns!"

Henry said nothing. He knew Trish wouldn't get it, because *he* didn't either. It wasn't like he sat around comparing his friends. (He didn't have enough friends, for one thing.) But there was something he found compelling in Eden which he didn't find in anyone else. He liked the sorts of conversations they had together.

∴

The Sorts of Conversations They Had Together

"How do you feel about sultanas?" Henry asked.

"Well, I wouldn't look at one and yearn for it," said Eden.

Henry laughed for a very long time.

∴

Tomorrow

"I like how you always get the ones without sultanas," said Louisa, as they partook of their mid-afternoon muesli bars together.

"Sultanas are overrated," Henry said thickly, mouth full of apricot and cashew.

"Yeah, I'll cop that. Raisins are worse, though. Don't even get me started on raisin bread."

"The devil's bread."

"The proof that we live in a fallen world."

Henry chuckled. "Ah, Louisa, I'm glad I have you around to bounce my nonsense off."

She gave him a wry look. "Truly, that is the greatest of my virtues."

"No, I'm being serious. If not for people like you, I'd be frightfully boring. All I would ever talk about is memetics this and godstonks that, and be quite oblivious to the fact that no one asked."

She raised an eyebrow at him. "Now *that's* not true. You're fun! Aren't you going to a party or something this Saturday?"

He snorted. "Yes, I'm expecting it to be an absolute rager by every standard."

"That's the spirit."

∴

An Absolute Rager By Every Standard

"Dude, this party really sucks!" Trish yelled over the music.

"What did you expect?" Henry shouted back. "It's *Jackson's* eighteenth, it was never going to be the pinnacle of culture!"

"I can't hear you, I'm going to get a drink!" she yelled.

He watched her vanish into the crowd of sweaty bodies, then decided to go out for some air.

Eden met him in the yard, where the shadows from the bonfire touched the back fence. "Hello."

"Hey."

They stood in silence for a few minutes and watched their friends laughing and drinking by the fire.

"Are you okay?" Eden asked.

He didn't answer.

"I only ask because you have this…heaviness, like this weight upon you, like you're carrying something really big. I've felt that before. I was wondering if I could do anything to help."

Henry let out a long breath. "It's just…that I have all these things I have to worry about, and I feel like there's never enough time to invest in all of them, so no matter how well I'm doing in one area, I'm always letting myself down in another. Like, if I hang out with one friend, another one gets upset. If I focus on studying, then *all* my friends suffer, and if I *don't* study, my parents get mad. And the older we get, the more things we have to worry about, so it's just going to get harder and harder. So what's the point of trying at anything if I can't enjoy myself because I always feel guilty about something else that I'm neglecting?"

"Well, whose voice is that, speaking those things to you?" Eden said gently. "Is that the Henry who knows that he is good and people love him no matter what he does? Or is that the Henry who feels like he has to earn it?"

"It's the Henry who wants to stop *thinking* about these things and just be a good person without it being so much effort," he groaned.

She laid a hand on his arm. "It'll happen," she said. "With practice."

His skin prickled at her touch. He forced himself to meet her eye, and found her smiling at him.

My God, he thought, she's beautiful.

He reached out to touch her face, and she did not stop him.

Beautiful.

∴

Tomorrow

There came a knock at the office door.

"Come in," said Henry, glad to be temporarily rescued from the arduous task of drafting his abstract.

Lo and behold, in walked Joey.

"Hi!" quoth she.

"Joey!" said Henry. "Back so soon?"

"Yeah, I forgot something," Joey began.

"Was it this copy of *BIONICLE Legends 4: Legacy of Evil?*" Louisa enquired, producing that very item from beneath her desk.

"No! …Well, yes, I forgot about that too. But actually, Dr B., I've been meaning to ask – that is, I was just wondering…would you consider being my Ph.D. supervisor?"

Henry was floored. "I – well – I…yes, I'd love to!"

"Hurray!" said Joey. "Thanks a whole heap, Doc – thanks, Lou," (as Louisa threw the book at her and she caught it precariously with the tips of her fingers), "I'll let you go now, I'm actually running late to a protest, but we'll chat soon and work out all the details. Ciao ciao!" And she threw them a double peace sign and left.

"That's a bit cute," said Louisa.

"Maybe I am fun after all," said Henry.

"Of course you are, old man. Come this Saturday, you shall rise like a phoenix from the ashes, and become one with your past self."

Crikey, I hope not, Henry thought.

∴

When It Ended (The First Time)

He knocked twice.

Eden opened the door. "Henry, we have exams *tomorrow*, why are you here?"

"We need to break up," he said.

They stood on either side of the door for a long time and looked at each other.

"Why?" she finally asked.

He dropped his eyes. "It's just that…I have a lot on my mind, and I can't think when I'm with you."

"I don't understand."

"Neither do I!" he yelled, balling his fists in frustration. "That's the *point*, I don't understand anything about you – us – any of it! I'm trying to work out what my purpose is, and what I want to do with my life, and whether God comes into any of it – but when I'm with *you*, I can't even think about what to study after dinner – I can't think at *all*, except about how you make me feel – which doesn't make sense to me either, because you're not even my type, if I did have a type, which I don't, because I don't want a relationship, I don't want to get married, I don't want to be a father – *I don't want any of it!*"

"Fine," she said, angrily blinking back tears. "Go away and do your *thinking* then, if I'm such an obstacle to you. I'm sorry I'm not the fountain of clarity that you wanted. I'm sorry I came into the picture right when you *finally* hit puberty. But don't blame me just because you aren't ready to be an adult. That's your problem, not mine."

"Eden——"

The door slammed shut.

He turned to go, feeling even more confused than when he'd arrived.

∴

This Saturday (Morning)

Henry sat in his study alone, gazing blankly at the pages of a book of semiotic analyses of mid-2010s MMORPGs and not taking any of it in, his stomach churning faintly, and wondered why he was feeling so nervous.

After all, he reminded himself, heedless of the fact that he was grinding his teeth, everything that had happened back then, all that mess – it had been so many years ago. Surely it could have no hold over him now.

And yet…

∴

Years Ago

He knocked thrice.

The door opened, and there she was, looking much the same as she had always done. Neither of them acknowledged the last time they had stood here, less than a year ago. "I heard about what happened…" She didn't say 'to your parents.'

He nodded, carefully avoiding her eye. "May I come in?"

"Of course."

She moved aside to let him through, and closed the door behind them.

∴

This Saturday (Evening)

He knocked four times.

"Henry!" said Eden, joyfully throwing open the door. "I'm so glad you could make it. Come on in, and I'll introduce you to my other friends."

The guests were gathered in the lounge room, which was lit with scented tealight candles and decorated with sprigs of wattle flowers. Gypsy jazz played softly in the background, filtering in amidst the conversation in a warm, unobtrusive way.

Henry allowed himself to be guided towards a chair and plied with charcuterie and champagne. A pleasant hour or so ensued, in which he acquainted himself with the hodgepodge of friends and relations who had been summoned for the night's revels. By and by, however, people began to rise from their chairs and move about, and Henry seized the opportunity to pursue a conversation with Eden.

She stood by the window, which looked out upon the distant waterfront, and, as he approached, smiled up at him as though she had been waiting for him. "It's so good to see you again," she said. "You haven't aged a day."

He laughed. "That is blatantly untrue. The last part, anyway," he amended. "It's good to see you, too. Did you ever go back and finish your degree?"

"Not exactly. I took a couple of years off, then came back and switched degrees a few times, and ended up graduating at thirty with the most outlandish array of electives you ever did see. I worked a few different jobs, went to Thailand for a bit, wrote a memoir of *appalling* literary quality, then decided I just wanted to do something simple for a while, and that's when I started working at Kmart."

"Wow," he said. "And here I've been doing the exact same thing for twenty years."

She shrugged. "There's pros and cons in both. You always did seem like you were made for stability."

"But that's why I liked you so much," he said. "You brought out the spontaneity in me."

"Brought it out, or projected mine onto you?"

"If anyone was projecting anything, it was me."

She laughed. "*That's* true. You're all gentlemanly and dignified now, but you were a very angsty boy once."

"I'm still angsty now," he grinned. "You should hear me going off at Toni when I go up to visit her."

"I believe it."

"I think it's in my nature. Just like fear is in yours."

She turned away to face the window. "Is it?"

"That's what you said to me once. At that New Year's party."

"Oh yes," she said, "I remember."

∴

That New Year's Party

It was almost time for the countdown. He'd had one too many drinks, and was slumped in a beanbag in the corner, listening to someone's housemates screaming "Auld Lang Syne" at the tops of their lungs, even though it wasn't midnight yet. (They'd been singing it on and off since 6:00PM.) Trish was back in the library, studying. He was beginning to wish he'd stayed with her.

He thought he heard someone say his name. He looked up, but couldn't figure out who had spoken.

Then he saw her – Eden – standing in the doorway across the room, half-hidden by a knot of engineering students who were shoving cigarettes up someone's nose.

They locked eyes as the countdown started.

Ten…nine…

He clambered unsteadily to his feet –

Eight…seven…six…

And stumbled through the crowd towards her –

Five…four…three…

His hands scrabbled to catch hold of her – his fingers weren't working properly – he heard himself speaking her name –

Two…one…

The room around them erupted with cheering as the old millennium passed into the new, but he heard nothing save the pounding of blood in his ears as he kissed her.

∴

"I can't do this any more," she said, hours later. "It's always come and go with you. You come to me when you're sad, and you tell me about your feelings, and you love me. And then you leave. It's not fair."

He looked at her, and saw by the cold light of dawn how true her words were. A tear rolled down his cheek. "I didn't mean for it to turn out this way," he said. "I *want* to stay with you, Eden. But I'm scared."

"So am I," she said. "It's in my nature. But you can't keep messing me around like this. Every time you leave, you take a piece of me with you. Keep it up and one day there'll be nothing left for you to come back to."

They were both weeping now, hot tears mingling with the cold dew.

"I won't leave," Henry choked. "It'll be different this time."

She took his hand in hers, but shook her head gently. "I can't do this," she repeated, "any more."

He looked away. "Yeah," he said finally, his words little more than a strangled whisper. "Neither can I."

∴

This Saturday (Evening)

"Listen, Eden," said Henry, "I truly am sorry. About everything. I was an idiot back then, but I still should have known better than to treat you the way I did. I don't deserve it, but…will you forgive me?"

She smiled. "Of course."

"Thank you." Feeling suddenly awkward, he helped himself to a plate of hors-d'oeuvres and decided it was about time to change the subject. "So, how about that game this arvo? The Hurricanes played really well, I thought."

"I still love you, Henry," said Eden. "I always have."

Henry choked on his saveloy.

Chapter Nine – Henry Does In Fact Have Male Friends

Once a month, on a Sunday evening after dinner, Henry would get together with two of his closest friends, Mark and Donovan, and ponder life's great questions over a cup of tea and some Digestive Thins.

The three of them had met in their mid-twenties, through the commingling of various social and university circles, and, though divided on many points over the years, had remained united by their shared pursuit of Truth and their love of plain biscuits. They each took turns hosting their monthly gatherings, and consequently, Mark and Donovan were among the very select few people who knew about the Biddlesnoot-Bloomington ancestral curse.

This month it was Donovan's turn to host (something Mark and Henry always looked forward to, as Donovan had the nicest lounge room), and so it was he who, answering his front door and seeing in Henry's face that something was amiss, was the first to ask what had happened and receive a straight answer.

"I saw Eden last night," said Henry. "She's working at the Quartermaster's Arms now, and she invited me to her birthday party and told me that she's still in love with me."

Donovan blinked twice. "She what?"

"She said, 'I still love you, and I always have.'"

"And what did *you* say?"

"Uhm, well, I was in the middle of eating something when she told me, and at that point it went down the wrong way, and I sort of started choking to death, and by the time I'd recovered and she'd gone to get a glass of water, it didn't really seem like a good time to finish the conversation."

Donovan sighed. "We're going to need some *real* drinks for this."

He led the way through to the back of the house, pausing in the dining room as Henry exchanged greetings with the rest of the family. They entered the lounge, and Henry saw that Mark had already arrived and was sitting in the armchair nearest the fire, perusing a large volume of the collected works of Flannery O'Connor. He replaced this on the shelf as they hove in sight. "'A Good Man is Hard to Find,'" he said. "Discuss."

"He is," said Donovan. "That's why I had to settle for *you* two galahs."

"Says the guy who ordered cauliflower soup at the Fern Tree Tavern."

"That was *ten* years ago."

"And it's still a travesty."

"It was nice soup."

"You don't go to a tavern and order soup! You order a schnitty, or a parmy, or a big juicy steak!"

"Well I felt like having soup!"

Mark looked to Henry for support. "*You're* the expert on canon law. Tell this man how wrong he is."

Henry laughed and shook his head. "The Catholic Church has scant few teachings on the subject of cauliflower soup, I'm afraid."

"Add that to the list of reasons why I never joined," said Donovan.

"Don't be cheeky," said Mark. "One day you're going to stand before the Pearly Gates and explain to St Peter why you chose cauliflower soup over a nice chicken schnitzel with chips and gravy."

"An eschatologically dubious assertion," Henry offered.

"Don't think your fancy words are going to save you being lectured," retorted Donovan.

"I'm *defending* you!"

"Yes, but it's *you* that needs defending, which is what I was getting around to before Mark over here decided to interrupt and have a go at my dietary decisions."

"Why, what's he done this time?" asked Mark, as Henry threw up his hands in feigned despair.

"*This* feckless oik," said Donovan, producing a bottle of port from a nearby cabinet and gesticulating at Henry with it, "had a beautiful woman confess her undying love to him last night, and he just *ignored* her. Now what d'you reckon St Peter would have to say about that, Mark?"

"Dunno," said Mark, as Henry sighed and Donovan poured the drinks. "Depends on whether she was single or not."

"You're both making far too much out of it," Henry protested. "We were at a *dinner party*! You can't just go and make romantic declarations at a dinner party and expect them to be met with any sort of robust discourse! And why'd she have to say it, anyway? No one asked her to! *I* certainly didn't ask her to! I was just minding my own business, and then she had the *nerve* to go and…"

As Henry spluttered into incoherence, Mark took the opportunity to ask, "So who are we talking about?"

"Eden Thomas," said Donovan.

"*Oh…*" Mark stared at Henry. "Since when are you and *she* talking again?"

"We aren't 'talking again,'" Henry said testily. "I just bumped into her the other day, and she invited me to her birthday party."

"And you went," said Donovan.

"Yes, I went! I had no reason not to, and it was nice to see her again, *as a friend*."

"Did your mum chuck a fit?" asked Mark.

Henry let out a long breath of air. "She didn't ask about it when I got home last night. Just looked at me and went off to do whatever she does."

"What *does* she do these days?"

"Haunts the garden, mainly. She likes talking to the plants. We have the finest roses in the country, thanks to her. Or so I'm told, at least."

"You're both changing the subject," said Donovan. "You know you can't just leave that poor woman hanging, Henry. What are you going to say to her?"

"I don't know," Henry groaned. "What was she *thinking*, anyway? Surely she knows nothing's changed!"

"Well, *has* nothing changed?" asked Mark.

"*Yes!*" Henry said emphatically. "I'm perfectly happy being single, and I don't see why that's so hard for everybody to understand. I don't harass other people about *their* relationships, I don't care about any of that – I just want to look at memes on the internet and write papers about them. Am I hurting anyone by doing that? Am I failing to live up to my potential? No! Am I living out my vocation? *I* think so! Why can't women just leave me alone and stop being attracted to me? I mean, what did I do to deserve or encourage that, beyond showing the merest modicum of basic human decency?!"

"'Women'?" Mark echoed. "Are there *more* you haven't told us about?"

"No, that's not what I… Look, it doesn't matter. I just wish she hadn't said anything, that's all. Everything would have been so much easier if we'd just let bygones be bygones."

"Henry, old mate," Donovan said quietly, "you can't expect poor Eden to just *know* how you feel. You two haven't seen each other for nearly twenty years! Anything could have changed in that time, are you really going to blame her for taking a chance?"

Henry looked away. "S'pose not."

"Right. Well then, you'd better have a chat with her soon and sort things out, or you're going to have to find yourself a new pub, aren't you?"

Henry growled. "Let's just go back to talking about soup, I'm tired of this."

"Man doesn't appreciate fraternal correction," Mark said *sotto voce* to Donovan, who laughed.

∴

Henry returned home from his outing in a bleak mood. To be sure, he appreciated the truth of his friends' words, however mocking, and he certainly wasn't going to neglect his duty of care to Eden as her friend.

But holy dooley, he just *didn't* want to have that conversation! Why did these things have to be so much effort? Why must honesty be so uncomfortable? Why couldn't everyone just think in exactly the same way and be able to understand each other without having to *talk* about it? (He had once, during his late adolescence, overheard one of his peers on the school bus demand of her neighbour, "Why must we be burdened with human emotions?" And although he hated to admit it [for his philosophical convictions demanded a holistic view of the human person], there was a small, primordial part of him that sympathised with this lament.)

So he decided, in his wisdom, that he would think about the problem later.

It dawned upon him that yodelling would be a useful skill to learn, and he spent a happy hour or so in one of the more secluded drawing rooms, looking at YouTube tutorials and trying out their methods for himself, before Uncle Bertram materialised from beneath the floorboards and clapped him (imperceptibly) on the shoulder. "Henry, my boy, would you please come and help me water my orchids?"

Henry rolled his eyes, knowing full well that his uncle didn't need the help, but often asked for it as an excuse to spend time together. "*You* and Mum and your *bloody* plants, I've just about had it up to *here* with – no, I jest, of course I'll water your orchids for you, Uncle." And he cheerfully abandoned the beginnings of what might have been a long and illustrious musical career and followed his ghostly uncle into the greenhouse, where they walked quietly amongst the orchids for a little while, Henry carrying the watering can and Uncle Bertram administering gentle directions as to how much water each specimen needed.

Presently, however, Uncle Bertram said, "Your mother spoke to me earlier today."

Henry grunted and said nothing.

"She's a bit worried about you."

"As is her right and privilege as a mother."

Uncle Bertram affected a sigh, though of course he did not have working lungs any more. "You know I don't like to interfere, Henry."

"I know, Uncle."

"But I wouldn't be much of a brother-in-law if I didn't listen to her, at least."

"Yes."

Silence.

"*She* doesn't like to interfere either. Not with this, anyway."

Grunt.

"That's why she came to me instead of you."

Henry put down the watering can and looked his uncle in the ethereal eye. "Uncle, I believe that all of you care about me. I really do. That's why I've stayed here all these years. But I'm thirty-nine in September. I have my friends, and I have the Lord. I don't need you and Mum and Dad and everyone else all constantly checking up on me and asking about my feelings and thinking that my whole life is going to fall apart over some woman. Or women. Or lack thereof."

Uncle Bertram chuckled. "I know, I know. I wasn't the marrying type either. And believe me, they gave me a whole lot more trouble about it when I was your age than they give *you* now."

"Well then, what exactly are you trying to tell me, Uncle? What is the point of this conversation?"

"Just go and talk to your mum, Henry. She'd appreciate it."

∴

So Henry left Uncle Bertram in the greenhouse and went to find his mother in the garden. She was telling the roses the story of how her grandfather and grandmother had met: "And then, you know, he rode past on his motorcycle and said, 'Lady, I am a brigand, but I feel the enchanting power of your beauty. You are free!' Or something to that effect, anyway. Oh, Henry, darling, I didn't see you there."

"G'day, Mum," he said. "Still talking to the roses?"

She smiled at him. "They are such needy creatures. They crave constant intellectual stimulation."

"I can appreciate that."

He sat down beside her and contemplated the flowers awhile.

"Mum," he said slowly, "you know, everything that happened between me and Eden…it was a *very* long time ago. It's not going to happen again."

"I know, dearest, but…you weren't yourself when you were seeing her."

"Yes, because I was young, and because I didn't know who I *was*. Not because of her."

"Then what happened last night? You weren't yourself when you came home."

Henry looked down at his hands. "Nothing *happened*, exactly. It was always just going to be difficult, seeing her again after so long. But that's part of life, and that's alright." Bolstered by his own words, he stood up. "Anyway, I'm working tomorrow, so I'd best be off to bed."

"Goodnight then."

"Love you."

He made his way inside, feeling considerably less agitated than before, and, as he ascended the staircase towards his bedroom, opened up his phone and sent a message to Eden: *Perhaps we'd better talk soon.*

The reply was almost instantaneous: *Tomorrow after work?*

Sure, see you then.

Chapter Ten – All Is Well

The cock crowed three times. Louisa woke up to the smell of freshly baked bread, and knew that all was well. She yawned widely, tugged a knot out of her hair, threw on a big fluffy dressing-gown over her jumper and track pants (it was cold on the mountain), and made her way into the kitchen, where Nonna was pulling a tray of focaccia out of the oven.

"Good morning, *bambina*," Nonna said, smiling at her as she appeared.

"Morning, Nonna. That smells good. What did you put in it?"

"Rosemary, from the garden."

"Nice. I can't wait to try it." Louisa inhaled deeply, sighed with satisfaction, then went over to the side door, beside which stood a pair of old gumboots that had once belonged to Nonno but were now considered communal. She put these on and opened the door. Her breath fogged as she stepped outside, but the air smelled of pine and petrichor and woodfire smoke, and the crisp winter cold only added to her delight.

She grabbed a bucket of feed and squelched through the muddy yard to the chicken coop, where Chauntecleer, Penny, Bong, and Pertelote awaited her morning offering with indifferent scratching and ruffling of feathers.

"G'day, chookens," Louisa said, tipping a generous portion of grain into their bowl. (She had addressed them thus since the age of three, when she had vociferated her first sentence, "Chooken go cluck!") They did not deign to reply, but she was unoffended by their silence.

After that, she milked the cows, Annie and Clarabel, who showed significantly more gratitude for her attentions. When she returned indoors, Nonna had set the kitchen table for breakfast. They said grace, then Nonna heaped her plate with eggs, bacon, focaccia and mushrooms, while Louisa filled their mugs with strong black coffee.

"The woodpile is getting a little sparse, I noticed yesterday," said Nonna, after they had eaten awhile in silence. "I was wondering if you could…?"

Louisa nodded. "I'll chop some more before I head off to work."

Nonna patted her hand. "*Tu sei un angelo.*"

"*no u,*" Louisa grinned.

"And what are you doing at work today?"

"Well, I think we're on track to finish our paper, because all that's left is just revising the intro and conclusion, which Henry will do most of, while I go over and proofread the whole thing. Then we're going to submit it to the top-ranking technocultural journal, and we'll finally be done! Oh, and the new edition of /*REL*/ gets delivered today, so I'll bring back a copy and you can read my article on Aquinas memes if you want."

"Wonderful!" said Nonna. "I'll bake a cake and we can celebrate together when you get home."

"Sounds good!" said Louisa. "Alright, I'd better get moving. Thanks for breakfast; the rosemary was a great addition."

She stacked the empty plates and deposited them in the sink, before donning the gumboots again and heading out to the woodshed, where she spent a happy half-hour splitting logs and thinking about nothing of consequence. Academia would always be her first love, but she nonetheless found great satisfaction in manual labour and how it drew one out of the mind and into the body – which was one reason why she, of all her siblings and cousins, had elected to stay on the farm with Nonna and keep her company in her old age. A colleague had once suggested to her that all acts of charity are really based on self-interest. She wasn't entirely sure whether she agreed, but either way, there seemed to be a connection between self-sacrifice and human flourishing, which had always filled her with fascination and gratitude.

When she had finished stacking the woodpile, she went inside, had a shower and got dressed, kissed Nonna goodbye and drove down the mountain to work, knowing still that all was well.

∴

Upon her arrival, Louisa was astonished to find Henry's desk empty, and showing no signs of recent habitation. She checked her watch, just to be sure that it was in fact 8:30AM on a weekday. It was! And yet the office was deserted? This was unprecedented! Was he ill? Was he *dead?* Had Trish Mackenzie flown in from Sydney in the middle of the night to strangle him as he lay sleeping?

Thoroughly disoriented, she pulled out her phone and messaged him: *where u at??* But there was no reply. So she tried calling him, and again received no answer. This was worrying. However, he was a grown man and could look after himself; and she had work to do, regardless of his whereabouts. So she threw her coat over the back of a chair, opened up her laptop and began reading mechanically through their nearly-completed paper (which by this point they'd christened 'Gold Yamre: An Origin Myth'), checking for typos.

By and by, there was a knock at the door and Joey Carter appeared.

"Hi Lou!" she said. "Where's Dr B.?"

"Not here yet," said Louisa. "Talking about Ph.D. things?"

"Yeah," said Joey, taking a seat by the door. "He said to meet here around nine."

"That's okay, I'm sure he'll be in soon. How was *BIONICLE Legends 4?*"

"Bro, the Piraka really slap, but it feels a bit redundant to have an entire novel devoted to the backstory of characters who are sidelined immediately, like, two books later."

"Yeah that's true, they kind of just get turned into snakes and then fused into a guy who's entirely irrelevant and never appears in any of the books, so you have to wonder what was the point."

"The point was to make six dudes responsible for a massive amount of stuff in-universe, which, if you ask me, totally undermines the whole appeal of the franchise, which is to create this immense sense of scale."

"Mm, I always liked bonkle as an example of multimedia narrative, but not as an actual thing to read for fun. Give me *Nicomachean Ethics* over that any day."

Joey laughed. "Modern philosophers like Farshtey will never live up to the classics."

"Not until Farshtey acknowledges that the Barraki were by far the best villains, anyway. But enough of these trivialities! Have you decided on your thesis topic yet?"

"Well, I'm still in the middle of narrowing it down, but I want to do something on lolcow discourse as a way of social engineering."

"Oh, like scapegoating?"

"Yeah, basically. Although there's more to it than that, because the memetic indices add to the layers of metanarrative, which allows the scapegoating process to happen on multiple levels of cultural consciousness."

"Huh," said Louisa. "Solid."

"Thanks!" said Joey. "I think it's a winner."

"What's a winner?" asked Henry, tromping through the door in a state of bleary dishevelment. "Hello, by the way. I'm so sorry I'm late, I didn't sleep very well last night. Joey, so good to see you again. Let's chat in the staff room, I'm really craving an instant coffee. Excuse us a moment, Louisa." He tossed his bag and jacket onto his desk and left as abruptly as he'd arrived, with a bemused Joey in tow.

Louisa watched them go, a feeling of unease creeping into the pit of her stomach. Although her colleague had spoken cheerfully enough, she could tell by the rapidity of his movements and the unfocussed look in his eyes that all was not well. What had happened that had kept him awake last night? What could be so pressing that it could distract him from his work at the critical hour, and drive him to seek the pallid comforts of instant coffee? It almost didn't bear thinking about.

She sighed and went back to her proofing, but found it more tedious than before. Usually she didn't have any trouble getting into flow state, for she took her work just seriously enough that she could give it her best effort, but not *so* seriously that she was ever in danger of overthinking it. But she just couldn't shake the growing certainty that something was really bothering Henry, and she couldn't *not* care about that, even if it wasn't her place to do anything about it.

Henry re-entered the room some thirty minutes later, looking calmer, although still with a slightly glazed expression. "Joey's thesis *does* sound like a winner," he said.

"Mm," said Louisa.

He sat down and stared at his computer for a very long time, drumming his fingers against the desk in an uncharacteristically arrhythmic pattern. Weirder and weirder, thought Louisa, struggling to concentrate on her own screen.

Morning segued into afternoon, and neither of them spoke much, but after a long time of agonising, 'Gold Yamre: An Origin Myth' was finally completed – and for the first time that day, Henry looked completely himself again as they held their breath and, each with one hand on the mouse, hit 'send' on the email that would present the fruits of their labour before the highest-ranking technocultural journal in circulation.

The email was sent.

"HURRAY!!!" our heroes cried, jumping up and down with glee.

"I can hardly believe it's finally finished," Henry gasped, gripping Louisa by the shoulders in maddened ecstasy. "And it would have taken so much longer if I hadn't had you to help me. Louisa, thank you. Thank you for everything."

Louisa looked up at him and felt a wave of emotion which seemed ludicrous in proportion to the actual event. She had always loved her work, and invested in it to her fullest ability, or so she'd thought. But Henry was on a completely different plane of existence. The extent of himself which he put into his work, sincerely and unabashedly, and somehow without ever seeming self-absorbed, was something she had never seen in anyone else; and it opened up a whole new realm of emotional possibilities which she had never before encountered. It was as if knowing him and working with him had somehow increased her capacity to feel joy – and sorrow – beyond what she had ever experienced before. And part of her embraced that newfound intensity of emotion – and part of her couldn't help but recoil from it.

She looked away, suddenly embarrassed to meet his gaze. "Hey, no worries, man, I'm just happy to help. Tell you what," she said, perking up again, "why don't we head down to the Arms and grab a cold one?"

To her surprise (although, then again, maybe not), Henry's shoulders slumped, and the light faded from his eyes. "I wish I could, but, um…I have some other business there this evening."

Louisa hesitated. Although she considered him more of a friend than a colleague, and had taken frequent liberties in teasing him and prodding him out of his curmudgeonly shell, she did not *really* want to pry too deeply into his personal affairs; and she knew from experience that he was more emotionally unpredictable than she.

But in the end, whether out of self-interest or not, her desire to help him won over caution, and the words slipped out: "Henry, are you okay?"

To his credit, Henry did not seem taken aback by the question. "I'm okay, thanks. I'm just…frustrated." He stopped there, perhaps thinking he'd said too much already.

"Is that why you couldn't sleep?" asked Louisa. She did not add, 'And were late this morning and didn't answer your phone.'

"More or less," he said, without any particular inflection. "I just need to have a conversation with——" (he did not say 'my friend who works at the bar,' but Louisa made an educated guess that that was who it was), "——someone, and I'm not looking forward to it."

"Why, what sort of conversation?" she asked, in too deep now to maintain any pretence of tact.

He chuckled mirthlessly. "It's not that I don't know how to say it… It's just that I don't know how to say it without sounding like an arrogant prick."

Louisa gave a small smile. "Don't worry, I've worked with you long enough to know that you're not an arrogant prick…or at least no more than anyone else, anyway. I mean, it doesn't matter, it's none of my business, but…you just seemed so off today, and I wish…that I could do something to help."

Henry laughed again. "It's not that kind of… It's just – there's this woman who told me that she loves me, and I don't know what to do with that, because I'm not looking for a relationship, and she should *know* that I'm not looking for a relationship, and, yeah, you know, I can let her down gently, and I suppose that's what I'll have to do, but we all know these things don't pan out as smoothly as we want them to, and, and – it just *frustrates* me that I have to feel responsible for her emotions, and to worry about whether this is going to turn into a big complicated mess, when all I wanted to do was be her friend and mind my own feelings, and she'd mind hers. Is that terrible? Am *I* the callous one here? I know these situations can happen to anybody, and it shouldn't be such a big deal, but I just feel like it *is* a big deal, and I never asked to be put in this position, and I never did anything to make her love me – or if I did, it was twenty years ago – so why do *I* have to be the one to solve the problem?!"

There was a silence in which he stared at her maniacally, and she took a step backwards and tried to process all of this.

"Wow," she said at last. "There's a lot going on there." (She did not try to add levity to the conversation by saying, 'Maybe you *are* an arrogant prick.')

He took a deep breath. "I'm sorry I dumped it all on you like that. But," he grinned wryly, "you did ask."

"Yeah," she said. "I did." A pause. "Well…I wish I could solve your problem for you, but this one's beyond my expertise, I'm afraid."

"That's alright," he said. "Thank you for listening." He kicked idly at his laptop bag on the floor. "Anyway, I'd better go and get it over with. But we'll celebrate soon, certainly." He slipped on his jacket, gathered up the bag and stowed his computer inside it, and turned towards the door. "Take care, Louisa. And thank you, again. You've been more of a help than I ever could have asked for."

"You're welcome," she said softly, as he left.

∴

Louisa drove up the mountain that night in a pensive mood. She was unsure why she didn't feel more satisfied with how the day had gone. They'd finished their project! All that hard work had finally paid off! And yet…there was this emptiness inside her that grew more insistent the further into the darkness she drove. True, this meant the end of their collaboration, which was something to be mourned. And…damn it, she had forgotten to bring the new edition of /REL/ home with her. But neither of these facts seemed sufficient explanation for what she felt.

True, she thought, it saddened her to see him feeling down, when the completion of the project had been so important to him. To both of them, in the end. It was like they'd both been waiting for some point of catharsis, and – they had *tasted* that catharsis for a fleeting instant, and perhaps it had been taken away too soon, or somehow marred by the existence of life beyond the academic sphere. But even still, there was *something* else that was weighing upon her, and she was irritated that she couldn't figure out what it was.

She parked her car in the yard and entered the house through the side door, where she found Nonna spreading the last of the icing onto an enormous chocolate cake. "*Buona sera, bambina,*" she said, beaming at Louisa as she came in. "You're just in time to come taste this cake I made you!"

Earlier that day, Louisa had thought that her capacity for joy had been stretched to the utmost limit by her friendship with Henry. But now she realised, as she rushed over and threw her arms about her grandmother, that she had been wrong.

Perhaps, she thought, a tear trickling down her cheek as she laughed and reached for a knife to cut the cake, all was not well.

But perhaps, in some greater, truer sense, all *was* well.

Chapter Eleven – A Busy Monday Night

It was, for once, a busy Monday night at the Quartermaster's Arms, and for this, Eden was grateful. She had spent the first part of the day playing with Churchill, the ageing long-haired German Shepherd she had inherited from her father, and reorganising all of her cupboards and shelves. Neither of these activities had proved as refreshing as they'd been wont to in the past, and she had finally been forced to admit to herself that she was nervous.

There wasn't any identifiable reason for it. She was not, after all, particularly worried about the outcome of tonight's conversation with Henry – just as she hadn't worried about the outcome of her confession to him at her birthday party. The time had long gone wherein she'd desired a specific direction for their relationship to move in. Now, after all these years, the only thing she desired was clarity.

But then why was she nervous? It didn't make sense. In the end, she'd been unable to fathom the source of her unrest, and had proceeded to work that evening dreading the prospect of standing idly at the bar for hours until her old friend finally arrived.

So when it turned out that a festival in the city had brought an unusually high number of patrons to the Arms on this Monday night, Eden embraced the opportunity to set aside her muddled feelings for a time and be fully present to the conversations that came her way.

∴

The first conversation was with a young woman named Jen, who patronised the Arms semi-regularly, was drinking alone, and was in a good mood.

"How's your day been?" Eden asked.

"Really good, thanks," said Jen. "I had this huge existential revelation watching *The Graduate* last night, because I watched it for the first time when I was sixteen, and I couldn't relate to Ben, and I thought the whole thing was really gross. But then I watched it again, and this time I *understood* what it was like to graduate and feel totally directionless and depressed, and I could *see* how he might get himself into that situation, and even though it was tragic, there was something really cool in being able to connect with it like that, and I just woke up this morning and thought, damn, I'm so glad I watched it again!"

"Mmm," said Eden, nodding slowly as she digested this. "I had a similar experience once when I watched the *Shaun the Sheep* movie with my nephew. There's this scene where the farmer reunites with his sheep, and it spoke to me profoundly about the nature of fatherly love."

Jen burst out laughing. "Nice."

∴

The second was with a man named Kev, whom she'd seen a couple of times before, and who was slightly agitated.

"I just don't understand why it's called 'Robbo's Chicken & Meat,'" he said, as she poured him a beer. "Why 'Chicken *and* Meat'? Why does Robbo separate the chicken from the other meat? Does he *specialise* in chicken and *dabble* in other meat? I just can't get my head around it."

"You're preaching to the choir, brother," said Eden. "I've been asking this same question for years."

"He doesn't even have that much chicken when you really think about it!" Kev went on. "All the other meat combined easily outweighs the amount of chicken he has! So *why* is it 'Robbo's Chicken & Meat'? I mean, what was Robbo thinking?!"

Eden threw up her hands in solidarity. "What *was* he thinking?"

"You can't just go and call yourself such a redundant name and expect people not to question it!"

"How can a successful business model be based on such a concept?!"

"How does Robbo make any money? Surely people are too confused by the name of his shop to ever go in there and *buy* any chicken *or* meat!"

"This man needs to rethink his brand strategy!"

"He needs to open a dictionary and look up what a tautology is!"

∴

The third was with a group of friends who wanted to know where she stood on the topic of wearing socks to bed.

"Well," said Eden, "I must admit, I do it myself during the winter months. But I always make sure they're clean."

"*See*, Jerome?" said one guy, giving the guy next to him a shove. "You can't just go to bed in the socks you've been wearing all day, that's so manky!"

"But if you wear clean socks to bed, they're only going to get sweaty in your sleep anyway," Jerome retorted.

"Yeah, but not as sweaty as when you wear them for hours and go around doing stuff and you're wearing shoes over the top!" said the young lady opposite him.

"But——"

"The barkeeper has spoken, Jerome. Stop wearing dirty socks to bed."

"Hold on now, I didn't ask to be a pawn in this political gambit," protested Eden, shaking her head at them. "Jerome did nothing to deserve public outcry against his sock-wearing habits, and I will not be made accessory to his character assassination."

"Aw, *come* on," said the girl who had posed her the question.

"The lady speaks truth," said Jerome. "Better to wear dirty socks than to have a dirty heart."

Eden grinned. "Couldn't have put it better myself."

∴

The fourth was with an old man whose name she didn't know.

"If I recited the longest number I could think of right now," he said, "like 3,497,034,112,054…what do you reckon are the odds that no one else has ever said that number out loud in human history?"

Eden smiled at him. "Dunno, but I'm gonna be up all night thinking about it."

∴

The fifth was with an author of about Eden's age who seemed vaguely depressed.

"I've been working on the sequel to my book for fifteen years, and I *still* feel like I'm only just barely making a dent in it," she told Eden. "Which is not to say I haven't made progress, of course. But it's like…imagine buying a 5,000-piece jigsaw puzzle, and on the box, you have the picture of what it'll look like when it's finished. That's my book, in my head. But what I've had on paper for the last decade and a half is a pile of jumbled-up jigsaw pieces, and even though I've been working away at it, and I've even finished putting all the edge pieces together, it still *feels* like I've done nothing, because I have this massive pile of pieces that I don't know where to put yet, and even though the edges are finished, I just keep looking at the middle and all I see is this big empty hole."

"Damn," said Eden. "That's a pretty good metaphor."

The woman laughed bitterly. "Yeah, well. I wouldn't be much cop as a writer if I couldn't at *least* come up with a metaphor every now and then."

"That's fair," said Eden, pouring her another coffee stout.

The woman sighed. "Sometimes I have to wonder why I keep at it, you know what I mean? There's no money in it. The last one barely sold two thousand copies in ten tears. Mass media is dying, so I'm not gonna get famous during my lifetime. And I reckon the literary canon'll be on its way out by the time I'm dead, so…I mean, what's the point?"

"Fun?" Eden suggested.

The woman gave a real, honest laugh this time. "No," she said. "Not for fun. I haven't had fun writing in years. I don't mind that though, I've never cared that much about fun. It's just…I *wish* if I were going to spend so much time doing it, that I knew *why*. It would be a lot easier to stay convicted if I knew the reason."

Eden considered this quandary. "Well," she said at last, "I'm not you, so I don't know. But I think it's easy to feel like you have to either do something for external gain, or because you get some kind of emotional satisfaction out of it. But maybe, sometimes, you should just do a thing because it's good to do."

"Hmm," the woman said. "Maybe."

∴

The sixth was with a man who, she was pretty sure, was named Robert Jones and had shared a history elective with her during the early days of her undergrad. But it was possible she was mistaken, and he didn't seem to recognise her, so she did the polite thing and pretended not to know him.

"What can I get you?" she asked.

"I'll have a schooner of the Stone & Wood, thanks."

"No worries."

∴

By the time the seventh conversation came, the bar was closed.

Eden had just locked the door and turned towards the car park when she saw him standing outside in the open road, one hand in the pocket of his coat and a wistful look on his face. She felt something tighten in her gut, and yet, in her mind, she was perfectly calm.

Truth be told, it hadn't been as hard for her, seeing him again, as she'd thought it would be. When it had ended the first time, she'd felt like something inside her had shattered. But when it had ended the last time, she'd known, even then, that although the pain he'd caused her was very real, she would always carry within her the desire to love him and forgive him. And now, after so many years of living, of encountering other joys and other sorrows, that pain, though still real, seemed suddenly so distant that it hardly mattered any more.

As he approached, and a nearby streetlight threw his face into sharp relief, she could see that he, too, was nervous – and a warmth rose up inside her, and she couldn't help but smile. Back then, she'd been drawn to him because of his gentleness and fragility. Now it gave her comfort to see that however much he might have changed, time hadn't hardened him completely.

"How long have you been waiting?" she asked.

"I just got here," he said, smiling back. "What did you have in mind?"

"I might ask *you* the same question. Walk me to my car?"

"Alright."

They walked several paces to the car, got in, and she drove. It had started raining, and the city lights reflecting off the glistening wet surfaces around them made the world feel shapeless and transient.

It was several minutes before Henry spoke; but to his credit, he got straight to the point. "I'm really touched," he said quietly, "that you said what you did."

"For what it's worth," said Eden, "I didn't mean that I've been pining away for you for the last twenty years, or that the sight of you has reignited some burning passion deep within me. I just meant… Well, what I said. There's just some little part of me that's always loved you, and probably always will."

"I don't deserve that," he said, even more quietly, as though his words were so weighed down by emotion that he could barely get them out.

"Is love deserved, or is it a gift freely given?"

"Either way, I can't accept it."

She looked at him. "Why not?"

"Because…I just can't be the person that you need me to be. I can't be that person to anyone. I don't know how to be. I don't think I'm *meant* to be. You're very important to me, and I value our friendship———" He broke off, clenching a fist. "That sounds so insipid. I'm sorry. I…cherish my memories of you, and I'm so grateful that I got to see you again and have a second chance at friendship with you. But I can't love you the way you need to be loved. I need you to know that, or else I risk leading you on again. And I refuse to do that. Not again."

He fell silent. She could hear him breathing heavily. It had cost him a great effort, to say this much, and remain so calm.

"So you're just going to be on your own forever?" she asked.

"Yes."

"Well…" She paused for a long time. "Alright then, no hard feelings."

He looked at her. "Really?"

"Yes, really. I think love *is* freely given, so I just wanted you to know how I felt, and that's why I told you the other night. But it doesn't have to *mean* anything, or require any particular response. It just is what it is." As she spoke the words, she believed them. But, she would reflect later, as she lay sleepless in her bed, that didn't necessarily make them true.

"Hmm," said he. "You are truly excellent."

She chuckled. "I know."

They drove around the block, and then she dropped him off at his car.

"Take care, old friend," he said.

"Thanks," she said. "You too."

Chapter Twelve – Knowing

"How do you make friends with someone you've never met before?"

"You talk to them," said Barista Frances, handing Mathilda back her loyalty card.

Mathilda scowled, tucking the card into her wallet. "You can't just up and *talk* to someone out of the blue."

"Yes you can," Barista Frances averred. "I do it all the time."

"But you're a barista! That's a function of your role! People understand your place in society, and they expect you to behave in conjunction with it! That's *worlds* apart from someone like me just moseying up to a person in the street and demanding intimacy with them!"

"Crikey, calm *down*, darl," said Frances. "You're going to give yourself an aneurysm thinking like that. Go on and grab a seat, and I'll bring your drink over."

Mathilda heaved a weary sigh. "You're right, you're right, sorry." She dawdled over to her second-favourite table (she became very self-denigrating when frustrated with the world, and often persuaded herself that she was undeserving of such trifles as first-favourite tables), set up her laptop, and looked at her watch. It was a quarter to eleven, and she was unsure whether Double-Park George (whom she refused to call Henry until formal acquaintance obliged her to do so) was going to make an appearance. He hadn't last week; and considering the variance in his routine over the last month or so, there was really no telling what would happen today. Anyway, it didn't matter, because she probably wouldn't talk to him even if he did turn up.

She sighed again and opened up the word doc, which still lingered miserably on an unfinished sentence in the opening paragraph of chapter twenty-three, right where she'd left it some weeks ago. Barista Frances came by presently with her latte and she murmured her thanks, feeling her eyes turn glassy as she stared at the screen.

Since her epiphany on the fourth Saturday of June, she had moved through all the five stages of grief (her usual response to a new piece of self-knowledge), and then proceeded to take no action whatsoever. Mathilda was the kind of person who had a lot of thoughts and feelings about a lot of different things, and placed absolutely no importance on any of it. So what if she was in love with this man whom she knew almost nothing about? Was it *really* love? What *was* love? Did it necessitate action? Would it still be here tomorrow? Would *anything* be here tomorrow? None of it really mattered anyway.

And yet.

She couldn't stop thinking about him.

Fundamentally, she was pretty sure that what she was feeling was the desire to *know*, more than anything else. George was a mystery to her, and she longed to comprehend him. She could intuit that they were similar somehow, and she could observe certain things about him, and project other things onto him – yet she had been proven wrong before, on that day when he'd brought his friend into the café with him (which he hadn't done since, so how significant *was* she to him, anyway?), and that had caused her to question everything else she'd surmised about him.

And anyway, there was a difference between knowing *about* and simply *knowing*. The behaviours she observed in him, the causes she ascribed to them, the assumptions she made, the contradictions she faced – they were all meaningless data points. Even if she could weave them together into a coherent theory in her mind, it was still just a theory. What she wanted was axiom: self-evident truth.

Actually, maybe what she wanted was just to *talk* to the guy.

But did it really matter what she wanted? What about what *he* wanted? What if he wanted to be left alone? What if he came to this place as a means of relaxation and escape, and not to be bothered by some maudlin artist who had no reasonable claim on him other than the inexplicable urge to fathom his interiority?

And yet she felt so *warmly* towards him, and she was certain that if he would only let her, she could give him the affection, care and acceptance that, deep down, most of us crave, just as he could give her the opportunity to come out of herself and be present to another person. Was that not worth taking a risk for, at least?

But really, her feelings didn't matter, except insofar as they fuelled her artistic expression – and even the value of *that* was debatable, come to think of it.

Sometimes she wished that she were more like Barista Frances, who never seemed to need to think about herself at all.

At this moment, George walked through the door.

Mathilda glanced up as he passed by. He was less animated than he had been the last few times she'd seen him – not dejected, exactly, but more like how he'd been when he'd first started coming to Corner Shop: introspective and sedate. He greeted Frances amicably, ordered two piccolos and sat down at his usual table, with only *David Copperfield* for company.

Mathilda was torn. On the one hand, he obviously wasn't doing anything of import, so it surely wouldn't matter too much if he were interrupted. But on the other hand, if he had gone to the trouble of bringing a book with him, then he probably didn't want to be engaged in conversation.

So should she speak to him or not? What would she even say? There was no point in trying to talk to him about Dickens, since she'd never read Dickens (although she told herself perpetually that she would get around to him one day). And anyway, she didn't like the thought of starting an arbitrary conversation for conversation's sake. It was like being accosted by those charity volunteers who prowled around in public spaces wearing lanyards and fluorescent T-shirts and harassing people for money, but who always began by asking her how her day was going or by complimenting her outfit, when they both knew that wasn't the real purpose of the interaction. So was she going to do the same now to poor old George?

No, she decided. This was a situation that, however desperate, called for authenticity and candour. There would be no beating about the bush.

So she saved her document (even though she hadn't actually done anything to it, besides inserting a comma and then removing it a minute later), closed her laptop and marched over to George's table, where he was chuckling quietly at his book. Her shadow fell over the page, and he looked up, his expression politely quizzical.

"Hi," said Mathilda, smiling sheepishly, "I'm Mathilda. I'm sorry to bother you, it's just – I see you come in here all the time, and I was wondering…what's your name?"

He stared at her, surprised, but perhaps (she hoped) pleasantly so.

"Henry," he said at last, relaxing slightly as he realised, perhaps, that she wasn't wearing a lanyard and wasn't going to ask him for money.

Emboldened by her success, Mathilda held out a hand. "Lovely to meet you, Henry."

"You too." His handshake was steady, which she took as a good sign because if he were secretly wishing that she would go away, then his reluctance would certainly have come through in his grip. So she abandoned all veneer of propriety and spoke from the depths of her heart.

"Listen," she said, stammering a bit at first, then speaking more forcefully as she warmed to her theme, "I know I'm being astoundingly socially dense right now, but rest assured that I do so with full knowledge of how I must come across to you, if that makes it any better, which maybe it doesn't. But…I just can't help but notice that you have excellent taste in cafés, and you get on with my friend Frances over there, and you must love a good yarn, if you're reading Dickens, and…I don't know why, but it just brings me so much joy that you order your piccolos two at a time, and, and, what I'm trying to say is, I think you must be a very interesting person, and I would love it if we could be friends."

There was a split-second of silence – and then Henry burst out laughing.

Mathilda felt her insides convulse. That's it, she thought. I've stuffed it. I can never show my face in here again.

She turned to go.

"Wait," said Henry, arresting her shameful flight before she'd so much as taken a step, "I'm sorry, I didn't mean to laugh, I was just so unprepared for that." He chuckled again, closed his book, and placed it on the table. "Please, have a seat."

Numb with shock, and with a rising sense of embarrassment as her brain caught up with her actions, Mathilda sat.

"Tell you what, Mathilda," said Henry, regarding her with an amusement that was sincere, unfettered, and totally free of condescension, "I reckon *you* must be a pretty interesting person to have the guts to say all that to a perfect stranger. How about we order another round and see where the conversation takes us?"

Mathilda beamed. "I'd like that."

Chapter Thirteen – Eternal Flame

The instant Trish stepped off the plane and beheld the distant mountain, a fire was lit within her heart. It was good to be home.

As she drove towards the city, the mountain loomed closer upon the horizon: a hulking dark mass of greens and greys emerging bold, majestic and alluring against the sparkling morning sky, calling to her a silent welcome, as though it could sense her presence somehow and had recognised her as one of its own. She kept her eyes on the road, yet felt it permeate the edges of her awareness in a way that was both comforting and surreal. The pull of the mountain on her mind and heart was something she found hard to explain or even describe, especially to outsiders. It was the totem of her youth, the metonym for home, intrinsically linked somehow to all of her primordial memories. She loved Sydney, but it was vast, sprawling, and *flat*. It was good to leave it once in a while, especially as a reward to self for a job well done. She careened elatedly down the freeway, and the fire inside her glowed bright.

The first item on her agenda was to procure breakfast at the nearest servo: a steaming hot National Pie. This was a holdover from her early undergrad days, during which she had worked part-time in a builder's yard – her memories of it now a cacophonous haze of hi-vis and ambient cursing and instant coffee and smoko breaks when no one actually smoked, and 6:30AM starts on bitter cold winter mornings when there was no time to eat before leaving home and the only way to survive was to stop by Mood Food and grab the hottest, fattiest, most filling thing she could find.

Her supervisor had reprimanded her for this on more than one occasion. "A meat pie," he'd said brusquely, "is *not* breakfast."

She'd bought one every morning after that, just to rile him up. And to this day, although her digestive tract was more inclined to vindicate him, she still had the occasional pie for breakfast, and considered it symbolic of her moral victory. Now, as she wolfed it down in a couple of bites and continued driving, she could feel the fire in her heart flare up again, as the heat from her stomach rose to join it. (*Heat moves upward*, she remembered learning in primary school.)

∴

She parked on the outskirts of the city and took a walking tour through the CBD. Its smallness and provinciality gave her a feeling of tender, maternal amusement. Its sandstone buildings filled her with delight. The plane trees had shed their leaves, but even their skeletons huddling in the streets were poignant, somehow. She meandered along the waterfront, admiring the yachts. She explored new fixtures and fooderies, knowing that they were new, yet not quite able to remember what had come before. She wandered through a series of old haunts: alleyways, vending machines, takeaway shops, plazas – all of them imbued with echoes of past Trishes, doing past things, with past friends. All of them the same, yet devoid of the significance they had once carried.

As she stood and surveyed the games shop where she had once played D&D with her college friends (now converted into a bar/café, with a shelf of board games standing forlornly off to one side), she realised that her home town, while still home, had also become the graveyard where all of her past selves were buried. Every time she came back, she was a new person, and the last Trish that had visited was dead.

Trish, however, was not prone to melancholy, and found the thought of having evolved through a number of different iterations on her way to her final form rather bolstering. She saluted the games-shop-turned-bar/café and went on her merry way, the fire burning brighter than ever.

∴

With her smaller, more immediate tasks out of the way, there was only one place left to visit: the university.

She barged into Henry's office without knocking. "Hey *nerd*, long time no see!"

He looked up from his desk, startled. And in the split-second before his eyes, dull with shock, lit up in jubilant recognition, Trish understood four things: 1) He had changed since she had last seen him: there were more lines on his face; he was wearing a thick woollen cardigan (a garment he had scorned in his youth); he'd parted his hair on the other side; the half-eaten muesli bar suspended in his hand mere inches from his mouth was coconut and pistachio, and he'd always hated pistachios; 2) All of these differences were irrelevant – merely the shedding and taking up anew of various accidental forms of Henry, which came and went like waves on the seashore; 3) The essential form of Henry remained intact beneath the surface; 4) It was *so* good to see him again.

He grinned at her, his essential form winking into view for a moment. "What the hell?" He sounded like he'd just awoken from a dream.

"That's a fine way to greet your friend and rival."

"What are you doing here?"

"I'm here to challenge you to a penalty shootout," declared Trish, blithely casting aside all other semantics and pragmatics which the question might have contained. "You and me, *mano a mano*, just like old times."

He gaped at her. "What?"

"You heard me! I've got gear waiting in the car, and the street is calling my name. Social comp doesn't cut it any more, Henry, I want a *real* challenge."

"But I have to——"

"Aw, don't gimme *that*, you're not doing anything important here! I know you've already submitted your project, so what's one afternoon spent with one of your oldest chums? Are you a winner, or a weenie?!"

"But," said Henry, laughing now as she grabbed his arm and began dragging him from the room, "I haven't played in years! There's no way I'd be able to match you now!"

"That's exactly the point! After I've thrashed you on the street, I'll thrash you again on paper when our articles come out, and my victory over you will be complete!"

"Oh, we'll see about *that*, Trish Mackenzie. I won't lose to you that easily!"

They were both laughing by this stage, and left the building in a state of shared merriment which completely undid the effects of time's passing, as though their friendship was not something marked by temporality, but something which had always existed – and always would – in the realm of eternity.

∴

The rules were simple: they would each take five shots, while the other defended. Whoever scored the most goals won. They flipped a coin and Henry found himself shooting first. He gripped the stick tightly, testing its weight in his hands, familiar yet unfamiliar, and tried to focus on the bin, placed on its side on the asphalt twenty metres away, that was his target – and not on Trish, who was guarding it. It was a clear, cold day. He gritted his teeth and fought the urge to shiver.

It took him some time to line up his first shot, circling slowly around the puck a few times to get used to the feeling of being on skates again. It had been a long time since he and she had played together in the university hockey club.

"Whatcha waiting for, old man?" Trish called out.

"You're two weeks older than me!" he retorted.

"Yeah, but that doesn't make you less old. C'mon, have at thee!"

"Alright then," he said – and, taking a deep breath, nudged the puck forward and began skating erratically towards her, picking up speed as muscle memory kicked in and he grew surer of his balance. He deked once – twice – fumbled the puck and missed, nearly colliding with Trish in the process.

"Damn it," he panted, bringing himself unsteadily to a halt.

"Go again," said Trish with ostensible charity, although the corner of her mouth was twitching. Henry, not deigning to reply, picked up the puck and returned to his starting position.

Next he tried a snap shot, which in bygone years had served him well – but he miscalculated the follow-through and shot wide, barely missing the front passenger window of a battered red Toyota Camry parked nearby.

"If it makes you feel any better," said Trish, "your skating isn't as garbage as I thought it would be."

"Yeah, yeah, don't say I didn't warn you," he grumbled. "Now quit laughing and help me look for the stupid puck."

Three shots later, he'd scored twice, although one of those was because he'd skated straight into Trish and knocked her clean out of goals, somehow managing to flick the puck into the bin with his foot as he did so. After giving her a hand up and checking to ensure that he hadn't seriously injured her, he handed her the stick, unlaced the skates, and put his shoes back on, accepting gloves and helmet from her once he'd finished.

He felt his heartbeat quicken as she circled the puck and began her first wind-up, but he wasn't sure whether it was because he was nervous or excited. Both, he decided, and was glad.

After five shots taken in rapid succession, she'd scored thrice (one loss being due to an actual save he'd made, the other to a botched attempt at a slapshot, but who could blame her for that?), and they came together and shook hands with a mutual satisfaction that was palpable. Their face-off hadn't exactly been a game for the ages, but it had reaffirmed what was most important: that no matter where life took them, the foundation of their friendship, eternal and not temporal, would never change.

∴

They had lunch at a nearby sushi restaurant which had popped up during their postgrad years, and which had become a staple of their diet for a feverish six months or so until they'd tired of fish and moved on to some other place. They ordered platefuls of takoyaki and spicy tuna rolls, and spent a pleasant hour or so reminiscing about the past and remarking on the present in fairly equal proportion.

Finally, Henry asked, "So why did you decide to throw down the gauntlet again after all this time?"

Trish gestured airily with her chopsticks. "No particular reason. I watched *The Mighty Ducks* again the other day and it gave me a yearning."

"I'm talking about you doing a yarn on Gold Yamre at the exact same time as me."

"Oh, that." She smiled, uncharacteristically demure. "Well, it'd been such a long while, and I felt like I'd done all I could do on the Meme Wars, and I missed going up against you. So when I heard about Gold Yamre, I thought, 'There's no way Henry's not going to write about that,' so I took the chance and decided to throw my hat in the ring, like we used to."

"Like we used to," he said dreamily. "We did have some good sparring matches, didn't we?"

"Wrote some decent papers, too."

He chuckled. "I liked your work on the Meme Wars. I was sorry when it ended."

"Yeah, yeah, very funny."

"No, I mean it," he said. "I'm a big fan of everything you've written. I always have been. It seems a shame to limit you to doing whatever *I'm* doing, just for the sake of competition."

Trish stared at him, almost wondering if he was joking. But he was serious: she could see it in his eyes, ablaze with whatever fire he carried in his own heart, mirroring hers.

"Although," he added, breaking into a grin, "I *do* love competing with you."

She grinned back. "We'll see if you still feel the same way when I whomp you in the spring editions."

"I'm not gonna lose to you this time, Trish."

"Well I won't lose to you, either!"

They stood simultaneously and shook hands, knowing there was nothing more to be said. He declined the offer of a lift back to the university, and she watched him walk up the street, still limping slightly after having crashed into her during their match. As he disappeared over the horizon, she felt the fire inside her flare up again, spreading through her, warming every part of her body.

And in that instant, she understood:
5) The fire was burning for him.

Chapter Fourteen – Narrative and Subculture

Joey was walking down the street with some of her friends, halfway through singing the *Arthur* theme in four-part harmony, when she glimpsed the time on the clock tower and realised she was going to be late for her meeting with Dr Henry.

"Aw, nuts," she muttered, abandoning the alto line and veering sharply to the left.

Her friends came to a startled, bumping halt, and the song's final notes were lost to the aether.

"Dude, you threw off the Emperor's groove," said Dave.

"Sorry guys," said Joey, "I've just remembered I've got a meeting with my Ph.D. supervisor. I'll meet you at the rodeo when I'm finished!" And she took off running back the way they'd come, leaving mass disgruntlement in her wake.

∴

There was no formal impetus to be meeting with each other at this stage, since Joey was not slated to begin her Ph.D. until the following February. However, they had both agreed that since Joey was relatively unfamiliar with the technocultural landscape, it wouldn't hurt for Dr Henry to give her some tips about where to begin in terms of background reading.

"So, how's your thesis idea coming along?" he said, once she had collapsed into a chair opposite him (having sprinted three blocks without stopping to the underground hot pot restaurant which they'd nominated for their rendezvous point) and recovered sufficient breath to apologise once again for her tardiness. "Still thinking about social engineering?"

"That's part of it," Joey said eagerly. "I had the idea after I watched a four-hour video essay on Ivan Ooze from the 1995 *Power Rangers* film, which argued that he would be totally insufferable if he were an actual person, and it got me thinking about how lolcow discourse is often imprinted with moralistic language which points to an objective standard of behaviour – so if a big enough community is created around a specific lolcow, it becomes a structure that reinforces certain social characteristics in the broader population. Which is obvious enough to anyone, if you think about it for two seconds. But *then* I thought, what if I used D.W. Brooks's Typology of Lolcows to create a model of memeticultural indices which could predict which individuals are likely to become emergent lolcows? And *then* what if I did a meta-analysis of social codes within contemporary communities to get an idea of which behaviours are most likely to be reinforced in the next ten years or so – and then see if there's any interaction between those two variables?"

Henry gave a low whistle. "That's an *enormous* undertaking."

"I know," Joey beamed. "Go big and go home, that's what I always say."

"'Go big *and* go home?'"

"Precisely. Work hard and give it your all – and when the day's done, go home and have a big fat nap, because you've earned it."

Henry chuckled. "I like that."

∴

He didn't have much to do in the office these days. It was quiet with both Joey and Louisa gone. (It wasn't that he was unhappy by himself; after all, he'd spent half a lifetime craving solitude, and would doubtless continue to do so for the rest of eternity once he joined his ancestors beyond the grave. But still.)

He was nervous about his article being reviewed. He always felt nervous, even though he hadn't received an outright rejection in years. But this time he was aiming for the top – for *Forward*, which had by far the highest impact rating of any technocultural journal in academic history. And his chances of getting into it were entirely dependent on the whims of just two people: Laz Buhrmann and H. R. Kimble.

Henry had met both these gentlemen at a futurist conference some years ago, and the three had reviewed each other's work back and forth throughout the majority of their careers. He knew from experience that Buhrmann would give him no trouble – would perhaps suggest a minor tweak to the concluding statement, but nothing more substantial than that. Kimble, on the other hand, was as volatile as a Metro bus on a Friday night, and whether or not he suggested major edits or even rejected the work altogether was entirely dependent on external factors such as the weather, what he'd eaten for breakfast, how easy it had been to find a parking spot that morning, and whether Collingwood had won on the weekend.

So, as usual, Henry was nervous.

And so, being nervous, he was glad of the distraction when it came.

His inbox pinged.

Hi Dr B, the email read. *Could we please catch up again soon? I have a few more ideas I'd like to get your thoughts on. Cheers, Joey*

∴

"I just don't get what the core difference is between our disciplines," she said, gesturing violently in a way that made sense in her head but probably didn't signal anything visually coherent to him. "I mean, yeah, I understand what it is you do, versus what it is I do – but this is a question of *being*, not *doing*. I mean, what is the *essence* of your field, and what is the *essence* of mine?"

He nodded slowly. "Mmm, I see what you mean."

"If I could just conceptualise the difference more clearly, that would make it easier to adapt the theoretical framework in my head, so I don't accidentally write this weird mutant thesis that's trying to be technocultural futurist but is actually a media studies project in disguise. Do you know what I mean?"

"Yes, I do," he said.

"So what *is* it?" she demanded, almost knocking over her bottle of Milkis in her frenzy. "Give me the answers I seek, Dr B.! You're a wise and learned man, so surely you can solve all of my life problems for me?!"

"I think," he said, laughing now, "I think your answer is bound to change, depending on what level of conceptualisation you're looking at."

"I *know* that," she said bitterly. "At the most abstract level, all fields of study are simply about seeking knowledge. But at their most surface-level, they're completely different. So what I'm asking is, what's the *most* abstract level we can think on, while still retaining a meaningful difference – and what does *that* level tell us?"

"Hmm," he said. "Well, what do you like most about lolcow studies? What does it do for you?"

"It's about *narrative!*" she all but shouted, making more incomprehensible hand gestures like some dyspraxic TEDx orator. "Narrative and *subculture!* It's about looking at the lives of individuals and the meaning we make from them as a collective!"

"Right!" said Henry, who was beginning, despite his laughter, to be swept away in the current of her enthusiasm. "Lolcow studies is to history as quantum mechanics is to astrophysics!"

"Yes!" she yelled. "It's about the microecology of culture, and the *specificity of being!*"

"That's so cool!" he cried. "So then if that's true, then technocultural futurism is all about applying those same mechanics of narrative and subculture to the question of *what next?* It's about seeing the patterns in that microhistory and extrapolating from that to predict what comes afterwards! Like reading a thousand different murder mysteries until you can pick up the latest Agatha Christie knock-off and guess the identity of the killer just by reading the title! Except instead of a single book, we're reading a complex, multimedia canon with a thousand plotlines and plot-twists, and by guessing even just one of those plot-twists, we obtain a deeper understanding of what that plot actually means!"

"But it's not just a *story* we're looking at either, because we're not just looking at people," she reminded him, "but we're looking at societal structures and technologies as well, and how they feed back into the narrative and the culture and the people within them! It's like we're trying to bridge the gap between how we *see* life and how we *live* it!"

"That's exactly it!" he said. "Everything is connected, and everything has meaning! That's what I've always loved about this work! No single meme on the internet is insignificant, because it gives us the tiniest glimpse of the overall Truth!"

∴

He sent her home with a pile of recommended reading, and she stayed up all night, skimming through books and journals, soaking up the different slivers of Truth until her eyes began to burn as if from gazing at the sun. There were so many different subfields and subcategories that she despaired of ever getting a handle on them all. But there was much to love, and much to think about.

Dr Henry had omitted, perhaps out of modesty, to recommend her any of his own work; but she tracked down a number of his articles nonetheless and enjoyed them greatly, which added to the pride and satisfaction of having helped him on his latest project.

There was one technocultural researcher, however, whose work she enjoyed even more than Dr Henry's, and that was T. C. Mackenzie, whose writing on the Meme Wars and other subcultural narratives spoke to the very core of Joey's being. She dived deep into the rabbit hole of Mackenzie's writings, and found herself further and further enamoured the more she read and understood Mackenzie's way of thinking.

When at last she fell into a sleepless stupor, with fragments of findings and conclusions and abstracts seeping in and out of her fading consciousness in a maelstrom of ambient thought, she felt a profound sense of gratitude at having had even the tiniest hand in a piece of research that would be pitted against T. C. Mackenzie's own work – and a sudden desire to meet this T. C. Mackenzie, if she ever got the chance.

∴

"How did you go with the readings?" Henry asked.

"Trish Mackenzie is *so cool!*" cried Joey, almost leaping out of her seat with excitement.

Henry was too surprised to say anything at first.

"I read nearly all her work the other night," Joey continued happily, "and it gave me so many new ideas for my thesis! The way she thinks – the way she *writes!* I wish I could write like her. No, I *will* write like her one day. That's my goal, to be as cool as she is when I'm her age."

At that, Henry smiled. "That might be the greatest endeavour of them all, Joey. But if anyone could do it, it'd be you."

∴

Over the course of several meetings, their discussions became less work-focussed but still just as fun. And this was fine, they told themselves, because their working relationship didn't officially resume until February anyway.

"My housemates and I had a party on Saturday," said Joey one afternoon, "and it was almost a disaster, but it was saved by a real *bona fide* hero of the people!"

"Oh?" said Dr Henry. "Pray tell."

"Well, you see, I was the only one home, because the others were coming home late from work, so I was getting the house ready and everything, and I'd just put a tray of banana muffins into the oven, when I remembered that we didn't have any ice! And obviously that was going to be a problem, because people were due to show up in the next five or ten minutes, and the bevvies weren't cold enough! So I ran down to the servo – I didn't think to drive, because it was only a block away, and I hate driving if it's going to be less than ten minutes, and in my head we only needed one bag of ice, so I was pretty sure I'd be able to carry it without any problems.

"But then I got to the servo and looked inside the ice locker, and I realised that one five-kilo bag wasn't going to be enough, so I thought perhaps I'd better get two. But then I saw they were $4.20 each, *or* three for $10! And I wasn't going to spend $8.40 for two bags when I could spend $10 and get three. So I picked up three bags of ice and carried them inside and paid for them, and

I was beginning to feel a bit like a fool for not bringing my car, but it was too late because I'd already paid for them. And then I started walking back home carrying *fifteen kilos of ice*, which apart from anything else is just very difficult to keep a grip on, especially because it was freezing outside, and my fingers were going numb. And by the way, the street that leads from the servo to my house is *uphill*, which made it even harder!

"So I was *staggering* up this hill with my fifteen kilos of ice, feeling like an *absolute* fool, and I could barely even see where I was going because the bags were heaped up that high, and my legs were really hurting, and I was just cursing my entire existence – and *then*, would you believe, some *plonker* had the audacity to drive right into my path, because they were pulling out of a driveway! I couldn't see the driver, because they had tinted windows. So I just stood there in the cold for a few seconds, screaming at this person internally because surely they could *see* how much more difficult they were making my task, making me wait for them while they moved their slow-ass car… But then the car stopped! And the driver wound the window down, and I saw it was a lady! She was a bit older than me, and had bright blue hair, and a lot of tattoos and facial piercings, and before I could get a word out, she said, 'Hi, I don't know you. But can I give you a lift to wherever it is you're going?'"

"No way!" said Dr Henry.

"Yes way!" laughed Joey. "I almost cried, I was so grateful – and so humbled. So I got into her car and she drove me the rest of the way to my house, and we had a good chat, and I thanked her for her troubles. And when I got inside with my fifteen kilos of ice, nobody had arrived yet, and my muffins weren't even burned! So it was a good night, in the end."

"I should hope so, after all that."

"It was," she said blissfully. "And I learned an important lesson: never judge the intentions of a driver with tinted-glass windows."

He smiled. "Beautiful."

Chapter Fifteen – Words of Wisdom

Whap.

The ball landed squarely in the rough.

"Typical," said Henry.

"You're not angling your wrist enough on the backswing," said Toni.

"I must be getting arthritic."

Toni snorted and pushed him aside so she could set up her approach. She wasted little time in calculation, and with one deft swing sent her ball neatly onto the green.

"Nice," said Henry.

Toni was the type of person who forgot birthdays, including her own. Each year, Henry would remember and give her a call, and she would dismiss him impatiently once she realised his reason for phoning. But this year she was forty, so Henry had insisted on their taking the day off work so they could go golfing.

"If you stuff up this shot, you owe me a pint," said Toni.

Henry sighed and switched to a 4-hybrid, then ambled down the hill towards his ball, which was sitting forlornly where he'd hit it, several metres into the rough. He lined up his shot with care, swung, and with some effort landed it back on the fairway, about three feet from the green.

"Not bad," said Toni. "Keep going like that and you might get your average up to double-bogey instead of triple."

"Whatever, I'm just here for banter. I don't care who wins."

"Good, 'cause it's gonna be me."

"You're only good at this because you act on instinct," he grumbled. "A thinking man like me has trouble with golf for the same reason he has trouble with power tools – because he spends too much time in his brain, and his body betrays him."

"I do plenty of thinking, you clown."

Henry laughed. It was true, of course: although she had left school after year ten to pursue a trade in cabinet-making, Toni was by far one of the smartest people he knew. It was just that she often couldn't (or couldn't be bothered to) find the words to clearly articulate the contents of her head.

"Alright then," he said, as she pulled a putter out of her bag and inspected it carefully, "today you have entered a new decade of existence. So tell me, what words of wisdom have you attained at your ripe old age that you would be happy to share with the rest of us lowly mortals?"

Toni gave the ground a couple of experimental taps with her clubhead. "Never take a trolley through the self-serve checkouts at the supermarket."

"Truer words were never spake by man," he said solemnly.

She putted her ball with expert ease into the hole. "Dunno about that."

Time passed.

They made their way to the end of the course.

Toni scored an eagle on the eighteenth hole.

"Well, you know what the Lord said on the sixth day…" said Henry.

She nodded. "'Very good.'"

∴

Afterwards, they went to the nearest RSL and ordered the traditional five-dollar pints of the local lager, which they sipped quietly on the outdoor veranda. It was late enough that the shadows were lengthening, but the day had not yet lost its warmth. The heavy afternoon air was punctuated by the distant sounds of industrial machinery, which provided an oddly comforting counterpoint to their silence.

Henry looked at his friend, who had turned away to gaze at nothing in particular, and was suddenly overcome with gratitude for her existence. They had met each other as tiny children, when their mothers had attended the same playgroup. She was a phantom figure who flitted in and out of his earliest memories, almost more of a feeling than a person. But as their paths had crossed repeatedly over the years, her role in his life had grown to one of vital importance: not because of anything she did for him, but just because she was who she was. Her presence was like that of a sibling: dependable, comfortable, understated. Easy to take for granted, if he wasn't careful.

"Toni," he began.

She cut him off with a gesture. "None of that, Hen."

"None of what?"

"You know…sentimental stuff. I don't like it."

"But it's your birthday!"

"Yeah, so why should I care then? It's not hard to make a fuss of someone on the one day you've been given to do it. I mean, I don't doubt that you're being genuine, but I just, I hate the structure of the thing. Pisses me off. If you really want to make a fuss, do it tomorrow, or some other day, when I'm not expecting it."

Henry chuckled. "Alright."

∴

So, the very next day, he turned up at her house with a bunch of flowers and a handmade card that said simply, 'You go alright.'

She burst out laughing when she saw him.

"You idiot," she said.

He shrugged. "I am what I am." Then he took her by the hand. "Now come on, let's go sailing."

Chapter Sixteen – Henry Thinks Everything is Fine, but is Wrong

In a third-floor corner office, in a mid-tier university somewhere in Central Europe, an ancient, bent-over man with bushy white brows and a face like an overripe cherry tomato finished penning his review of a technocultural futurist article on the emergence of Gold Yamre, King of the Godstonks.

His name was Laz Buhrmann, and his wizened old heart had been lifted that day by the offering which Drs Henry B. and L. Honeysett had laid upon the altar of his reviewership. His words to them were few, but kind.

How wonderful, he thought, his gnarled leathery finger poised to hit 'send,' that the younger folks are so alight with passion to continue the search for knowledge and wisdom in these troubled and turbulent times in which we live. How beautiful. And how brave.

∴

In a similar office back in Australia, H. R. Kimble, a wideset man of stern countenance and poetic disposition, sat at his desk in a haze of contentment after a lively couple of hours spent lunching with his old drag racing comrades, and regarded the same article by B. and Honeysett with an indulgent eye.

It's a'ight, was his final comment, which he submitted a moment later.

∴

On a warm sunny morning that signalled the beginning of spring, Trish Mackenzie made her sleepy way from her childhood bedroom to her parents' lounge room, and was met with thunderous salutations: far more noise, in fact, than one would expect from a couple of pensioners – but then, they *were* her parents.

"HAPPY BIRTHDAY!" they clamoured, applauding wildly and crowding in to embrace her.

"Thanks Mum, thanks Dad," she croaked, rubbing sleep from her eyes and graciously accepting the purple-wrapped box that was pressed into her arms. Opening it, she beheld with delight a finely crafted 600mL German beer stein, with lid.

Forty-odd years ago, her father, a timid, bespectacled anthropologist with a fondness for travel memoirs and exotic cuisines, had fallen in love with her mother, a riotously sociable skater-surfer and reformed juvenile delinquent; the result of their union was Trish, who embodied most of these characteristics to varying degrees. It was typical of them to present her with a gift steeped in cultural aesthetics, yet undoubtedly geared towards debauchery.

"Wow, great pick," said Trish, feeling its weight in her hands as she turned it over to admire the intricate patterns carved into its clay surface. "Whose idea was this one?"

"His," said her mother, winking at her father. "*I* wanted to get you a hookah, but he said you had enough vices already without us adding to the list."

"Except I put it more politely than that," her father added, laughing.

"Well, I mean, you're not wrong," Trish admitted. "Speaking of which———" She looked at the clock. "Is nine o'clock too early to start day-drinking?"

Her father looked at her mother and shrugged.

"Nah, not on your birthday," her mother said.

"Excellent – then I'm gonna christen this bad lad right *now*." And she made her way to the kitchen, pulled a couple of James Squires out of the fridge, and filled her new stein to the brim. As she took her first sip and heaved a blissful sigh, her phone buzzed. It was an email from *Currency*, the journal to which she had submitted her project after long and careful thought about which markets were ripest for cryptonomic research. As expected, 'The Seven Mysteries of Gold Yamre' had received glowing reviews, and would be featured prominently in their spring edition!

Trish smiled and returned to her beer. She hadn't been too worried about the reviews, but it felt good to have her work appreciated. *Currency* had traded second and third place in the rankings with *TeCH* since its maiden issue in 2001 (although its impact rating had declined recently over the publication [and subsequent retraction] of a controversial study of mating rituals within black-market dating sims). Out of all the high-ranking technocultural journals, it was the perfect balance between guaranteed publishing and reaching the widest possible audience.[1]

"Trish, are you coming to play indoor lawn bowls, or are you just going to sit in there quaffing pale ale all day?" her mother yelled from the lounge.

"Yeah, I'm coming, I just need to make breakfast," Trish called back.

She was halfway through scrambling some eggs when her phone buzzed again.

It was Henry!

Her smile broadened, and she went to open the message, which contained three simple words:

Happy birthday, LOSER!

Her stomach dropped. Could it be…?

∴

"HURRAYYYYYYYYYYY!!!"

The ear-splitting cry rent the air of the Social Sciences ground floor as Henry and Louisa pranced around the common area, dizzy with joy. They'd rushed to meet each other as soon as they'd received the news.

---

1   Cheers Jacinta <3

"Front entry in the spring edition of *Forward*," Henry gasped for the third time, grabbing her hand and squeezing it, "*and* featured on the cover too! I've *never* had a piece of research promoted so highly!"

Louisa grinned at him. "Don't act so surprised! You deserve it, you've really outdone yourself this time."

"I?" he said dramatically. "I did nothing in and of myself. It was thanks to our creative chemistry that we were able to climb so high. Even Kimble had good things to say about our yarn! In fact, Louisa, I have an apology to make that is long overdue. When I first met you, I thought you were going to be the kind of loose-unit maverick who would drag down a fiddly, pain-in-the-neck project like this one. But you aren't that at all – or at least, if you are, then you're the kind of loose-unit maverick a stuffy old codger like me needs around, to broaden his horizons and spur him on to greater and greater heights. Thank you, again, truly, from the bottom of my heart."

"Aw, cut it out, man," she laughed, "you're embarrassing me." Once again, she couldn't help but admire his naked display of emotion, which seemed so alien to her own, more measured existence. But it was an easy thing to admire from afar. The thought of *partaking* in said emotion – of being drawn into it, even, against her will...*that* was what spurred her hasty retreat behind the walls of false modesty. "So...am I hearing 'celebratory pints'?"

Henry's face fell. "Oh...I'm so sorry, I can't. I have a meeting with Joey, and after that I'm taking my sad, washed-up rival out for her birthday. Raincheck, though?"

"Aw, come on! That's the second time you've done this to me, you absolute dog-act!"

"I know, I know, I'm sorry. Tomorrow night. On my honour."

"Yeah, yeah, what little you have left. Alright, it's a deal. Why don't we——"

But Louisa was cut off as Joey burst through the double sliding doors on a skateboard, looking sweaty and dishevelled. "Hi folks!" she said, skidding to a halt and dismounting with a flourish. "Long time no see, Lou! Hi Dr B.! Ready to go?"

"I am," he said, smiling at her. "Just a sec – let me get my wallet, I left it in my office." He took off running up the stairs, humming something by Takeo Ischi under his breath. Joey and Louisa turned to face each other.

"Back into skating?" Louisa said.

"Yeah." Joey looked sheepish. "I've been in hibernation mode all winter, and it was starting to feel pretty grotty. So I've been trying to get back into more physical activities, and I've gotta say, it's lifted my mood *heaps.*"

"That's so good!" Louisa said. "I feel like that whenever I work on my nonna's farm. It really helps you get out of your head and back into the world, doesn't it?"

"Yeah, it does! I've been thinking a lot lately about this whole question of *being* versus *doing,* and I find that, for me, even though physical tasks are technically *doing,* they feel a lot more like *being,* because they're not tied to any external goals or deadlines, so it's like I can just relax into it and enjoy the feeling of being alive, you know what I'm saying?"

"For sure. So then, do you think it's only like this for people who have office jobs?"

"What do you mean?"

"Well, if you do manual labour for a living, like say you're a bricklayer or something, then do you feel like you're *being,* or *doing,* when you're at work? Does it feel different from when you do manual labour in your spare time? And how do you feel when you're just sitting down reading a book or watching a movie?"

"I don't know, it probably depends on the person."

"Yeah, probably."

"Probably what?" Henry asked, reappearing with his laptop bag slung over one shoulder.

"We're talking about manual labour," Joey said. "Oh – that reminds me! I did some volunteer work in a cemetery the other day, and I learned how to use all these different power tools, and I was trying to use a brush cutter to trim the grass around the graves, but I couldn't get it to turn on! I was pulling the starter cord heaps, and I swear I'd followed all the steps to start it properly, but it just wasn't turning on... And *then*——" (she started laughing, and could barely get the rest of the story out), "——I heard this ambient voice – from behind a hedge or something, and it was an old man – and he said, 'That girl's trying to start a whipper snipper!' – and his friend said, 'Give it a good pull!' and I was like, 'I *am*!' and I have never felt so emasculated in my entire life." (She was crying with laughter by this point.) "It was mortifying. But I had a hearty chuckle about it later."

Louisa and Henry laughed along with her…but Louisa couldn't help but notice that throughout the duration of her tale, Joey had made eye contact only with Henry. And this irked her. Had she not been the one to start the conversation? Was her presence not worth acknowledging? But no…surely she was reading too much into it.

"Well, Lord bless old men and their comments that no one asked for," said Henry.

"May He preserve you from becoming one of them someday," said Louisa.

He winked at her. "Touché." Then he turned to Joey. "Shall we get going?"

"Sounds good. Bye, Lou! See you round!"

"Take care, Louisa. I'll text you about tomorrow night. Bye."

Louisa watched them go, feeling as though she'd been stood in the sun for too long. Her skin felt hot, and her head was spinning.

Joey had made eye contact only with Henry.

Was it just a matter of respect? Was she irritated because a basic rule of courtesy had been violated? Or…?

People don't just look at a person the way Joey looked at Henry, unless…

The anger she felt was immediate, unexpected, and consuming.

But she still didn't understand why.

∴

"You seem super happy today, Dr B.," Joey said over lunch.

"How can I not be?" he chortled. "Our article *destroyed* Trish Mackenzie's, just like I said it would."

"No way!"

"Yes way! We got front pages in *Forward*, and she only got a measly centre-feature in *Currency*! Sucks to be her right now." He raised his glass. "And you were part of that too, Joey! Thanks so much for all your help."

"Aw," she said. "Well, I'm sad for her. But I'm so happy for us! Congratulations!"

"Thanks," he said. "Anyway, I'll commiserate with her this evening when we go out for her birthday."

Joey's eyes widened. "She's *here*?"

"Oh. Yeah, she's down for a couple of months working remotely, to spend some time with her parents. I saw her the other week – played her at street hockey, in fact." (He omitted the part where he'd lost.)

"THAT'S SOOOOO COOL!" she said, nearly jumping out of her seat with excitement. "Do you… Do you think, maybe, you could introduce me to her?"

"Oh," said Henry. "Well. Yes, why not? I'll send her a message right now, if you like." And he did just that. "But anyway, we didn't come here to talk about me and her. So, tell me, what new ideas have you been brewing up for your thesis?"

"*Well…*" Joey took in a deep breath. "How much do you know about multivariate memeconomic stream theory?"

∴

Trish sat upon her bed in a haze of depression.

When the message came from Henry, she was almost too dejected to answer it. But it was *Henry*, and the fire in her heart still burned for him, even if now it was a small, sorry mass of faintly glowing coals.

Hey Trisho, was just wondering if you'd mind me bringing a guest tonight. I'm supervising her Ph.D. next year, and she's a BIG fan of your work. I think you'd enjoy meeting her. - H

Trish was surprised. Henry wasn't normally one for networking, or for overlapping different sets of relationships. Whoever this person was, she must be something special. And who was she, Trish Mackenzie, to scorn a person's wish to meet someone they admired? Anyway, it would distract her from her current desolation.

So she resigned herself and replied: *sure thing, see you at 7.*

∴

Evening fell, and Eden was shocked to see Henry and Trish enter the Arms together, accompanied by a much younger woman whom she didn't recognise.

"G'day!" she exclaimed, as they approached the bar. "What's all this about?"

"Eden?" said Trish. "I didn't know you were back!"

"I could say the same for you!"

They gaped at each other in amazement.

("Let's go and find a table," Henry murmured to Joey, who readily acquiesced.)

"So, how's life?" Eden asked Trish.

Trish did not generally have the capacity to feel more than one emotion at a time. Currently, her self-pity had been displaced by surprise, which in turn was slowly tending back towards her default optimism, so she was more open to conversation than she had been an hour ago. "Not bad, thanks. I've been working in Sydney, writing on this and that, playing hockey, and just generally having a jolly old time. You?"

Eden smiled. "I had a turbulent few years after I left, but life is pretty serene now. I serve people drinks, and I listen to their yarns, and I like to think that I inject a tiny modicum of joy into their day…and then I go home and spend time with my dog."

"That does sound serene," said Trish, slightly envious. Her natural disposition forbade her from sitting still, even in her scholarly profession, and she had yet to spend a day in any state remotely bordering serenity.

"Mm, she goes alright," said Eden.

Trish laughed. It was strange for her to encounter this new, grown-up Eden after so many years. She had never exactly disliked her, but she'd resented the effect that Eden had on Henry – and by extension, on Trish's friendship with Henry. But the tension had never been strong enough to manifest itself outwardly, and now that its basis was both distant and irrelevant, Trish felt a sudden burst of gratitude at having the opportunity to know Eden as a person, and not just as a concept which sparked vague animosity.

"Well, while I'm down here, hopefully I'll see you around," she said.

"I'd like that," said Eden.

Trish ordered a round of drinks and departed to find her comrades.

Eden watched her go, and, though she knew not why, thought back to her conversation with Henry some weeks ago, and found herself wondering how sincere his words had been – and, worse, how sincere *hers* had been.

∴

"You shouldn't have bought the first round on your birthday," Henry objected, as Trish set their glasses down on the table and took a seat.

"Well what was I supposed to do, you numpty? You just up and *left* me!"

"Yeah, because you and Eden were talking, and I didn't want to interrupt! I was just going to grab a table, but I would've come *back* to get drinks once you'd finished."

"And you just expected me to know that?"

"Obviously!"

Trish rolled her eyes and turned to Joey. "Sorry about him, he's a menace. So. You're Joey."

Joey nodded eagerly. "Yes."

"And by some great misfortune," Trish went on, "you've been landed with this buffoon for your Ph.D. supervisor, yes?"

"That's no way to talk about the guy who's getting featured on the front cover of *Forward*," Henry teased.

"Shut up," she rejoined. "We're still only tied, and I'll beat you next time."

"Actually," Joey piped up, "I asked him to be my supervisor."

"Oh," said Trish. "Well, fair enough. You could do worse than someone who just got on the front cover of *Forward*, I guess…" A sudden wave of depression cascaded over her, and she reached for her glass.

"Well," said Joey, "I don't know too much about all those rankings and whatnot. I just think it's amazing that both of you got published! The only thing I've published so far is my master's thesis. But your work is *so good*, though! I'm just so happy to be able to meet you! Thank you so much for sharing your birthday celebration with me, by the way – oh, and happy birthday! Sorry, I can't seem to get my paragraphs to flow properly today, I'm obviously out of practice…"

Trish found herself warming to this peculiar young lady and her mile-a-minute sentences. She liked how Joey was so unabashed about her emotions – it reminded her of herself. Although, being a stubborn and highly competitive person, she was slightly confronted by the ease with which Joey displayed her admiration of others and desire for guidance. "I know what you mean," she said, "I've always had trouble laying out a logical order of ideas myself. My writing is a bit like 'HERE'S A LOT OF DIFFERENT THINGS WHICH HAVE NO RELEVANCE TO EACH OTHER BUT ARE ALL EQUALLY INTERESTING,' whereas Henry writes more like *'Here's a gradual progression from A to B.'*"

"Mmmmm," said Joey, nodding more vehemently, "I noticed that when I was reading both your works, but I hadn't really put words to it before. I think I'm probably somewhere between those two extremes. With academia, at least. With everything else it's just kind of nebulous chaos."

"Oh, that's not true," said Henry. "You tell an excellent anecdote. Tell Trish the one about the old lady and the mulberry tree!"

The conversation wore on, rambling capriciously from topic to topic in the way that all the best conversations do. Joey enjoyed herself immensely, although at certain points she felt the faint stab of insecurity at being in the presence of an old and obviously well-established friendship. But Trish and Henry were very open in their interactions, and by the end of the evening, they might all three of them have been old friends.

∴

Henry arrived home that night feeling pleasantly overloaded with sensations and memories from what felt like a thousand different conversations – and was startled to find himself surrounded by a number of his ghostly relatives: Doreen, his triple-great grandmother; Uncle Tompkin, his grandfather's older half-brother; Lucibelle and Mayflower, his twin third cousins twice removed, who had always worn thick black woollen stockings even in summer; and a half-dozen others besides, all shouting at the tops of their voices.

"Henry!" Uncle Tompkin thundered. "What is the meaning of this?"

"The meaning of what, Uncle?"

"Of gallivanting around the town with this woman and that, that's what!" said Cousin Lucibelle, poking him in the chest with a long-nailed finger that might have hurt if it had possessed material substance.

"What do you mean by flitting about hither and yon like a giddy schoolboy, promising everything and delivering nothing?" Great-Grandmother Doreen snapped. "A sensible lad of your age should know better!"

"But——" said Henry.

"You can't just go and traipse around with one girl in the morning, have lunch with another in the afternoon, and have drinks with *three* different girls in the evening!" she went on. "It simply isn't done!"

"Not to mention that other one he talks to at the café," Cousin Mayflower interjected.

"How do you *know* these things?" Henry cried.

"Your grandmother's right, Henry," said Tompkin fastidiously. "A real man knows what he wants, and he gives it everything he's got. He lays his life on the line for it, and doesn't let anything, or any*one* distract him."

"But I *do* know what I want!" Henry shot back. "I want to do my research. I'm *committed* to my research! And the only thing distracting me is *you* people, and your incessant meddling in my affairs! I don't know how it is that you have so much insight into my social calendar, but this needs to stop! I'm not doing anything wrong, and I'm under no obligation to anybody. If I want to sustain a few different friendships with a few different people who just *happen* to be women, then that's my business, and it doesn't mean anything. My mind is as made up as it's always been. I'm *not* getting married, and that's that."

He stormed upstairs, pausing only to turn off the hall lights, and took himself exasperatedly to bed, where he lay awake, fuming, for a very long while.

∴

When he went out the next evening with Louisa (having suggested a different pub this time), his spirits had once again plummeted to the lowest possible depths.

Louisa, observing his subdued movements and speech, was conflicted. On the one hand, her desire to help him was as strong as ever. On the other, she felt slightly hurt that he had seemed so happy in the company of others, and was now so melancholy in hers. Was there something wrong with her? Did he not enjoy being around her any more? Or was it entirely coincidental?

In the end, however, the desire to help won out, and, emboldened by the fact that she'd got a response from him last time (even though that conversation had left her feeling equally ambivalent), she asked, "Everything alright, Henry?"

"Hm?" he said, scowling into his amber ale.

"You seem down in the dumps again. Is it that friend of yours?"

He looked up, startled. He'd forgotten he'd talked to her about that. "Oh…no. Nothing like that. Just family stuff, that's all."

"Ah."

A pause.

He took a very long drink, almost emptying his glass in one go. He was fed up with decorum. After a moment, he shrugged, made a vague gesture of contempt, and continued. "They want me to get married and produce an heir and all that stuff, but I'm not interested. I keep telling them, but they never listen. It's been a point of contention for about as long as I've been alive."

"Oh," said Louisa. This was the issue with asking about these things. His problems, much like his emotions, were unfathomable to her. Their lives, their experiences, were polar opposites. She had no idea what to say to him. "That's rough."

He shrugged again. "It's not that bad, mostly. It just builds up every now and again. I'm sorry, I've not been much of a colleague to you recently."

"No, you're…" She broke off, unsure what she was trying to say, unsure if her words were convincing even to herself. "You're fine."

He smiled wanly. "Thanks."

∴

When they parted ways later that evening, she finally understood why it was that she'd been feeling so unsettled of late, and why his actions, and hers, and Joey's, and everyone's, were so difficult to process.

A colleague. That was all she was to him.

The truth was, no matter how much time passed, and no matter how close they became, he would never see her – never value her – as anything other than a means of furthering his research.

And that was devastating.

Chapter Seventeen – Three Interviews

Sarah had never met Dr Trish Mackenzie in person before, though they had corresponded several times in the last couple of years, during which Dr Mackenzie had written a series of research articles on the Meme Wars and Sarah had reported on her findings. Sarah admired Dr Mackenzie's work immensely, but had always imagined that she would be intimidated by her, should they actually meet.

Now, as they shook hands for the first time over a couple of short macchiatos, Sarah was surprised by how drawn she felt to this older woman who had cut such a striking figure upon the academic scene, whose short black hair and bright red glasses gave her an almost aggressive appearance, and yet whose demeanour, though forceful, was warm and inviting – magnetic, even – like that of a born leader.

"Thank you for coming to meet with me," Sarah said, overcoming the temptation to shyness and giving the doctor her most winning smile. "I know you're not often in the state, and your time must be precious."

Dr Mackenzie took a sip of coffee and returned the smile. "Not at all! I love sharing about my work, I'll talk about it with anybody who'll listen."

"That's fair," said Sarah. "I appreciate that." She paused, almost not wanting to ask the question and potentially spoil the mood. "From what I understand, your most recent project on the godstonk Gold Yamre will be published in the upcoming issue of *Currency*, which is the third-highest ranking technocultural journal. How do you feel about these results?"

Dr Mackenzie shrugged. "Well, I'll be honest, I was pretty disappointed I hadn't just taken the risk and submitted to *Forward*, especially when my arch-rival snagged the front cover. But you have to learn to cop these things if you want to survive in academia. Some people think it's a frivolous occupation, but I'm telling ya, it's a blood sport. You don't get very far if you can't handle a loss every now and then."

"Were you happy with your work overall, though?"

"Oh, absolutely! I think it turned out really well, given its scope was more ambitious than a lot of my other projects. And it allowed me to experiment with a couple of different methods than the ones I've used in the past. It got good reviews, too. It just happened that Henry outdid me this time." She took another drink, totally unselfconscious.

"Do you have any ideas about your next project?" Sarah asked.

Dr Mackenzie steepled her fingers. "Not sure. I'm thinking I might go back to my roots, maybe look into some multimedia depictions of emergent technologies…but we'll see. The beauty of the field is that there's a lot of topical crossover, so you don't have to worry too much about specialising yourself into a hole."

"Then do you think your research will continue to overlap with Dr B.'s?"

Dr Mackenzie smiled. "I have no doubt of that. We're fated rivals, he and I. We inspire one another to improve through our competition. That's how it's always been. That's how I came to love technocultural futurism in the first place, really. I always found it interesting, but I would never have stuck with it for so long, if I hadn't been competing with him."

"I'm sort of surprised you aren't more upset by your recent loss, since you feel so strongly about this," Sarah admitted.

"Then you haven't known the pleasure of a battle hard-fought between friends."

Sarah was taken aback. "Sorry?"

"Well, he's a friend first, and a rival second," Dr Mackenzie said, as though this were the most obvious thing in the world. "I salute him for his victory; it was well deserved."

Sarah, who found nothing so agonising as her own failings, couldn't help but feel touched by the ease and grace with which Dr Mackenzie seemed to have accepted her defeat. She was currently trying to improve in this area herself, by reading a book called *How To Accept Defeat*. But now she wondered, sitting across from this woman who seemed the epitome of self-assurance, whether she might just be able to learn a whole lot more from her than could ever be found in any book.

As if reading her mind, Dr Mackenzie winked at her. "Anyway, I'll beat him for sure next time."

Sarah chuckled.

∴

"How do you think your experience working with Dr B. on 'Gold Yamre: An Origin Myth' will benefit your own future research?"

Dr Honeysett deliberated for a moment, taking a large bite of her Hawaiian parmy with extra cheese before answering. "Well, I've always been a fan of interdisciplinary projects, so I find any collaborative work rewarding. And I think a broadening of one's perspective is always going to strengthen one's solo research. But I've never worked in a field with as much potential for practical application as technocultural futurism, so I think that's opened up a lot of new doors, which is really exciting."

"There's been some speculation that your contribution to the project is the reason it's been so successful, since none of Dr B.'s other work to date has been published so prominently. What are your thoughts?"

Louisa blushed faintly. "I dunno about that, I mean…I think, in life, you have visionaries, and you have doers. I'm more of a doer, personally, and I probably brought some specific skills to the table, which maybe helped us to execute Dr B.'s vision in a way which he mightn't have been able to by himself. But it was still *his* vision, do you know what I mean?"

"I do," Sarah conceded. "Then do you think, if you're a doer, would you ever switch fields to something, in your own words, more practically applicable, like technocultural futurism?"

"Nah, man," Louisa grinned. "Futurism might be practical, but media studies is so much more fun."

Sarah blinked.

"Huh," she said. "Fair enough."

A pause ensued, broken only by the clink of cutlery against plates.

"Would you work with Dr B. again?" asked Sarah.

It was only a slight thing, and only for a second – but Louisa frowned. "Dunno," she said. "Depends on where our different paths of research take us."

Sarah decided not to press the issue. "Makes sense."

∴

"Congratulations!"

Dr B. smiled. "Thank you, Sarah. I'm very proud of the work we put into this one, so I'm glad the folks at *Forward* were as pleased with it as we were."

"Tell me about your findings."

"Well, as you know, our objective in the beginning was to find the origin of Gold Yamre and an explanation for its rapid ascension amongst the other godstonks. But after we decrypted the YamreAU Beta Fan Forum and followed the trail of breadcrumbs to its very inception, what we found was that Gold Yamre actually doesn't exist!"

"What?"

"Exactly. The whole concept, and the discourse surrounding it, was an elaborate ruse dreamed up by some high schoolers, intended to parody the mechanics of real existing godstonks, but not actually having any real-world effects. But the power of the narrative became so great, and so many people bought into it, that the phantom currency began acquiring an actual monetary value. Much like how *Pingu in the City* was briefly voted the number-one anime of all time."

"That's incredible!"

"Isn't it just?" he said excitedly. "It opens up a whole new field of memeconomic possibilities, from phantom currency to psychosocial consumerism to semiotic capital catalysis! I'm having trouble just deciding what to do for my next project!"

"You've beat me to my next question," Sarah laughed. "I'll have to come back later and interview you again."

"I wouldn't be complaining if you did."

Sarah felt her cheeks grow hot.

"Technocultural futurism is a field that doesn't get a lot of coverage," Dr B. went on, heedless of her agitation, "so I'm very grateful for people like you, who've taken such an interest in it."

Ah, of course.

She cleared her throat. "Was there anything you did differently while working on this project that you think might have improved on your previous research?"

"Well, I think I was a lot more open than I normally would be to changing the scope of the article as the results came in. And obviously, collaborating with Dr Honeysett meant that we could get a lot more work done in a shorter space of time."

"How was it working with Dr Honeysett?"

"Oh, she's fantastic. We have a really good working relationship, and I found that she challenged me to improve in a lot of ways that I hadn't considered before."

"Would you work with her again?"

He hesitated. "I'm not usually the collaborating type, I must admit… I think I'd like to refocus and continue honing my skills on my own for a while."

Sarah could understand that.

"But I hope so," he added. "Someday, in the not-too-distant future. It was a fruitful dynamic, while it lasted."

She smiled. "Thank you so much for your time, Dr B."

"No," he said, "thank *you*."

They shook hands.

"Busy day?" he asked.

"Yeah," she said, faintly aware of a rising anxiety now that the formal structure of the conversation was over. "Might go home and crack open a cold one, maybe watch *The Castle*…"

"*The Castle*," Dr B. mused. "Good choice."

She nodded, grinning despite herself. "It's my go-to for the end of a long day. I'm one of those people who watches the same five movies over and over again, and *The Castle* is my favourite, because…" She realised she was babbling, and stopped.

"Because why?" he asked.

Her face was on fire. "Because…it helps me believe that life is actually good."

"Beautiful," he said quietly.

The silence that stretched out between them seemed longer than a day in the Antarctic.

"Well," said he, standing up to leave, "I hope you enjoy it, as always."

"Thanks," she murmured.

He reached the door, and –

"Henry?" she said.

He stopped.

"Do you think…" she began. "Would you ever… Would you want——"

His eyes met hers. "Would I want…?"

She could feel herself beginning to panic – and then the words came tumbling out, almost of their own accord: *"Would you want to go out for coffee sometime?"*

He looked at her – startled – hesitant – confused –

Her vision clouded over.

"Never mind," she started to say.

Suddenly, he smiled – and it was as though the clouds had split and the sun had broken through to touch the earth.

"I'd like that," he said.

Chapter Eighteen – Thirty-Nine in September, Part I

Here sits Henry at his desk, quietly working.

Little does he know of the events being set in motion, soon to rear up and perturb him, like peasants with pitchforks come to wake the giant from its slumber. Little does he know of the conversations being had even now, revolving around him like the flotsam and jetsam of a sixty-year Space Race orbiting the earth.

∴

"We should do something for Henry's birthday," Mark mused.

"Like what?" asked Donovan, grunting slightly as he wrestled with a particularly stubborn patch of Spanish heath. It was a Saturday morning, and he'd offered to help Mark with some gardening.

"Well, that's the part I was hoping you'd be able to help me with."

"Am I not doing enough for you already?" Donovan demanded, pulling the weed free at last and brandishing it before his friend's eyes.

"I'm giving you the opportunity to grow in charity, Don. You should be thanking me."

Donovan snorted. "Anyway, what makes you think he'd want to do anything?"

"I just think he needs a break; he's seemed really out of it lately. I rang him the other day, and he couldn't make up his mind how he felt about being so out of routine the last couple of months. So I think it would be good if we got together and did something different, help him to refresh and recentre himself."

"Hmm," said Donovan. "You might be right."

"But I'm stumped for what to do," Mark sighed, attacking a fresh clump of weeds as though they were the source of all his woes. "My idea of a good time is sitting in the garden doing sudoku."

Donovan frowned into space for a while, poking idly at the ground with his trowel.

Then he brightened. "Why don't we go camping?"

∴

At the corner of the eastern wing of Biddlesnoot-Bloomington Manor, there is a tall, rickety tower. At the top of this tower, there is a parlour room with windows on every side. It is known as the Murder Room, for reasons which the first generation of Biddlesnoot-Bloomingtons have never cared to share with their descendants. In this room, the family patriarchs and matriarchs have conducted their private business for centuries, unnoticed or unheeded by the younger generations.

On this particular day, a number of Biddlesnoot-Bloomingtons had gathered in the Murder Room to discuss what should be done about Henry, their wayward heir. Chief among them were his parents, Samson and Adelaide; his triple-great grandmother, Doreen; his Aunts Rosalind and Rosalinda; his Uncle Bertram; and his ten-times-great-grandfather, John, the very first Biddlesnoot-Bloomington, who, at the age of six-and-twenty, had become the richest alpaca farmer in the known world, and had subsequently changed his name from Smith because he didn't think it distinguished enough for a man of his position.

A reverent hush fell over the spectral assembly as John Biddlesnoot-Bloomington wafted through their midst to assume his place at the head of the room. A short man, barely four-foot-one, and almost as wide, John had always had a looming presence, like storm clouds gathering on the horizon: even before he spoke, one could not help but feel his shadow cast over everything which lay before him. He was an impressive man, with bushy white whiskers and a black velvet jacket. Even now, in his immaterial state, he was like a heavenly body with immense gravitational pull, drawing all eyes and ears to himself, exerting the weight of his being upon the universe.

As the silence in the room thickened to the point of solidity, John broke it easily, like a child breaking a stick in its hands. He affected a clearing of the throat that was, of course, entirely rhetorical.

"What seems," quoth he, "to be the problem?"

Two dozen voices answered eagerly, clamouring at him, bawling and blustering, screeching and clawing at each other in their desperation for his attention, piling together in a cacophonous throng until the East-Wing Tower had become its very own Tower of Babel, erupting at the seams in a howling, frenetic pandemonium that would have made poor deaf Beethoven weep.

John held up a hand, and his kindred were still.

He pointed to Adelaide. "Speak, Granddaughter."

Though nervous, Adelaide did not hesitate. "It's about Henry."

John closed his eyes and nodded slowly. "Hoom. I might have known."

"It's just that," Adelaide went on, "he's been seeing a lot of different women lately, but we – some of us, anyway – are worried that he hasn't really committed to anyone, and if he doesn't make up his mind soon, his companions may well lose interest and leave him right back where he started."

"We didn't want to meddle," Samson chimed in, "but the lad doesn't know his own heart. Left to his own devices, he'd sooner run than make any sort of decision."

"I don't think that's quite fair——" Uncle Bertram began.

John cut him off with a gesture. "Enough. I have heard tell of these things which you speak. I think it is high time that something be done about the boy. Otherwise, our legacy which we have worked so hard to build may be doomed."

There was a solemn pause.

"Then what do you suggest we do, Grandfather?" asked Rosalinda.

"Hoom," said John. "I think perhaps we had better give him some encouragement."

∴

Elsewhere in Biddlesnoot-Bloomington Manor, Cousin Phillipus sat before a congregation of aunts, uncles, cousins, and step-siblings, and read out a series of numbers from a little black notebook:

"A-right, a-right, listen up, listen up – odds on the young Ph.D. hopeful are ten to one – ten to one, I said – any bets on the young Ph.D. hopeful? Very good, Cousin Engelbert. A-right, short odds on the rival researcher, at the moment she's sitting on one to three – one to three, I said – any bets? Now, there's been a bit of fluctuation lately, but I'm told it's one to one for the research partner, and two to one for the old flame – bet with care, lads and lasses, those numbers may change again shortly. A-right, odds on the old friend are five to one – bit reclusive, hard to get any data, but time will tell if loyalty wins out. Any bets on the old friend? Five to one, now – any bets? Ooh, a handsome wager from Uncle Victor and Cousin Emmaline! Jolly good. Now, odds on the precocious young journalist…"

∴

Meanwhile, in the observatory, Uncle Tompkin, having received instructions from Great-Grandfather John, had assembled a strike team of relations to carry out the patriarch's master plan.

"It's very simple," he said pompously, pacing up and down the room with his ghostly hands in his waistcoat pockets. "Grandfather John has it on good authority that Master Henry's friends are planning to take him on a camping trip. This should provide more than adequate opportunity for relationship-building if we can just get some of his lady friends to go with him. But since neither Henry nor his friends will think to invite them, *we* shall simply have to do so on Henry's behalf. So, I've procured the names and addresses of the ladies in question——"

"Why, Uncle Tompkin, how *ever* did you manage that?" said little Cousin Timothy, staring at his uncle with slack-jawed admiration.

Uncle Tompkin smirked. "Ah, Timothy, perhaps you have not yet realised that we spirits are no longer bound by material laws."

"I see," said Timothy, not seeing at all.

"Very good," his uncle said. "Now, if there are no more questions, I have assigned each of you an invitee, and I want you all to put your very best efforts into writing an invitation that will surely persuade your target to accompany Master Henry on the trip."

As the other ghosts got to work, Aunt Perpetua raised a hand.

Tompkin rolled his eyes. "Yes?"

"Wouldn't it be more effective to concentrate our efforts on just *one* target?" Perpetua enquired. "I can't imagine that the presence of several ladies all at once would lead very naturally to intimacy."

"Orders from on high," Tompkin shrugged. "Eggs and baskets and all that."

"Well, don't say I didn't warn you," Perpetua muttered under her non-existent breath.

∴

Henry sits at his desk, quietly working,
totally unaware of all these happenings.

∴

Louisa was astonished to check the letters one morning and find a handwritten note from Henry, inviting her on a camping trip that weekend to celebrate his birthday.

Whatever had happened to being merely colleagues? Had she misjudged his intentions all this time?

For a long while, she was hesitant to reply, not knowing what she wanted, and not knowing what was right.

∴

Trish was delighted at the prospect of a camping trip, particularly since she was to return to Sydney on Monday night, and there could be no more fitting way to say goodbye.

She read the invitation over again, and the fire in her heart burned fierce and bright.

∴

Mathilda was dumbfounded. *She?* Invited on a *camping trip?* With a man she'd barely *met?*

But then again, what else was she doing with her life right now?

∴

Sarah was scandalised. They hadn't even had that coffee yet!

∴

"Wahoo, Dorothy!" cried Joey, bounding up and down the stairs with unbridled elation.

"What is it this time?" one of her housemates called from the kitchen.

"I'm going *camping!*"

∴

Toni smiled and shook her head.

That *idiot.*

She fished around in her jacket pocket for an old Woolies receipt and scrawled a brief reply: *Sorry Hen, but you know I can't stand these get-togethers. Maybe next time.*

∴

Eden felt her heart rate rising exponentially with each sentence that she read.

Could this mean…?

Was it possible that he had changed his mind?

Surely not, she rebuked herself.

But then again, there was no telling – not with him.

Chapter Nineteen – Thirty-Nine in September, Part II

Henry was enjoying a nice quiet Friday afternoon, sitting serenely in his office and daydreaming about potential topics for his next research project, when all of a sudden, he was beset by a veritable avalanche of text messages which sent his phone into a spasmodic fit and startled him so violently that he almost fell out of his ergonomic green pleather swivel chair.

Hi Dr B, thanks so much for the invite, wrote Sarah Banks. *Unfortunately I'm busy this weekend, so I won't be able to make it.*

Make what? thought Henry, brow furrowed.

see you soon, nerd! wrote Trish.

HAPPY BIRTHDAY DR B! Joey practically screamed at him through her violent and altogether unnecessary use of all-caps. *I LOVE CAMPING! I'LL BE THERE.*

Henry was starting to feel a bit like a damp sock, clinging pathetically to the walls of the washing machine when the rest of the load has been hung out to dry. *Camping?* What was going on?

A deluge of thank-yous and yes-pleases swiftly followed from Eden, Mathilda Smythe (how had she got hold of his number?!), and Louisa Honeysett, each of them expressing in their own way how pleased they were to be joining him on a camping trip of some description.

Henry was utterly lobotomised by the enormity of his situation. He had no time to wonder what to say – what to do – who was behind all these messages – when someone knocked at his office door and then strode on in without taking the trouble to wait for an answer.

It was a small acne-ridden youth.

"Courier service for you, Master Henry," it mumbled indistinctly through a wad of fluoro-pink bubble gum.

"I beg your pardon?" Henry managed after a tense couple of seconds.

The child rolled its eyes. "A note was left for you at your house, so your mum aksed me to come bring it to you."

"If it was sent to my *house*, why couldn't it just wait there until I got home from work?!" Henry exploded.

The youth shrugged at him and held out the note (which seemed to be inscribed upon the back of an old shopping receipt), popping its gum as it did so.

Henry took it with a sigh.

"That'll be five bucks," said the youth indifferently.

Henry growled and shoved some coins in its general direction. "There, now *please* leave me alone, and don't accept any more job offers from my mother."

"Fine," the child snapped. "Don't aks *me* for any help when you need it, then. Beastly ole sod." And it stuck its tongue out at him and left.

Defeated, Henry read the note. It wasn't signed, but the handwriting was Toni's. He almost laughed at it despite himself, it was so like her. He envied her ability to say 'no' without feeling the need to cushion it with social niceties (although he also wasn't sure whether such behaviour was compatible with his moral principles: a dilemma which he had oft contemplated during the wee hours of the night, after those ill-fated days when he'd indulged in one too many piccolos).

At this precise nanosecond, Mark and Donovan came lolloping through the door (which the small acne-ridden youth had left ajar [deliberately, Henry was certain, although he tried not to be in the habit of judging the disposition of his fellow men's hearts]), both of them bedecked in party hats and streamers and other festive frippery. "HAPPY BIRTHDAY!!" they chorused, executing a war dance around his desk and generally making complete fools of themselves.

Henry glowered at them. "It's *tomorrow*, you dumb molls."

"We *know* that," said Mark, taking him by the elbow and placing a party hat on his head, "but there's this wonderful little thing called 'anticipation,' which perhaps you've heard of. No? Well then, allow me to introduce you, I think you'll make a lovely couple."

"Don't stuff me around, Mark, I've had a rough day," Henry complained. (He hadn't, mind you; his entire day sans the last five minutes had been refreshingly uneventful. But we might forgive him his sweeping generalisations, given the heat of the moment.) "What are you *doing*, anyway?" For they had seized him on either side and begun dragging him from the room.

"We're taking you camping for the weekend," said Donovan. "Down at my old man's shack."

"What?" said Henry.

"For your birthday," Mark grinned. "You've seemed a bit off lately, so we thought it would cheer you up."

"And so you just decided to gather all of the women in my life in one place and make me spend an entire weekend with them all at once?" Henry demanded as he was led downstairs, out of the building, and bundled into the backseat of Mark's Toyota SUV. "How is *that* supposed to cheer me up, exactly?"

"What?" said Mark and Donovan simultaneously.

Henry made an impatient noise and showed them the messages on his phone.

Mark and Donovan gawped at each other – and suddenly, Henry understood what was really going on. He cursed himself for not having thought of it sooner, for it *should* have been obvious from the beginning. "Hold on," he said curtly, and dialled the Biddlesnoot-Bloomington landline, while his friends drove on down the highway in a sort of stupor.

It was his Cousin Flora who answered. "Biddlesn——"

"Flora, it's me," said Henry, loath to suffer the dreadful name to be uttered. "Can you put Mum on, please?"

"Fine, whatever," his cousin said.

There was an oppressive silence, during which Mark tried to play Suzi Quatro on the CD player, but Donovan turned it off again.

Then Henry heard his mother on the line: "Henry, sweetheart, what's wrong?"

"Don't 'what's wrong' me, Mum!" he squalled. "You know perfectly well what's wrong! Are you and the others trying to ruin my birthday? Are you trying to ruin my *life*? Why did you invite Trish and Louisa and everyone else to come *camping* with me, *without* my knowledge or consent?!"

"Oh, that," his mother said vaguely. "You don't need to worry——"

"*Yes I bloody-well do!*"

"Don't speak to me like that, Henry. The family and I just want you to have a wonderful birthday with all your friends, you know. And since you weren't likely to organise anything on your own, we just gave you a bit of help, that's all. Oh – now do excuse me, darling, I believe your grandmother wants me to come and help her haunt those rats in the cellar." With that, she hung up, leaving Henry speechless with rage.

"So," said Mark. "What are we gonna do, chief?"

"Tell 'em there was a mistake and they should go home," Donovan suggested.

"We can't do that!" said Henry, appalled.

"Why not? It's the truth."

"Yes, but – you can't just – I mean, what am I supposed to say? 'Thank you so much for taking time out of your week to celebrate my birthday with me, but I actually don't want you here, and it wasn't really me sending the invites, it was the ghosts of my family ancestors'?"

"Something like that, yeah."

"They'll never believe it!" Henry wailed. "They're just gonna think I'm some kind of schizophrenic maniac who doesn't know if he loves or hates them!"

"That's the truth too, isn't it?" Mark teased.

Henry scowled at him. "No. We're just going to have to pretend that the invitations were legitimate, and that nothing is amiss. It'll be far less awkward that way."

"For *you*, maybe!" Donovan said, outraged. "*We're* married! We planned this camping trip on the understanding that it was just going to be the three of us! What's Katie going to say when she finds out I actually spent the whole weekend with a bunch of random women she's never met?!"

"Don't worry about it, Don, they're all in love with Henry anyway, so there's no danger," said Mark.

"You are both impossible," Henry snapped. "This is why I *hate* surprise birthday parties."

"Well excuse *us* for trying to be charitable," said Mark.

The argument waxed and waned until they reached their destination: a half-acre block of bushland, heavily populated with wattle and banksia trees, which backed onto a high narrow hill. They passed the letterbox, which was hewn from an old tree stump, and travelled slowly up the long gravel driveway until they reached a low, red brick building which sat lopsidedly at the edge of the block as though it had fallen off the back of a passing lorry. Seeing there were already a couple of cars parked outside, Donovan hastily turned off the engine and excused himself to go and call his wife. Mark gave Henry an apologetic glance, then trailed after him.

Henry alighted reluctantly from the car and went to greet Trish and Joey, who, having arrived some time ago, had wandered through the scrub towards a nearby dam, and were admiring the ducks.

"I think ducks are the most overrated *and* underrated animal," Joey was saying as he drew near.

"Hmmm," said Trish, "I can see that."

Henry cleared his throat. "Evening."

They whirled to face him.

"Happy birthday, Dr B.!" said Joey, bounding over and saluting. "Oh! Wait on, I got you a present, just one sec——" And she skipped away to her car, abrupt as ever.

"G'day, loser," said Trish.

"Thanks for coming," Henry said nervously.

"Well, thanks for having me," she beamed, looking around her and breathing in deeply. "It's been ages since I went camping. Although, are we proper camping, or——" (with a derisive glance towards the low brick building), "*weenie* camping?"

"I'm not——" Henry began, feeling his pores erupt at the thought of cramming so many people into such a small house…

"I brought my mum's old tent just in case, so I'm good to go either way," Trish went on, oblivious (as usual) to his discomfort.

At this point Joey came half-running, half-waddling back, carrying a large cardboard box which appeared slightly damp at the bottom, with a bright red ribbon tied around it, and a number of suspicious-looking holes bored into the top. "Here you go!" she said triumphantly. "From my heart and home to yours. Be careful though…" As she pressed the box into his arms, Henry peeped awkwardly through one of the holes, and descried a small goldfish in a bowl.

"Isn't he beaut?" Joey sighed blissfully, as Henry gazed upon the fish, aghast, and beside him Trish went into fits of helpless laughter. "I'm not normally good at giving presents, but *this* one was inspired, if I do say so myself. I thought he could keep you company in the office now that Lou and I are both gone."

By and by, Mark and Donovan came to greet the party. "Hullo!" said Mark. "What've you got there, Hen?"

"It's a fish," Joey exposited needlessly, so pleased was she with her perfect gift that she even forgot to introduce herself. "I gave him to Dr B. for his birthday. He doesn't have a name yet, though. What are you gonna call him, Dr B.?"

"I," said Henry, "I don't——"

"Speaking of names, mine's Mark," said Mark. "And this is Donovan."

"Oh," said Joey, blushing slightly, "sorry – I'm Joey, I'm from the uni."

"And *we're* from the real world," said Donovan, shaking her hand.

"Don't be cheeky, Don," said Mark. "Trish!" he added. "Long time no see."

Trish greeted Mark and Donovan with her usual enthusiasm, having of course known them on and off for years. The conversation continued, and presently another couple of cars pulled into the driveway. Recognising them as Louisa's and Eden's, Henry gingerly handed the fish back to Joey and trotted towards the house to meet them.

"G'day, thanks for coming," he said, embracing them in turn as they emerged from their vehicles. "You two have more or less met, haven't you?"

Louisa and Eden eyed each other with dim recognition.

"I'm Eden," the latter said, smiling.

"Louisa," that worthy replied. "Nice to meet you, Eden. Happy birthday, Henry! I got you something." Henry went taut at the sight of another cardboard box; however, on opening it, it proved to be filled with… "Homemade muesli bars! Nonna and I made them this morning. They're all different flavours, local-grown ingredients, mainly from ours and our neighbours' farms. *Basically* gourmet, not that it's a big deal or anything…" She pretended to inspect her fingernails.

"I truly don't deserve this," faltered Henry. "I'm only turning thirty-nine, after all!"

"A humble age," Eden mused, albeit with a twinkle in her eye, "but still worth celebrating."

"I agree," Louisa said brightly. "Life is pain, and we gotta scrape the joy out of it."

"I never thought I'd hear you say something so nihilistic," Henry remarked.

Eden laughed. "It's from a movie, you nong. Also, here, I got you something too."

She handed him a small red envelope, which he accepted warily, wondering what emotionally-laden trinkets lay within – then cracked up laughing upon the discovery that it held nothing more than a couple of Tatts tickets. They had often used to joke about the cultural significance of gifting scratchies and lotto tickets on Christmases and birthdays.

"Thank you both very much," he said. "I couldn't have asked for anything better."

"Hey, Henry!" yelled Trish, as the rest of the party began to make their way back from the dam. "I've got something for you too!"

"What?" cried Henry "Please, no more! You're all making me feel terrible I never got any of you anything, I——"

"Don't worry," Trish chuckled, "you wouldn't have been able to top this one if you'd tried." She handed him a small package wrapped in green tissue paper, which turned out to be a handsome leather-bound book, with gilt-edged pages and gold-embossed lettering on the cover which read: *The Complete Scholastic Works of T. C. Mackenzie, First Edition.*

"You're joking," said Henry.

Trish grinned at him. "Nope! I know a lady who owns a printing press, and she owed me a favour. It's got every single journal article I've ever published, as well as the forewords I wrote for a couple of anthologies. I thought it might inspire you to up your game whenever you saw it on your bookshelf."

Henry had begun laughing hysterically, and was unable to answer for several moments. "That's *awfully* rich," he wheezed at last, "coming from you, who only got printed in *Currency* when I got front cover of *Forward*——"

"With *help*," Louisa reminded him.

"Ah," Trish said wisely, ignoring the interruption, "that was but a single battle, my friend. The *true* victor wins the war."

Henry wiped his eyes and shook his head slowly. "Well, you've outdone yourself this time, Trisho, this is an absolutely unforgettable present."

Not knowing where to put all the items he'd been given, he stacked them neatly in a pile on the ground, then put his hands on his hips and surveyed the motley crew before him. "Rightio, then, I guess we'd better have a look round the place and figure out where to put everybody, and then we'll get some dinner ready while we wait for Mathilda, who I think is still coming."

"Who's that?" asked Donovan.

"A woman I met at Corner Shop the other day," said Henry.

"And you invited her to go *camping* with you?" Trish said, narrowing her eyes.

Henry pretended not to hear, and Donovan was kind enough to change the subject by taking them all on a tour of the property.

In the end it was decided that Henry, Mark and Donovan would take the four-man tent which was kept in the house for such purposes, while Trish and Eden would share Trish's tent.

Joey and Louisa were given one of the two bedrooms in the house, and the other was left for Mathilda – who finally rocked up just as the sun was setting and dinner was cooking on the campfire.

"I'm sorry I'm late," she gasped, seeming oddly out of breath for someone who had just spent two hours in the car. "Happy birthday, Henry. Hi all, I'm Mathilda."

"We've met before," said Eden, winking at her.

"What? Oh, yeah. Good to see you again." Mathilda took in a few deep breaths, then handed Henry a large bottle wrapped in brown paper tied with string. "With compliments on your birthday."

Henry stopped himself from saying 'It's actually tomorrow,' realising in the nick of time that such a statement, though factually accurate, would be ungracious. He thanked her and unwrapped the bottle, which was ornate, unlabelled, and had a glass stopper. It contained a pale-yellow liquor of some sort.

"It's a type of fruit brandy you can only get from this one monastery in Hungary," Mathilda explained, in response to his quizzical look. "I have a friend living over there who sends me a case every now and then, and it's become my go-to gift. I recommend mixing it with Little Fat Lamb."

Henry couldn't quite muster the words to form a reply. But he embraced her by way of thanks, and showed her to a vacant chair by the fire. He hadn't felt so overwhelmed with care and affection in many years – perhaps not since he'd been a child. It was almost disembodying, like reality had turned in on itself and become something ontologically *other*. But he could feel his nerves beginning to steady, and reflected to himself as he took his own seat that perhaps the weekend would be fun after all.

The sun set, and the party ate, and stargazed, and played soft music on someone's portable speaker until, one by one, they made their way to bed.

Chapter Twenty – Thirty-Nine in September, Part III

Friday Night

"Hey, Trish," Eden whispered.

"Yeah?"

"Do you reckon Henry's changed?"

A pause.

"Nah, not really. Maybe on the outside, but not underneath. Why?"

"Well…you'd think he would have. Everyone does."

"I don't think so."

"Don't you?"

"Nah."

Silence.

Maybe that was the problem, thought Eden. He hadn't changed, and so she couldn't relinquish the conviction that after all this time, there was still something between them that was *right*. They belonged together. Even though they hadn't been ready when they were younger, maybe there was a reason why they hadn't grown apart, and, perhaps…finally, the time was right.

But still, he'd said it himself: he couldn't be that person, not to anyone.

But *why* couldn't he? Didn't he understand what they were capable of building together, given the chance? What was he seeing that she wasn't seeing? What was she seeing that he wasn't? …And why did he still look at her like that, the way he used to?

And if she was wrong, and he was right, and they really weren't meant to follow that path, then why couldn't she just accept it? Was there something lacking in their friendship? Why was there the need to turn it into something else? Was there any point in trying to tie two separate lives together now, after so many years spent in peaceful solitude?

She sighed and rolled over, unable to sleep. Her eyes burned with frustration. What was wrong with her? What quality was she missing, that she wasn't good enough for him? And *why* couldn't she let him go?

∴

Louisa and Joey played Snap late into the night, neither of them speaking.

Do you really like him? Louisa asked silently, unsure whether the question was directed at herself or Joey.

I don't know, thought Joey.

You're a child next to him. You inhabit different worlds; your lives are chapters apart.

I don't know why I feel like this.

He's not interested.

But he's so good to me.

But he's not interested.

I don't know how I should feel.

But I wish he were.

∴

Saturday Morning

Dawn lifted her weary head, shaking colour into the world like a housewife shaking out a tablecloth. Trish was up with the sun, and crawled out of her tent to see Mathilda slumped against the base of a tree, looking mildly concussed.

"Are you okay?" she said, alarmed.

Mathilda turned blearily towards her. "Oh, yeah. I'm fine, it's just…I didn't sleep amazingly, because I finally had some ideas for my next chapter, so I was writing them all down, and then I was pinging so much I couldn't sleep, and now I'm here and I feel like a walking corpse (minus the walking part of course), and normally I would have had three or four coffees by now, so my body's screaming with rage at its own existence, and I thought maybe sitting in the sun would help me wake up, but I just feel kind of hungover."

Trish chuckled. "Sounds like my entire undergrad experience."

"I can imagine."

"So, what's your book about?"

"Oh, it's just about this guy who's running from his past, but he can't remember it, but he knows it was bad, so he doesn't *want* to remember it, and it's sort of about how he makes peace with it, but without letting it define him."

"Hmm, sounds good. I'd read that."

Mathilda gave a watery smile. "Thanks. I've been stuck lately because I just can't think of a catalyst for the emotional revelations he needs to have. Like, I know the next stage he has to reach, but I can't think of a plot event to actually get him there. But last night, I had this idea that maybe he could just be chatting about life with someone at the pub, because even though that feels artificial in a book, it's actually how we come to a lot of our revelations in real life."

Trish nodded. "Yeah, makes sense. Well, good luck finishing it."

"I'm gonna need it," said Mathilda.

∴

Henry was the last to wake, having had a fitful night's sleep. He'd dreamt of a village populated with large anthropomorphic pastel-coloured bears, each of whom had spoken with one of his friends' voices, and each of whom had philosophised to him at length about their values and principles, as though some cataclysmic ideological battle were taking place and no one had bothered to inform him of the fact.

He woke up just as a baby-blue bear with Louisa's voice (or what seemed like her voice in the dream world) was offering him a choice between two brightly-coloured jellybeans – and then he was blinded by sunlight, with the sound and smell of breakfast cooking on the breeze, and Donovan sitting up on the camping mat beside him, reading *1984*.

"What time is it?" Henry yawned.

"Time doesn't exist when you're camping," said Donovan.

∴

Eden helped Mark with breakfast.

"So, how have you been travelling?" she asked.

"Aw, pretty well, thanks," said Mark. "I had a couple of weeks where I felt like I was stagnating for a bit, you know, my life was all just work and family and sudoku puzzles – and I love those things, don't get me wrong, but I still thought maybe there was something missing, and I was starting to wonder if I was having a mid-life crisis, like maybe I should buy a sports car or pick up a gambling habit or something – but then I planted some beans in the garden and I felt a lot better, so I reckon it was just a false alarm."

"Mmmm," said Eden, eyes widening in agreement. "I think it was Lewis who wrote about how we exist in tension between stability and change, and that's why we have the four seasons. Maybe you were in a winter period, and you're finally coming into spring."

Mark laughed. "Yeah, you hear a lot about the springtime of youth, but the springtime of middle-age is totally underrated, if you ask me."

The billy boiled, and Eden made tea. "It's eucalyptus and dandelion," she explained as the unusual aroma permeated the air.

"What the hell is wrong with you?" asked Mark.

"Nothing; it was a present from my grandma and I wanted to honour her memory."

"Oh, I'm sorry."

"Nah, she's not dead, I just haven't seen her in ages."

∴

Henry named his fish Martin, and knew
that he would make a fine companion.

∴

They walked to the beach. Trish and Donovan went surfing. Joey, Louisa and Henry built an enormous sandcastle big enough for Joey to crawl inside. (The castle promptly collapsed, and they had to rescue her from imminent suffocation.) Mathilda observed crabs in a rock pool and yearned to cast off her worldly cares and become one with their community. Eden collected shells. Mark told everybody to put on more sunscreen. No one listened to him, and they all got dreadfully burnt.

∴

"Wanna race from here to the top of the hill?" Trish asked Henry after lunch.

"No way, I'll do my ACL."

"You are such a lame old man."

"No I'm not, I'm able-bodied, that's the *whole* point."

"Weenie." She gave him a shove.

"Don't be such a child," he said, irritated from sunburn and shoddy sleep.

She narrowed her eyes at him. "I'm not a child. I just don't feel the need to take everything as seriously as you do."

"Excuse me? You gave me a self-published *leather-bound* anthology of journal articles you wrote in the mid-2000s! You dragged me out of my workplace to play street hockey with you! You take life more seriously than *anyone*!"

"That was different."

"Your mum's different."

"You leave Jodie out of this!"

"Sorry, Jodie."

They both laughed.

∴

"I dunno what he thinks he's doing," Donovan said to Mark, watching Henry play Irish Snap with Eden, Mathilda, and Joey. (Louisa and Trish were sitting off to one side under a blue gum, drinking Gatorade and debating the merits of sustainable memes versus single-use memetics.)

"He seems happy, though," said Mark.

"Happiness is an illusion," said Donovan.

Mark rolled his eyes. "Back on the Orwell again, I see."

∴

"Surely we have a bush doof?" said Joey.

Henry checked his watch. "It's 3:00PM."

"So?"

"It's not even dark yet!"

Joey sighed. "After dinner?"

Henry was an indifferent dancer. But he felt that to repress Joey's spirits would be roughly akin to taking a tour of Rottnest Island and drop-kicking a quokka off a jetty.

"Maybe," he said.

Joey ran a victory lap around the encampment, tripped, and fell into the dam.

∴

Louisa caught herself watching Henry in the distance
and felt a tremor in her chest, like a mine shaft collapsing.

∴

They walked through the bush to the top of the hill.

"So, what's your book about?" asked Mark.

"A quest to find self-knowledge," said Mathilda.

"Sounds groovy."

"It's also set in space."

"Oh, neat. How far off finishing are you?"

Mathilda shrugged her shoulders helplessly.

Trish, observing the interaction from behind, could not understand why this writer person seemed so depressed about her work.

∴

Eden found a lizard. "Hello there, friend."

The lizard stared at her.

"Let me ask you a question," said Eden. "Have you ever felt rejected by someone you loved?"

A pause.

"Of course not. Creatures like you are spared both the pain and joy of being in love."

The lizard flicked out its tongue.

"But if you could feel what I am feeling," Eden went on, "and you were in my position, what would you do about it?"

"Are you talking to a lizard?" Donovan demanded, coming up behind her.

"Yes, I enjoy processing verbally with animals. I find they make good listeners, because they don't care about what you're saying, so you needn't worry about burdening them with your emotional baggage."

"I don't know why, but that just makes me think of the scene in *Garzey's Wing* where Christopher Senshu falls off a horse, and everyone asks him if he's alright and he says, 'I intentionally fell off to protect the horse's feelings,'" said Joey.

Donovan shook his head. "Struth."

∴

Dinner was a magical concoction of stewed meats and spices and fortified wine, which Donovan, inspired by a Tarantino film, had boiled together in a large stock pot. It had a bold, savoury flavour that no one could quite pin down, and a disproportionate number of bay leaves.

Louisa watched Henry talking and laughing with Eden, and wondered why this grated on her so, when the truth shot through her like a myoclonic jerk at 2:00AM: he lacked integrity. His words did not align with his actions. He professed contentment with his singleness, and scorn towards romantic relationships – yet he was so attentive, even flirtatious towards women, without ever stopping to think about how his words and actions affected the hearts of those around him.

Did that make him callous? He, who was so courteous and gentle in nearly all other aspects? Would it not have been easier if he had been eccentric and cantankerous, as he sometimes seemed at first glance? And what part of this was *her* fault, for reading so much intention into all that he had said and done? If she felt rejected by him (and she still wasn't ready to admit that she did), then had she only herself to blame, for allowing those feelings to develop and grow when she'd already known the outcome? Or could he have treated her differently, more distantly, more carefully, to prevent those feelings from arising in the first place?

Then, as Louisa finally acknowledged her feelings after so many months of denial, she was gripped by an immediate and overwhelming desire for solitude. Excusing herself, she rose from the fire, fled to her room, buried her face in her pillow and wept. Better to have kept the door closed on desire, she thought miserably, than to have opened it and been disappointed.

But it was too late: the door had opened, and she was powerless to close it again.

∴

They held a bush doof up on the hill that night. Everyone danced except Louisa (who was still in bed) and Henry, who was sitting by himself on the pretext of being in charge of music (which was a blatant lie, since they were using one of Joey's playlists and Henry knew nothing of modern rave music).

Eventually, Joey wriggled her way out of the mosh and stood before him, breathless and sweaty, the moonlight glistening on her bare arms and legs and making her look ethereal and childlike. "Come dance?" she shouted over the speakers.

Henry smiled and shook his head. "Nah, I'm fine, thanks."

And in that moment Joey saw herself, at last, as he must surely see her: like a child demanding affection from an amused parent; like a girl who suffers from want of attention and must seek it at all cost, heedless of her naked heart laid out upon her sleeve, baring her pain to all who pass her by.

Her eyes stung. She nodded and disappeared back into the mass of bodies, unable even to leave, for fear that she should be seen, and pitied.

∴

Sunday Morning

Henry, frying eggs for breakfast, felt peaceful.

This was good, he thought. It was a fun weekend, after all.

He was wrong, of course; but we'll let him think for now that he is right.

Chapter Twenty-One – Four More Saturdays

If it occurred to Henry, during the weeks that followed, that Louisa and Joey and Eden were being rather distant, he didn't bother to question it.

∴

One Saturday Morning

"What's the deepest desire of your heart?"

Henry nearly spat half his second piccolo onto the table. "Sorry?"

"Well, this isn't a date," said Sarah, secretly appalled at her own daring, but unwilling to back down, "so surely no questions are off-limits?"

Such directness! His synapses were imploding in their effort to comprehend what was being asked of him, let alone to reconcile the reality of the conversation with his expectations of how it ought to have gone. And yet, he reflected, as he finished his coffee (and regretted for the second or third time that morning having not taken Sarah to Corner Shop…but he was beginning to feel like he had already introduced too many new people to that delicate, untapped ecosystem; to bring more bodies into such a place would be to reduce one of nature's greatest marvels to a stifled, gasping tourist haunt – to plant thousands of grubby footprints through the pristine wilderness, formerly unseen by human eyes, now torn up by the roots and flung across the virtual world – pixelated, pinioned against post after post and filtered through a thousand, thousand media feeds…and so it was only right and just that he die to himself and partake of a sub-par piccolo every now and then), there was a part of him that welcomed the question – was pleased, in fact, to have a challenge to rise to.

"I suppose," he said slowly, "the deepest desire of my heart would be to grow in virtue."

Sarah turned the ancient word over in her mind. "Care to elaborate?"

He shrugged. "It's an abstract goal, but it's the one that underlies all others. I want to form my thoughts and words and actions into habits that are good for me and everyone else. Simply put, I want to love people – y'know, in the rational Thomistic sense, not that vague, anaemic 'love and peace' stuff they came up with in the '60s."

She laughed. "I dunno, I have a soft spot for the love and peace stuff myself. But I know what you mean; it sort of gives the impression that you can have love and peace without actually doing anything to attain it. But you'd think that love would require effort of some kind."

"Pretty much."

"I can get on board with that. I'm not sure virtue ethics is the conceptual framework I would use…but then, I don't know what framework I *would* use. I just want to be a good person."

"I don't think you can divide people into good and bad."

"You don't?"

"Well," he admitted, "I s'pose, technically speaking, I believe the person is an inherent good. But that's not what we usually mean when we talk about a good person. I think people have value in and of themselves, but it's their actions that are good or bad, and it's too complicated to try and measure all of a person's actions in hopes of finding some kind of sum total."

"So you don't reckon Hitler was a bad person?" she asked, knowing the fruit hung low, but interested to hear his response.

Henry grimaced. "I reckon he did a lot of bad things."

"Hm."

"Don't you find this in your line of work, though?" he asked. "Like, have you ever gone to interview someone, and previously you've thought them a good or a bad person, and then when you've actually talked to them, they've surprised you?"

Sarah pondered. "Maybe once or twice." She was beginning to feel drawn to all this talk of inherent goodness and virtue. She hadn't thought about such things since she'd taken a philosophy elective in university years ago.

"What about you?" he asked.

"Huh?"

"What's the deepest desire of your heart?"

Sarah was silent for a very long time, given that she had asked the question first and really ought to have had an answer prepared for it. "Truth, I think," she said at last.

Henry smiled. "A worthy cause."

"I think that's why I read so many self-help books," she said. "It's partly that I want to be a good person, and to make the most of my life, and be productive and successful and all that… But also, I feel like so much of myself is unknown, and the truth of who I am is so confronting, that if I can just control it, make it into something other, better — then facing that truth wouldn't be so bad." She spoke the words in a rush, articulating her findings almost before they came to her — keenly aware that she was speaking not for his sake but her own, yet needing him to hear her, to bear witness to her revelation, to gaze upon her with human eyes and reassure her that she was not alone with this terrible truth.

He looked at her, unwilling to breach the sacredness of the moment — embarrassed by her vulnerability, yet touched by her courage.

She looked away, exposed, thinking she had said too much, wishing she had been less selfish, more measured.

"Sarah," he said.

Her eyes met his.

"The truth of who you are is good," he said. "There's no need to fear it."

His words pierced her like thorns; but it was one of those rare moments when pain and joy are intertwined.

∴

The Following Saturday Afternoon

It was near closing time, and the café smelled of dried sage and savoury scones. Henry and Mathilda, sitting at the corner table, took little notice as Barista Frances began cleaning up in the background, trusting that she would eject them when the time was truly right.

"So, what's your book about?" asked Henry.

Mathilda scowled. "Let's not talk about the dumb book."

"What? Why not? You're a writer, doesn't that mean your whole identity is built upon your literary works?"

"The only one here whose identity is built on their work is *you.*"

He laughed. "Yeah, I'll cop that. So, what would you rather talk about?"

"I don't know," she sighed. "Everything seems so bland and meaningless."

"How can you say such a thing, when the sun shines so sweetly outside yonder door?"

"The sun is free from mankind's woes; he may shine as he likes, but the rest of us must toil away for the next fifty or sixty years until Death finally comes for us and we're allowed to clock off this wretched mortal shift."

A slight pause.

"Forgive me for asking," said Henry, "but are you…depressed?"

Much to his surprise, Mathilda burst out laughing. "Of course not, you goose. I just talk like this to let off steam."

"Oh," he said. "Well, that's good, then."

She shook her head, still chuckling. "It takes more than a bit of existential dread to make me depressed."

"Why the existential dread?"

"I dunno, man, I think it's just my default state. But enough about me – let's talk about *you*. Tell me three bullet points about yourself."

"Uh… I drink piccolos because I enjoy them more than lattes, but I always get two of them because one isn't enough, so sometimes I lie awake at night wondering why I don't just cave and order a latte.

I really like yodelling, and I wish that it were among our standard cultural practices. And I love my work."

She grimaced. "That makes one of us."

"You don't love what you do?"

"Nah, not really."

"I thought that was the whole point of being a writer."

She made an exasperated sound. "I say I don't 'love' it because I don't get any pleasure or satisfaction out of it whatsoever. But I know that it's a good thing to do, and I keep having these ideas and feeling convicted to write them, so I guess I write them in case no one else will. But it's hard to stand up in the face of one camp of people who say you should do what you love, and another who say you should do what's realistic, and you know that you're not really doing either, but you're just doing what you have to."

"Struth," he said.

"Yeah, you're telling me. So, why do you love your work so much, then?"

He grinned. "I just like exploring all the weird ideas people come up with, and looking at how different sets of ideas interact, and trying to see all the different patterns that keep evolving out of the chaos. It's not particularly world-changing stuff, but there's an audience for it, and an endless variety of topics to work with, so I'm never bored."

"Okay, but that sounds more like reading than writing. What about when you have to actually *work*, and turn your observations into readable results?"

His grin turned wolfish. "That's when it gets *really* fun."

Mathilda stared at him. "You're mad."

And he was, too. But there was something captivating in what he said as well; she could feel his words enkindle a new vigour within her – and for the first time in months, she felt the irrepressible urge to go home immediately and *write*.

She stood up. "Thanks for this, it's been very useful."

Surprised, he checked his watch. "You're going already?"

"I've been in this business long enough to know to ride the wave when it comes. Next time you see me, I'll be sitting on a finished manuscript, I'm sure of it!"

He waved. "Good luck!"

∴

The Following Saturday Evening

Henry didn't often phone people just to have a chat, but when he did, he phoned Trish. In the early days, after they'd reconnected at college, they used to call each other almost every day, sometimes for hours, when they were at home, and bored, and still had landlines. He would ring her from his big lonely manor house, and she would answer from her parents' kitchen, and they would talk about all sorts of things which seemed important then, but which had long since passed out of recollection.

That was before Eden, of course. After Eden, he hadn't called Trish nearly as often; and then they had all started university together and spent nearly all their time in each other's company, and Trish had been there to pick him up and dust him off when Eden had gone. After Trish moved to Sydney, they'd begun to call each other again, once in a while – often a long call, now on mobile phones (which were less expensive), to catch up on each other's lives and to while away the lonely evenings. But it was never quite the same as it had been in the early days, on their parents' landlines; and there was still a part of him, faint and detached, which mourned the loss of that era, holding tightly to the remnants set in amber memories.

"How was your flight home?" he asked.

"Pretty good," she said. "I didn't put down a seat preference, so they put me between these two nice old men. And we were each given those little Lindt chocolates with our dinner, and I ate mine, and then the man on my left asked me did I want his – and to be honest, I didn't, but I thought better to eat it than it get thrown away, so I said yes, and I ate it, and felt *so* full – and then the man on my right asked me did I want *his*, and by that point I was in too deep to say no, but I couldn't actually eat it, because you know how rich they are——"

"I do know," he reassured her.

"Right? So anyway, I put it in my jacket pocket for later, but I didn't realise how hot the plane actually was, and it MELTED."

Henry started laughing. "That sounds like a Joey story."

"Well it's not, it's a Trish story," she said bluntly.

"Of course; forgive me."

But she had already moved on. "Remember that one weekend we flew to the Gold Coast, and our flight got delayed till 2:00AM?"

"And we played airport hide-and-seek?"

"Best idea ever."

"I died once we got on the plane though. I was an *actual* corpse."

"Yeah, but that's the price of joy, after all."

"Theologically, I have to disagree."

She chuckled. "Fair enough."

A pause.

"So, how's the family?" she asked.

"Yeah, they're alright, same old, same old, really. The dead don't change much; that's sort of a prime feature of being dead."

"Maybe."

"You don't reckon?"

"Well, I'm just not convinced that *we* change all that much, either."

"Is that so?"

"Nah. You're still basically the same as when I first met you."

"I don't know if I like that."

"No, it's good! I mean, you're older, obviously, and you're different on the surface and everything, but your *essence* is the same. You know what I mean?"

"Sounds very Aristotelian."

"But it's good, because it was your essence that made me like you in the first place. It's what makes you *you*. If that changed, you wouldn't be you any more, and we might not still be friends."

"Crikey, that's a lot of pressure."

She smiled, and he could hear it in her voice. "Diamonds are made under pressure."

"So is excrement."

A sharp intake of breath. "That remark, Henry Biddlesnoot-Bloomington, was beneath your dignity."

He grunted. Only Trish was allowed to call him by his full name without reprimand, and even then… "It's not beneath my dignity at all. I'm an embodied soul, and it's all part of the experience. Even Our Incarnate Lord had bowels, you know."

"Ugh, 'list of things I didn't want to think about today'…"

"Humanity takes itself far too seriously."

"You are such a muppet."

"I could think of worse things to be."

A pause.

"You know," he said, "I've never thanked you for being one of the few people I can just empty my brain to. With most folks, I'd plan out the conversation in advance, or at least have a couple of points in mind to talk about, but I never have to do that with you."

"So, what you're saying is, I'm not worth the effort you go to with other people."

"No!" he laughed. "It's more like…we talk often enough that we're always up to date on the broad strokes of each other's lives, but I never run out of other things to talk about, because I feel comfortable enough with you to talk about the silly, mundane things that I wouldn't with other people. Do you know what I mean?"

"Yeah, I know."

A pause.

"So, what are you going to work on next?" he asked.

"Wait and see, it's gonna knock your socks off."

"Oh yeah? Not if I knock yours off first!"

"I won't lose to you, Henry B.!"

"Nor I you, T. C. Mackenzie!"

A pause.

"You're a good friend," she said.

"Back at ya," he replied.

A pause.

"I love you, you know," she said.

A fault line traced its way through the centre of his heart.

"Yeah," he said. "I know."

∴

The Following Saturday Night

He and Toni sat on her veranda, washed in starlight, smoking a pair of cigars. She was teaching him to blow smoke rings.

"Toni?" he said, after a long silence.

"Yeah?"

"Do you think…I overstep the boundaries in my friendships with women?"

Toni snorted. "What am I, your shrink now?"

He forced a laugh. "Send me an invoice any time you like and we'll make it official."

"I dunno, man, I don't sit around analysing this stuff like you do."

"Yeah, but…I'm just worried that maybe, sometimes, I make myself too much a part of people's lives, and then they come to depend on me, and then I get annoyed when that happens, even though it wouldn't have happened if I'd kept my distance."

"Okay, sure."

"But it's so frustrating!" he cried. "I'm just trying to be a decent human being, and practise words of affirmation and active listening and all that crap, and then next thing I know, I'm having deep, emotionally-charged conversations with news reporters in coffee shops, and childhood friends are making ambiguous 'I love you' statements, and *what am I gonna do?*"

Toni blew a smoke ring. "Just cut 'em loose and go join the monastery."

"Ha, good one."

"I'm not joking."

He tried to blow a smoke ring and failed.

"You're not moving your lips properly. Here, watch." She blew another.

He tried again, and almost got it.

The smoke dissipated, and they looked up at the stars for a while.

When he spoke again, his voice cracked. "I just don't know what to do, Toni."

She shrugged. "Well I dunno why you're coming to *me* for help."

"Because you're the smartest person I know?"

She turned to face him for the first time – and he shivered, for her eyes were cold and flat. "I can't help you with this, Henry."

"Why not?" he said, hating how small and petulant his voice sounded.

She looked away again, and let out a deep breath. But he saw her fingers curl into a fist. "Because I just don't care about any of it, and I can't make myself care."

He stared at her, unsure whether any other explanation was forthcoming – not wanting to take her words at face value. But she said nothing, and eventually he said, "It's not that you have to care about what happens with them——"

"Henry, you don't get it!" she yelled, startling him in her ferocity. "I don't want to talk about them at all! I don't even want to *think* about them, okay?"

"But – why?"

"Because it pisses me off, that's why! I don't want to think about all these weird emotional flings you've been having with a hundred different women! You promised me years ago that you were never going to be with anyone, and I took you at your word. All this time, I – I've been on my own because I never met anyone I liked more than you. And I was *okay* with that because I knew you wanted to be by yourself. But if you change your mind now, Henry, then what was all that waiting for? If you're going to change your mind, after all this time——" She broke off, clenching her fists again, too proud to say the words outright: *then you should be with me.*

Henry looked at her, throat constricting, and felt tears spring into his eyes.

He had no idea what she wanted from him in this moment – no idea how to comfort her, how to make her better. To see her in that much pain, and to be so utterly helpless to do anything about it, ruined him.

Hesitantly, he put his arms around her, and was astonished that she did not push him away.

They sat in silence for a long time, until finally she said, "Go home, Henry. There's nothing more to be said."

And, in his despair, he obeyed.

Chapter Twenty-Two – Feelings
(Are Just Feelings)

Toni refused to speak to Henry for some days after that conversation. He tried visiting her, but she had left on some mysterious errand and did not return until after he had gone. Naturally, this distressed him, but as there was nothing he could do about it, he lost all motivation for anything else and sat about at home for a week in his pyjamas, eating Pocky and listening to Daft Punk, and growing more and more miserable and moody and melancholy, until his family (who, being dead, had a fairly high tolerance for that sort of thing) began to find him unutterably vexing, and finally expelled him from the manor until he'd pulled himself together.

So, with nothing better to do, he returned to the university and took up his work again with renewed urgency. But he had a great deal of trouble thinking up a topic for a new project; he'd submitted a few different research proposals since 'Gold Yamre: An Origin Myth' had been published, and each of them had been turned down. The message was the same everywhere: his proposals sounded promising, but they weren't *quite* up to the standard which 'Origin Myth' had set, and the research bodies would much rather hold onto their grant money until he gave them something *really* good.

So he lounged in his office chair, spinning around and around aimlessly, scrolling day-old meme pages and lurking in decade-old discussion forums. He sent unhinged emails to schoolteachers, asking about what kinds of things their students talked about between classes. He leafed through books of philosophy and sociology; he stood on his head; he threw darts, rolled dice, and did all the things he normally did to try and find inspiration…and none of them worked. By 10:00PM, all he'd achieved was to reply to a few emails, tweak the opening paragraph of a unit outline for a course he was meant to be teaching the following year, and accept an offer to peer-review a couple of papers for next quarter's edition of *CULTure*. Consumed with ennui, he drove home, hoping that his family would take pity on him and let him back inside.

There was no one at the door to stop him entering the house, so he dumped his bag in the entrance hall and proceeded to the kitchen, stepping nimbly over a couple of rats which ran shrieking past him from the cellar (Grandmother Betsy was doing her manifestation thing again, no doubt). He ate two English muffins with raspberry jam, then wandered off towards the library, still hoping to find an idea for a project.

The Biddlesnoot-Bloomington Library was really just a small cupboard full of second-hand Mills & Boon novels, because the original library had burned down in a fire many years ago, and no one had bothered to restore it because no one in the family cared much about reading except for Henry, and Henry was too busy with his work to do anything about it – and anyway, the burnt-out shell of the original library was now being used by Uncle Bertram to store his plants.

Henry sat down upon a cushion on the floor, took up a copy of *Sugar Island* by Jean S. MacLeod, and began reading. Presently, his Cousin Pippin (who had died at the age of seven, poor thing) emerged from the back of the cupboard and floated there a moment, surveying him dispassionately.

"Hullo, Cousin," she said. "What are you reading?"

"A most enlightening tome," said Henry, showing her the cover.

"Pshaw," said Pippin, wrinkling her nose at it. "I've read that one before. It's not half so good as *Wife Without Kisses*."

Henry smiled wryly. "Careful I don't tell your mother you've been reading these."

"She wouldn't care," Pippin huffed. "She and Father read them together all the time. He does the voices of the ladies, and she does the voices of the gentlemen."

Henry flipped to the next page. "Well, one can't help being starved for entertainment in the afterlife, I suppose."

"Rude," said Pippin, crossing her arms.

"Sorry."

"So," she asked, "what are you so gloomy and glum about?"

Henry pondered how much of his predicament to share. Pippin meant well, and could generally be trusted. And although she still looked seven, she had died at least a hundred years ago, and was consequently, in a sense, much older than he. But he didn't feel like copping another lecture about his interactions with women right now, so he decided to stick to the immediate facts. "Well, I just can't think of what to write about next for my work."

Pippin thought for a minute. "Write about Vocaloid cage matches."

Henry blinked. "What?"

"You know, those virtual pop singers. They keep getting hacked by online fight clubs and being forced to duel each other to the death over livestream. Rumour has it they're gonna replace WWE as the biggest global sports entertainment enterprise by 2040. The revenue they're generating is insane. Given the rate younger generations are gravitating away from traditional competitive sports, I wouldn't be surprised if VocaLeague ends up becoming the new FIFA."

"How do you *know* all this?" Henry demanded.

She shrugged. "Some guys I follow on Twitch."

Henry stroked his chin. "That's not a bad idea…not a bad idea at all!" He leapt to his feet. "Thank you, Pip. I'll get on it right away – no, better yet, I'll ask Louisa to collaborate with me again! A topic like this should be *right* up her alley." And he dashed exuberantly away.

Cousin Pippin smiled to herself, remembering the large bet she'd placed a few weeks ago on Louisa marrying Henry.

That ought to sweeten the odds a bit, she thought.

∴

The next morning, Henry barrelled into Louisa's office without knocking, remembered too late that this was a tradition he held with Trish, not Louisa, then realised with relief – then dismay – that Louisa wasn't in. He waited a few minutes to see if she would return; she did not.

A media studies professor ambled by. "Looking for Lou?" Henry nodded. "She's on leave this week."

"Okay, thanks," said Henry.

Nothing daunted, he dug his phone out of his pocket and tried giving Louisa a call. She did not pick up. So he sent her a message: *Hey, sorry to interrupt your leave, but I have a proposal for a new project which I think you'll like. Call me ASAP!*

But there was no reply.

He resigned himself to waiting at first, assuming that she was enjoying a well-earned holiday and not answering correspondence until she got back. He tried to amuse himself with yodelling practice, and drafting the new research proposal, and shopping for new flavours of muesli bar. But in the end, his impatience (and perhaps the desire to distract himself from the imminent implosion of most of his other close interpersonal relationships) got the better of him, and so he drove up the mountain to her nonna's farm to enquire if she was home.

The farm was quite small – really just a cottage with a couple of paddocks attached, hemmed in on all sides by forest. But it contained cows and chickens and a large vegetable patch and a number of fruit trees, and was altogether the last place he would have pictured Louisa living in, and yet, somehow, he wasn't surprised.

He knocked on the door of the cottage, and it was answered by a little old woman with curly hair and bright eyes, who could only be Louisa's nonna. "*Buona sera,*" she said, looking up at him gravely.

"Er, hullo," he said, slightly nervous. "Is Louisa here? I'm a colleague – er, friend, and was wondering if I could talk to her."

The old woman's face softened. "You are Henry, yes?"

"Oh – yes, I'm sorry, I should have led with that."

"You seem a nice young man," she said, smiling knowingly.

(Henry couldn't remember the last time someone had called him a young man.)

"She's out the back, chopping firewood," Louisa's nonna said, showing him around to the other side of the house, which afforded a closer view of the two cows standing serenely in one of the paddocks, the hen house, and…Louisa, hard at work splitting logs, wearing a flannel shirt and overalls, her reddish-blonde hair tied up in a bun. She straightened and turned to him as he approached, her face flushed and sweaty, her expression wary.

"Hey," he said lamely.

She did not smile. "Henry, what's up?"

He cleared his throat, suddenly unable to meet her eye. "Er, I'm sorry to bother you when you're on leave. It's just, I had this idea for a…for a new project, and I was wondering if…you'd be interested." He felt his words become thinner, less substantial, as the conviction which had brought him here seeped away, leaving him stunned by the absurdity of his actions. *Why* hadn't he just waited until she'd come back to work?

"Oh," said Louisa. "Is that all?"

"Yeah," he said, even more lamely.

She leaned the axe against the side of the woodshed. "Well, what's your idea?"

Somehow, he hadn't expected to receive that answer, and it took him a moment to gather his thoughts. "Oh…well, er…basically, it's about VocaLeague, if you've heard of it, and the effect it's bound to have on the sports and entertainment industries."

"Hmmm," she said, nodding slowly.

I should've just waited, he thought.

"Sounds pretty good, actually," said Louisa, with just a hint of her old smile.

Henry felt as though his insides had been pumped full of helium. "Really? Then you're keen?"

Her face went slack again. "I'll…have to think about it, I'm not really sure what my next couple of months are looking like, work-wise."

"Oh." He paused. "Okay, fair enough."

She made no move to leave, nor to speak. So he turned to go… and then stopped.

"Louisa," he said, feeling his pulse accelerate, having no way of knowing if breaking the silence was the right thing to do or not, "if I've hurt you in some way, please tell me."

She stared at him, caught totally off-guard.

"You haven't——" she choked. "It's not – like that."

He held her gaze, his eyes on hers like a searchlight. "Are you sure?"

"Yes."

"Really?"

"*Yes.*"

He folded his arms. "Well, I get the feeling that you're upset with me."

"Henry, you haven't done anything to me," she snapped.

He gave way to frustration in a matter of seconds. "Then why are you being like this?!"

"Because – you don't make any sense to me!"

"What?"

"I don't understand you! You keep telling me you're not interested in family or relationships, so why do you spend all your time hanging out with women?!"

"What's *wrong* with that?" he said angrily, fed up with hearing this argument once again, yet part of him fearing, once again, that maybe there was a shred of truth in it. "Just because I don't desire romantic involvement with anyone, does that mean I'm not allowed to be friends with women? Am I not allowed to *talk* to them? I thought it was supposed to be healthy and normal to interact with people and not expect anything like that from them, so why am *I* the villain here?!"

"I'm not saying you can't have friends, Henry, I'm just saying, why stop at friendship? What are you running from?"

"I'm not running from anything! I have no problems with relationships as a *concept*. I'm just not interested in having one myself. It doesn't speak to me. Why is that a bad thing? Why do I need a reason not to want a relationship? Why does there have to be something wrong with me? I'm not repressed, I'm not asexual, I'm not anything – I'm just *not interested!*"

"Well, if you're not interested, then why do you let yourself get so close to people whom you have no intention of going the next step with?"

"Why shouldn't I?" he snapped. "Last time I checked, having meaningful emotional connection in a friendship wasn't an inherent evil. I can manage my own feelings, so why can't everyone else just do the same?!"

"It's not that simple!"

"Isn't it?"

"No, you idiot! Maybe you can keep *your* feelings under control, but you don't give any thought to how your behaviour affects *other* people's feelings!"

"Feelings are just feelings," he said coldly. "They don't mean anything, they don't entitle a person to anything, and they're not my responsibility."

"Well that's a great philosophy," she snarled. "That makes me feel so good about myself."

"Well – what?"

"You heard me. I'm this pathetic wimp who has meaningless *emotions*. I *like* you, Henry. Or I did, anyway, until you made me feel like the biggest clown on the planet for daring to be attracted to you. Well I can't *help* that, and I don't appreciate being belittled for it. And I know it's not your fault how I feel, but I wish…" She took a deep breath and let it out slowly, the anger bleeding from her voice, leaving her dulled and defeated. "I just wish you'd kept to yourself a bit more, if you'd known the whole time that nothing was ever going to happen between us. Maybe I should've known better, but…by the time you told me where you stood, it was already too late."

Henry looked at her for a long time, frozen with shock, grief, anguish.

"I'm sorry," he said, not knowing what else to say.

"I *said* it's not your fault, stupid," she growled. "And you're right, in a way. Feelings are just feelings. I just…wish you had some better reason for rejecting me than 'I'm just not interested.' It doesn't really seem fair."

Henry closed his eyes. There were so many things he shouldn't have said – wouldn't have said, if he had only known.

"The thing you have to understand," he said at last, "is that my family…well, they're dead."

Her eyes widened. "Oh! I'm——"

"No, no, I didn't mean that how it sounded. But what I mean is…" He broke off.

"What?"

"Well, you're not going to believe me, that's all."

"So what if I don't? My opinion doesn't really affect you one way or another."

He sighed. "Okay. Well. So, there's this curse on my family going back generations. I don't really know where it came from, I hear a lot of different stories about it every time we have a family gathering, but I've never got the authoritative version. But basically, whenever one of us dies, we come back as a ghost, doomed to haunt the family home forever after. So, I'm the last living member of my family, and I live with the ghosts of all my ancestors, who make it their sole purpose and pleasure to try and control my life. And they're always telling me to get married and have children and continue the family line and the whole wretched business, but I just can't be bothered. I think, 'No. Stuff you guys, don't tell me what to do with my life, I'm single and I'm going to enjoy it.' And anyway, who'd want to carry on a name like 'Biddlesnoot-Bloomington'? And…" He faltered. "How could I ask someone to marry me, knowing that would be her fate one day too?"

Louisa stared at him.

He shrugged. "If you don't believe me, that's fine. But I'd appreciate it if you didn't tell anyone else. I'm a bit sensitive about it."

"No…of course. Makes sense." She tilted her head. "Can I meet them?"

"What?"

"Your family. I've never met a ghost before."

He gaped at her. "I suppose so…?" A pause. "I really thought you wouldn't believe me."

"Well, I don't know if I actually believe you, or if I'm just too tired and emotional to argue." She smiled faintly. "Either way, living or dead, I'd like to meet the people responsible for your existence."

He laughed. "Yeah, alright, I'll see what I can arrange." Then he turned serious again. "And listen, Louisa… I am very sorry. About everything."

She tossed her head. "Don't be. It was no one's fault, these things just play out like this sometimes." She paused, and gave him a rueful look. "Would've been easier if you weren't such a frigging good bloke, though."

He laughed again. "I'm really very far from it."

"And he's modest too, can you blame a lady for trying?"

He looked away. "I'm sorry."

"Aw, c'mon, stop being sorry, you're just making me feel worse. Come in and have a cuppa or something, will you?"

"Oh, no, I – couldn't——"

"Don't be stupid, you came all the way up here anyway, and I'm sure Nonna's dying to get to know you. And Henry…?"

"Yes?"

She grinned suddenly, reminding him of when they'd first met. "I'd love to work with you on that project."

"Really?"

"Yes, really, it sounds like fun."

He felt dizzy. "Incredible! I'm so excited. I'll call you when you get back from leave and we'll sort out the details."

"You've got a deal."

They went inside.

Nonna greeted them in the kitchen with a stern countenance. "You *bambini* sort it all out?"

Louisa patted her arm. "Yes, Nonna."

"Wonderful!" she cried, pulling them both into a hug. "I baked a cake just in case. You sit down, I'll dish up." Smiling, they obeyed, and she fed them with cake until they could eat no more, and a jolly good time was had by all.

Chapter Twenty-Three – Equals

In springtime, the weather can be temperamental, especially in the morning. This morning, for instance, Henry awoke later than usual to the sound of rain against the window, and rolled his eyes. "How much longer until we finally get some sunshine?" he groused, flinging some fish food contemptuously into Martin's tank as though Martin was the one responsible for the foul weather.

Then, as he left the house, well-cocooned in his scarf and raincoat, the sun came out, and all at once he felt suffocated and damp with sweat. He sighed and removed his outer layers, deciding it was going to be one of those days where he would have to roll with the punches.

He arrived at the university and found Louisa waiting for him in his office (which they were sharing again for the duration of the project), two piccolos at the ready. A warmth rose up inside him which had nothing to do with the sun. "You shouldn't have," he said, taking the tiny paper cups from her with reverence, as though they were the visible signs of an invisible reality, the flagpole of friendship, the signifier of reconciliation and redemption. "I must owe you at least a dozen rounds by now."

Louisa shrugged. "'Tis a gift freely given; I don't keep track of these things."

"You are a ray of hope in a cold and heartless world."

"Yeah alright, quit flattering me and let's get to work."

So they did.

∴

It took some time for Henry, working steadily away with Louisa on gathering data and mapping out the scope of their project, to notice a) that something was bothering him; and b) what that something was. But when he came to the realisation, it brought with it an unexpected wave of grief: he missed Joey.

Now that he thought about it, frowning at his computer screen, eyes glazing over as he tried to concentrate on the fixtures for the VocaLeague summer season, he hadn't actually heard anything from Joey since the camping trip. Yet before that, they'd been in the habit of meeting for lunch fairly frequently, and now it was like there was something missing from his routine. Was there something wrong? Was she okay? Or was she just busy? Anyway, their professional relationship didn't start until next year, so he had no reason to expect her to contact him before then.

Except…they were friends now, weren't they?

But if he was her friend, he thought guiltily, then shouldn't *he* have contacted *her* by now?

But he'd been busy – so maybe she had as well.

Well, there was no harm in asking what she was up to, he thought. So he reached for his phone and sent her a quick message: *Hey Joey, hope you're well. How's things?*

She didn't reply; and to press her would be to stray beyond the scope of their relationship. So he tried to put her out of his mind – and failed – for the rest of the day.

∴

After several days without reply, Henry asked Louisa whether she thought their project might benefit from having Joey as their research assistant once again.

An alarm bell went off in Louisa's mind, but she pushed it aside and said that she didn't see why not. So Henry tried ringing Joey, and she did not pick up; whereupon he sent her another message explaining the scope of their project and asking if she was interested. Again, she did not reply.

∴

Louisa could see that Henry was disquieted in some way by Joey's absence. This annoyed her, for reasons previously stipulated. Nevertheless, her compassionate heart was not wholly untouched, and it was probable that having a third person in the room might alleviate some of the unease which existed between her and Henry still, however much they pretended it wasn't there.

(Even if that third person was Joey.)

After a time, and perhaps against her better judgement, Louisa decided (but did not tell Henry, in case it didn't go well) to pay Joey a visit and see what, if anything, was the matter. She had been to Joey's house for a number of social get-togethers, and although a drop-in would be unexpected, it would not, she supposed, be ill-received.

∴

Joey was in the garage, practising her kickflip, when she slipped and fell into a stack of moving boxes containing one of her housemate's continental philosophy textbooks. She was unharmed, for she always wore a helmet, thanks to the stringent teachings of her grandfather (himself an avid cyclist, who had once fractured his neck riding to work, and would have died if he hadn't been wearing a helmet. Even now, in those moments when her resolve weakened and she contemplated going for a skate without safety gear, she could hear herself at age thirteen, arguing with him: 'But Grandpa, I feel so uncool,' 'Don't worry about cool, Joey, worry about *safety*…').

However, the boxes hadn't been touched in months, and her impact raised a heavy cloud of dust which sent her into such a violent fit of hacking and coughing that a grubby old gentleman in the street, passing by the house and hearing her through the open garage door, crossed himself and mumbled a few words in her direction which sounded suspiciously like an exorcism.

Once her spluttering had subsided, Joey heard voices in the house and realised that they had a visitor. So she brushed herself off, put board and helmet back in the corner of the garage where they belonged, and wandered into the living room, where she found Anna, her housemate, talking to Louisa Honeysett.

"Hi Lou," said Joey, slightly dazed from her fall, and also from the abruptness with which her old supervisor had entered her home. "What brings you here?"

"She came to check that you hadn't died," said Anna (who was a part-time accountant and full-time wisecracker). "Which, judging from all that banging and crashing in the garage, was not an unlikely possibility."

Joey rubbed distractedly at a sore spot on her elbow, which had struck the floor when she'd fallen. "Takes more than a little tumble to kill me."

"I didn't mean to invade," Louisa said apologetically. "I was just passing through the neighbourhood and I hadn't seen you in a while, so I thought I'd drop in and see what you were up to."

"Aw, shucks," said Joey (as Anna bowed out of the conversation and returned to her bedroom to finish an argument on Discord about whether or not Derek Savage would end up releasing the new *Cool Cat* movie). "I've been going well, I guess. I'm only tutoring for one unit this semester, so I get a lot of time at home, which is pretty fun."

"Oh, sounds nice," said Louisa, wondering if she and Henry had both misjudged the situation and Joey really just had been busy. She decided that, seeing as she had taken the trouble to come all the way to Joey's house, she might as well be direct. "I'm not sure if you saw Dr B.'s messages, but he and I are starting a new project, and we were hoping you might like to come back onboard to help us with it."

Joey met her eye for the first time since entering the room – and immediately, Louisa understood. "I dunno, I…don't really think I add that much to the team, y'know."

Louisa was uncertain how to respond. They were friendly, as colleagues went, but they weren't strictly *friends*. Joey had never asked for any sort of guidance from her, outside of her thesis, and to offer unbidden advice was rarely the wise thing to do. Yet the way Joey had looked at her, and the inflection she'd spoken with…

"You're not worried…are you, that we don't take you seriously?" she asked, after letting the silence linger to the utmost extent of its natural lifespan.

"Something like that," Joey admitted. "It's just… I had this realisation, when we went camping, that I think…maybe I rely on Dr B. a bit too much, to feel good about myself. Because he's always so nice, and he gives you his full attention when he talks to you. I don't…have many people like that. Not like him. But it makes me feel like…we're not equals in the friendship, you know? And I don't like that, I don't like being needy. So I was thinking, if I'm still going to get him to supervise my Ph.D., then I've gotta back off for a bit so I can be normal around him when we start working together again." She gave Louisa a defiant look, as though daring her to disagree.

"You have a crush on him, don't you?" Louisa said, taking no pleasure in the accusation. But she realised as she was speaking that she didn't feel so vindictive towards Joey any more. It was almost a relief to find someone else like herself, to share in the pain of rejection.

Joey just looked at her and said nothing; but her chin trembled slightly.

"It's alright," Louisa said quietly. "You wouldn't be the first."

Joey looked down, brushing a tear from her cheek. "I just wish that – I didn't feel like – my feelings are worthless because next to him I'm…"

Louisa took her by the shoulders. "You aren't less than him, Joey. You and he are just two people, like anybody else."

"But——"

"No 'but's."

Joey sniffled, but did not protest further.

"Anyway," Louisa sighed, releasing her, "I wouldn't stress too much about it if I were you. Henry isn't interested in relationships, so it doesn't really matter what your motivation is for liking him. All are equal in his eyes, in that regard."

Joey made a sound that could, conceivably, have been a chuckle.

Louisa relaxed. "Look, Joey… There's no pressure, from me or him, for you to come onto the project if you think that's best. But he does value your help, and your company – as do I. So if you change your mind, just drop us a line and we'd love to have you back. Okay?"

Joey gave her a small smile. "I'll think about it."
Louisa grinned back. "Excellent."

Chapter Twenty-Four – Night of the Soul

"Drinking alone?"

Henry looked up from his schooner to see Eden standing before him, looking amused.

"Not at all," he said airily, gesturing to the three or four other patrons sitting nearby, "I'm on the fringes of communion."

She smiled at him: her old smile, the one which might have passed for gently mocking, but really meant *I delight in you.* (The smile he had once been so in love with, when he'd thought he understood what love was.) "I'm not on shift tonight; mind if I join you?"

"You hang out at your workplace when you're not even working? I'd call you sad, but that'd turn us both into kitchenware."

Eden grimaced. "Hello, my name is kettle, and I am an alcoholic."

"Not funny enough for you, ma'am?"

"That was the kind of witty literary quip my *grandpa* would make."

Henry chose not to rise to her provocations. "There's a lot of grandpas back where I come from. They must've rubbed off on me."

"Also," said Eden, disregarding his excuses and moving to take the seat across from him, "I will have you know that we get a hearty employee discount here."

"Yeah? What sort of percentage?"

"Trade secret."

"You're just scared I'm calling your bluff."

She smiled again, and raised her hands in surrender. "Maybe I just like it here."

"Can't blame you," he said. "You don't seem to have a drink, though."

"I saw you on my way to the bar and thought I'd say hello first."

He rose from his seat. "My shout."

"Quick, someone get me ABC News on the phone, I have to tell them chivalry isn't dead…"

Henry rolled his eyes. "It will be in a minute if you keep being cheeky."

"You know my poison," she called after him as he left.

He returned a little while later with a pint of milk stout. "Same as always."

"Thanks, Hen." She clinked her glass against his. "To grandpas, and grandpa-figures everywhere."

"Amen," he said. "May they age like fine wine, and not like dried grapes."

Eden snorted into her beer.

"So," he said, "how have you been?"

"Hmmm," she said. "Quite well, thank you. I've been reminiscing on my time at Kmart lately and have concluded that, while it may not have been my most golden era, there were certainly some golden moments in amidst the quotidian mean; and as I was talking to Churchill about it last night, I felt overcome with gratitude for having closed that chapter of my life before it reached the stage of bitterness, so that I can look upon it now with fond recollection."

Her words, chosen with care, were grand – even grandiloquent – at face value, but were spoken, as always, with a kind of self-deprecating caprice that betrayed her real intention: not to impress him or to project a certain image of herself, but simply to enjoy the experience of conversing, of framing the ordinary in extraordinary ways, weaving meaning into the mundane – without affectation, and without bestowing any significance that was disproportionate to the event itself. He had forgotten how much he liked listening to her speak.

"I'm happy for you," he said.

She grinned at him, suddenly childlike. "Thanks! Me too. So what's happening on your end of things?"

"I think I'm having a mid-life crisis."

She checked her watch. "Seems premature."

He burst out laughing. (It wasn't so much the gesture itself, but the *intentionality* with which she'd looked at her watch that had got to him.) "Toni says I'm not allowed to have one," he said, once he'd recovered. (He regretted saying this immediately the name escaped his lips: he was still trying not to think about that last conversation he'd had with her on the veranda.)

"She's a wise woman, that Toni. Better listen to her. An existential crisis of any kind will get you nowhere. I should know: I have at least three a day."

"Maybe that's because fear is in your nature."

"I dunno why you get so hung up on *that*, out of everything I've ever said to you," she griped.

"It was just *so* angsty. It was like a line out of a 2000s teen drama coming-of-age movie. Except this was right when the 2000s started, so you were ahead of the curve."

She laughed. "I did say some dumb things back then."

"We all did."

"And arguably still do."

He chuckled. "I wouldn't have it any other way."

"Really?"

"Absolutely. Who wants to have only serious and intellectual discussions all the time? Not me, thanks."

"Says the guy who intellectualises memes on the internet."

"Ouch," he said. "Work is work, and play is play." (As he spoke, he remembered Louisa once having said something to the contrary. He acknowledged the memory, and then put it firmly back in its box where it belonged.)

"Yeah, that's fair," she said. "So, what's your mid-life crisis about? Don't tell me you're afraid of dying; that wouldn't be very *memento mori* of you."

He started laughing again, this time until tears came into his eyes. "Stop making fun of me," he gasped, "I'm trying to share my heart with you, and you just keep throwing it back in my face."

She was laughing too by this point. "I'm so sorry, I shan't interrupt again."

They took a minute to collect themselves.

Then he said, "I think it's just that I'm starting to question my path in life for the first time in a long time."

She nodded. "Mm."

"I mean, I like my life how it is, and I love my work, and I don't really feel like I'm missing out on anything specific," he went on, "but I've just…had a lot of conversations lately, with a lot of people, and this question of what-am-I-doing and where-am-I-going just keeps *coming up*, and every time, I think I have the answer to the question – and then it comes up *again*, and I start wondering, do I *really* have the answer? Do you know what I mean?"

"Sure," she said.

"We were talking about grandpas earlier, for example," he said, "and part of me was thinking, 'I could *be* a grandpa right now in an alternate timeline…'"

"Whoa, hang on," she said, holding up her hands, "I don't know how many thirty-nine-year-old grandpas you've met, but *I* definitely don't know any."

"Yeah, but you know what I mean, though! It's not that I regret where I am now, or the choices that led me here. But it's just hitting home that I *did* make those choices, and so here I am."

"And this is bothering you?"

He paused. "It's not that it's *bothering* me," he said slowly, "it's just that sometimes I wonder if it *should* bother me."

"Oh," said Eden. "Well, it shouldn't. You've made your choices, and it's not like they were *bad* choices. And even if they were, you can't change any of them anyway, so why worry about it? There's no alternate timeline, only the present. And you have enough suffering to deal with in the present without creating more for yourself just by wondering what a different present would look like."

"I suppose so," he sighed, unconvinced.

Eden deliberated whether to ask him the question she had carried within her since their last big conversation – the question thrashing against the cage doors of her heart and mind even now, like a wounded animal. He had raised the topic of his own accord, so surely it was fair to ask… But was it *kind* to ask, now, when he was already wrestling with so much uncertainty and self-doubt?

But in the end, she asked, because she trusted him.

"What you said to me that night, about not being able to be 'that person' to anyone…"

He looked at her, and she could feel the weight of expectation in his gaze.

"Is it still true, Henry?" she whispered.

His eyes widened: anguish. "I don't know."

"You don't know."

"I want to believe that it's true," he said quietly, "but I can't know for certain."

She drew in a breath. "Then I need you to do something for me."

"What is it?"

Her voice hardened. "Reject me."

"What?"

"Reject me. Not relationships in general, but *me*, specifically."

"But – *why?*" he pleaded.

"Because," said Eden, "what *I* said, that night, about how my feelings didn't mean I wanted anything from you…wasn't true. I thought it was, but I was wrong. I wish that I could move on… but I don't think I can, unless you take from me this last little bit of hope, and rip it to pieces. Tell me that we can't be together, not ever. And then maybe I'll finally believe you."

Henry sat in stunned silence, so many emotions raging inside him that he couldn't even begin to identify them. When he spoke, the words came out in a strangled moan: "I can't."

"*Why not?*" she cried, suddenly enraged.

"Because that wouldn't be true either!" he said desperately. "I *don't* reject you. If anything——" He stopped himself, knowing that every word spoken only added to her pain. "This isn't about you. It's just my own lack of conviction. That's *all* it is. But don't ask me to speak against you——"

"I'm not asking you to *criticise* me, I'm just *asking* you to tell me that you're not in love with me!"

"Eden, my feelings are irrelevant to your happiness! I don't know what I feel today, and I don't know what I'll feel tomorrow! Being 'in love' is something that comes and goes, but relationships are about *commitment*, and I don't know if I have what it takes to make that commitment!"

"Then tell me you *won't* make it! Stop waiting for God to come down from the sky and tell you what to do with your life, and just *make a decision*!"

"Fine," he snarled, getting up from his chair. "I won't commit. And I never gave you any reason to believe I would, so I don't know why you wasted all these years hoping. I'll see you later."

He left without looking at her, regretting his last words but too proud to take them back. By the time he'd reached home, his rage had dissolved. By the time he'd reached the top of the stairwell, he was overcome with remorse.

He knew dimly that morning would come, bringing clarity and the hope of renewal. But as he was helpless to bring about the morning before its time, he threw himself upon his bed and wept bitterly, until sleep overtook him.

Chapter Twenty-Five – Epiphany

Henry woke up and rejoiced, for it was the Lord's Day.

Then he remembered his conversation with Eden the previous night and promptly returned to the depths of despair.

His first thought was to go to her immediately and apologise, if not for what he'd said (for his words had been true, after all), then at least for how he'd said it. But there was no time: Mass was in forty minutes, and Louisa was coming over afterwards for a tour of Biddlesnoot-Bloomington Manor. So he resigned himself to waiting, hoping that he and Eden would each benefit from the intervening time and space, and tried his best to put her out of his mind for the remainder of the day.

∴

Mathilda awoke and found herself lying on her lounge room couch, where she had fallen asleep watching reruns of *Full House* until her weak and weary eyes had closed and she had dreamt an endless procession of small, blonde-haired children whispering important life lessons sweetly in her ears.

She beheld the sun through her window, and decided to spend some time in meditation beneath the cherry tree to the left of her house (the one on the right not having quite the desired level of foliage with which to shelter the troubled soul of the artist). It was here that she had a revelation concerning the ending of her book: something she had known all along intuitively, and yet had never found the words to articulate – until now.

"He can't run forever," she murmured aloud. "Sooner or later, he has to turn back and face his fears head-on."

And there it was: the missing piece of the puzzle, the final turn of the Rubik's cube. Now that she had named the beast, its grip on her was broken – and suddenly, writing the story through to the end seemed nowhere near as daunting as it had been for the last fifteen years. She would berate herself later for taking so long to reach such an obvious conclusion, but there was no time to think about that now: she had to *write*.

She abandoned the cherry tree and raced inside, exultant.

∴

Louisa's first impression of Biddlesnoot-Bloomington Manor would have been favourable were it not for the faint scratching and scuttling of rats beneath the floorboards, and also the manifestation of more ghosts and ghouls and restless spirits than the naked eye could comprehend.

"I told you," Henry said with no particular inflection, as she gazed about her in dumbstruck awe and horror.

One of the ancient spectral mob descended like a cloud of smoke from the ceiling, where a number of them floated aimlessly about the chandelier, and stood (was that even the right word?) before Louisa, taking the shape of a young woman with curly dark hair and an eyepatch. "How do you do?" it (she?) said tersely.

"Uhm," said Louisa.

"This is my Great-Great-Aunt Yvonne," said Henry. "Auntie, this is my friend Louisa."

"Pleased to meet you, I'm sure," said the ghost, sounding not very pleased at all. (Unbeknownst to Louisa or Henry, she had wagered a substantial amount on Henry marrying Eden, so the sight of a competitor entering the house was thoroughly unwelcome to her undead eyes. But as she did not care to disclose such information to her nephew, she was doomed to appear belligerent and inhospitable, and sink lower in his esteem – as is sometimes the price we pay for prudence, alas.)

Louisa was too bewildered by the sight of an actual, visible ghost to feel offended by this rather frigid reception. "Pleased to meet you, too," she stammered.

Great-Great-Aunt Yvonne nodded and returned whence she came.

Louisa looked at Henry, who shrugged. "Come on," he said cheerfully, "it'd take all day for you to meet everyone. Let's go into the sitting room and I'll show you our record collection."

She arched an eyebrow. "Shouldn't we be finalising the scope of our VocaLeague project?"

"Certainly not; I don't work on Sundays. And besides," he went on as they took the staircase up towards the first floor, "I already settled on the scope on my way to Mass this morning."

"Is that so? And what, pray, might that be?"

"I'll tell you at precisely 12:01AM," he teased.

She groaned. "You are *so* annoying."

"'All have sinned and fallen short of the glory of God.'"

Louisa gave him a shove, and, laughing, they continued up the stairs.

∴

Trish Mackenzie sat at her computer in her office in Sydney, typing briskly. She had just made a breakthrough in her new project on phantom currency, and the fire within her was blazing. No doubt about it, *she* would be the one to take front cover on the next edition of *Forward*. And when that happened, she would soar across the Bass Strait on the very first plane just to run a victory lap around Henry's office.

Her head filled with visions of triumph, she smiled to herself.

∴

After Louisa had gone, Henry met Eden by the waterfront. She was wearing a dark green corduroy jacket and a long dress, like the ones she had often worn at college. She seemed ageless, somehow both older and younger than she really was. She looked at him, unsmiling – and he realised he felt shabby and awkward, standing before her in his scuffed Blundstone boots.

"G'day," he said.

"How are you?" she asked, with that politeness which is charming to new friends and excruciating to old.

"Penitential," he said, the corner of his mouth quirking upward despite everything.

She did not return the smile. "Oh."

He looked at her for a long moment, affection and remorse battling with each other inside him (as they always had, when it came to her).

"Words are cheap," he said. "But for what it *is* worth, I'm very sorry."

"Don't be," she said evenly. "I asked for the truth, and you gave it."

"Not kindly."

"When is Truth ever kind?" she asked – a note of bitterness creeping into her voice, against her will.

He didn't have an answer to that question, and he didn't know what else to say, so he was silent.

She looked down. "I don't think there's anything more to be said here, Henry. I'm grateful for your honesty, but…I probably need to be by myself for a while."

Remorse won.

(For now.)

"Okay," he said quietly.

She nodded at him and walked away.

∴

Sarah Banks sat in a plastic chair in the tiny communal backyard behind her apartment building, soaking up the late afternoon sun and reading a book called *(EQ)uilibrium*, which promised to teach her the secrets of emotional discipline.

'Take ownership of your emotions,' it reassured her. 'While emotions may arise in response to external actions or events, no one can *make* you feel anything. Placing the responsibility outside yourself will only leave you feeling frustrated and powerless.'

Sarah ruminated on these words, and was filled with hope.

∴

Henry met with Donovan and Mark at the latter's house that evening, over the usual tea and biscuits.

"You look depressed," Donovan accused as Henry entered Mark's lounge room.

"Cheers, Don."

"Wasn't a compliment."

"I *know*," Henry said crossly.

"So why are you depressed?" asked Mark, coming in with the tea things.

Henry threw himself upon the sofa and pulled a cushion over his head. "I'm not depressed."

"Alright, *don't* tell us, then," said Mark, pouring Donovan a peppermint and lime tea.

Presently, Henry emerged from beneath the cushion. "It's Eden."

Donovan rolled his eyes. "*Here* we bloody go…"

"Shut up, Don," Mark suggested. "Go on, Hen, tell us all about it."

So Henry related to his friends his most recent woes, and they listened with heroic patience and sympathy, given their position. When he had finished, however…

"I don't understand you two," Donovan said bluntly.

Henry sighed. "I'll let you know when *I* understand us."

"I just don't see why it has to be so complicated," said Donovan. "*Do* you like her, or don't you?"

"Define 'like'."

"Well I can't ask if you *love* her, or you'll start spouting that Thomist crap again!"

"He means, are you *in* love with her," Mark said helpfully.

"That's just another meaningless phrase we use for something vague, ephemeral, and of little consequence," Henry growled.

"Are you *attracted* to her?!" Donovan all but shouted, grabbing Henry by the shoulders and shaking him.

"Oh, for – *yes!*" Henry yelled back. "But that doesn't *mean* anything!"

"What do you mean, it 'doesn't mean anything'?!"

"Exactly what I just said!"

"Alright, settle down," said Mark, stepping in to separate them. "Don, you and I both know your philosophy on human love is more nuanced than this, so stop being a numpty. Henry, what Don's trying to ask, and not doing a great job of, is: *what* exactly is the barrier between you and Eden?"

"There *is* no barrier – that's what I was trying to tell her the other night! It's just that I don't want to get married, so any feelings I may have are irrelevant!"

"But if you *like* her, and there aren't any real, objective reasons why you shouldn't date her, then why not give it a go and see if you change your mind? You're not asking her to marry you just by asking her out for coffee, you know."

Henry pinched his brow. "I think we're well beyond the coffee stage by this point, Mark."

"He's right," said Donovan, surprising them both. "There's not much room in this situation for the getting-to-know-you part of the relationship. But," he added, "I don't think that means there can't be a trial-and-error part either."

"So you're saying I should gamble with someone else's heart?" Henry snapped.

"No, you idiot, I'm just saying that relationships aren't as absolute and categorical as you think they are! Everyone goes into it knowing there's a possibility it won't work out; that's just part of the deal. But most people, I think, would rather *know* it won't work than waste a bunch of time wondering what-if."

"Well, I'm not one of those people," Henry said shortly. "And I don't owe her anything just because she likes me, so stop looking at me like I'm the worst person in the world for wanting to be careful."

"*Are* you being careful?" asked Mark. "Or are you just completely, utterly crippled by your own fear?"

"I'm not afraid!"

"Then why are you *so* against the possibility that you and Eden might be right for each other after all?"

"Because..." said Henry, anger becoming anguish as the realisation struck him, "I just don't feel peaceful when I'm with her, that's all."

There was a slight pause. His friends' eyes widened, and he realised it was the first time he had admitted this, even to himself.

"I feel everything else," he went on, "love, hate, all the emotions in between – but not peace. I'm not myself around her. I *hate* myself around her." He paused, drew in a breath. "It's not her fault. It's just how it's always been. I love her, but…"

He stopped himself – the words hung in the air before him, the truth he was not yet willing to speak aloud: *I need someone I can be at peace with.*

Instead, he said, much more quietly, "It just won't work."

Wordlessly, his friends nodded. Mark poured him another tea, and it was understood that the discussion had ended.

But the words Henry had not yet spoken were still burning through the core of his mind, leaving him scarcely able to think or speak until he had left Mark's and gone home.

Because he had realised that there *was* one person, beyond all others, whom he felt at peace with. And he had never noticed it until now.

Chapter Twenty-Six – (Un)certainty

Henry lay awake, wrestling with the most profound identity crisis ever to plague him since the age of seventeen, when he had finally made the switch from Weet-Bix to Vita Brits.

Could this be real? he asked himself despairingly. Was he really feeling what he thought he was feeling? Was *this* who he was, after all? Was this what he really wanted – or needed?

He had spent so many years telling himself – telling everyone else – that he didn't need or want anyone – that he wasn't meant to walk that path – that he was happy the way he was. To admit any other possibility seemed a betrayal of his very self.

But something kept nagging at him.

Fear, Mark had said.

What are you so afraid of? everyone kept asking.

Was that it?

Was he afraid?

"Am I afraid?" he demanded of Martin the fish.

Martin didn't answer.

Henry sighed.

Perhaps he *was* afraid.

But then, if that was so, did he not owe it to himself…to *her*…to try to overcome that fear?

∴

The instant the very first ray of predawn light slipped between his curtains, he phoned her, knowing she would be awake.

"It's me," he said. "Don't go to work today."

"What?"

"I need to talk to you. I'll be right there. Just stay where you are."

He hung up.

∴

Later, he arrived on her doorstep.

He knocked.

Toni opened the door.

"Henry," she said, frowning at him, "what's going on?"

"Marry me," he said.

She blinked. "*What?*"

"You were right," said Henry, smiling, "and I was wrong. So marry me, Toni."

∴

(Joey woke up that morning and decided, after much uncertainty and deliberation, that it was better to face her fears head-on, rather than running away from them – and so she *would* help Dr Henry and Louisa with their new project. She tried calling Dr Henry, but he didn't pick up. So she called Louisa, who was delighted to hear the news.)

∴

Eventually she convinced him to wait.

"There's no point getting hitched till we know this actually works," she said.

"But we *know* it works," he argued. "We've been friends for my entire lifespan!"

"Yeah, but marriage is different, you silly dingo."

He sighed. "Alright. So what now?"

Toni shrugged. "Well I dunno about you, but *I've* gotta fix a man's pantry door."

"Okay... But after that, I'll – I'll take you to dinner."

A gleam entered her eye. "Five-dollar pints and schnitties at the bowlo?"

Henry surrendered his nascent hopes and dreams of five-star restaurants and sparkling rosés. "Done."

Toni grinned. And that was when Henry finally acknowledged the fundamental truth which had eluded his conscious mind for so many years: that she was quite, quite lovely.

∴

(It was wonderful to have Joey back in the office. Together, she, Henry, and Louisa made rapid strides in their research during the days that followed.)

∴

They sat on her veranda one night and watched the sun go down beyond the hills, neither of them speaking, which was normal.

But suddenly he felt self-conscious, which wasn't normal.

Did she expect something more of him now? Or was silence enough?

He turned towards her. "You okay, Tone?"

She looked at him, confused. "Yeah."

"Oh. Good."

The silence returned.

∴

He had taken her by the hand in the past, of course, and done so without a second thought. They were like siblings, after all. But now, for the first time, he *held* her hand: not for the sake of leading her somewhere, but for the sake of the gesture itself.

Toni's hands were cool to the touch, the skin coarse and slightly pinched. But they were not frail. She had the strong hands of a craftsman, of someone who had worked with power tools since before she could legally drink. He felt awed by her hands, somehow.

She noticed him looking, felt his fingertips against her calluses and scars – and suddenly, her usual placid expression contorted into something different –

Grief?

Henry met her eye. "What's wrong?"

She glanced away. "Nothing." A pause. "Time's just a bastard, that's all."

Few words, as always. But he understood her meaning: why had it taken them so many years to reach this point? Why couldn't they have come together when they were younger, more beautiful, with so much more time ahead of them?

"Toni," he said gently, "I don't think our time before now was wasted."

She looked at him.

"Those years you spent waiting for me…they're a testament to your love, and selflessness, and patience. They make you *more* beautiful to me, not less."

She smiled despite herself. "Sissy."

He let go of her hand.

∴

(Days passed; he lost count of how many. It was somewhere in November, he thought. So much time had passed…and so little.)

∴

"You still haven't touched me," he said one day as they were out golfing.

She almost dropped her 5-iron. "What?"

He blushed. "We're just…doing the same things we've always done. Nothing's changed. Don't get me wrong, I love friendship as much as the next guy, but I thought the whole point of this was to be more than friends. So how come you never touch me?" He smiled shyly. "I thought you liked me."

"I thought *you* liked *me*," she said crossly. "I was waiting for you to make the next move."

"I was waiting for *you*!"

"Why *me*?!"

"I dunno, I didn't want to be pushy… I haven't done this sort of thing in a while."

"Well neither've I, you great galoot," she said, laughing now.

He drew close to her, taking in the set of her jaw, the crinkling near her eyes as she laughed. She was perfect, he thought, feeling a burst of warmth and confidence and knowing that this was the right moment. He placed a hand on her waist, waiting as her laughter subsided and she fell still, the game of golf temporarily forgotten.

He reached up with his other hand and touched the lines on her face, wondering at how much – and how little – she had changed over the years. He felt her tense slightly, not with discomfort, but…apprehension? Surprise? He considered letting go, but felt somehow that this would be the wrong move.

So he cupped her cheek in his hand, feeling her skin flush hot with embarrassment against his palm: yet he saw in her eyes, locked on his, that she was open to what came next. And then he leaned in, closed his eyes and kissed her: gently, uncertainly, having almost forgotten what it was like to touch someone in that way. (He had only ever kissed one other person – but he tried not to think about that.) She went taut in his arms, although she kissed him back.

Neither was certain, when they'd pulled away, whether they had enjoyed it.

They finished the game in silence.

When he left, his thoughts were muddled: vaguely pleasant, but unclear.

∴

(Louisa and Joey each began to wonder – though they never talked about it with each other – why Henry seemed so distracted of late. An unspoken anxiety pervaded the office, eating away at the edges of perception, until they could hardly stand to be in the same room with him any more. But neither of them would ask him about it, nor would they back away.)

∴

"You never tell me how you're feeling," he said.

"You never ask."

"You never ask *me*, but I tell you anyway."

"Yeah, because you're a drama queen."

He knew she didn't really mean to be insulting, but her words still stung. "People in relationships are supposed to be able to tell each other things."

"There's nothing to tell," she said irritably. "I woke up this morning, I went to work, I came home."

"But how do you *feel?*"

"I don't know! I don't sit around *thinking* about my feelings like you do! I just feel them and then I move on!"

He exhaled slowly. "It just seems like I'm more open with you than you are with me, that's all."

She spread her hands helplessly. "I've been on my own for forty years, Henry. I've learned to sort things out for myself, I don't bring other people into it."

"But you wanted to bring me into it," he said sadly.

"Yeah…" she said, looking down. "I s'pose so."

∴

Eventually it became too painful
to touch each other, so they stopped.

∴

"Are you sure you even want to marry me?" he demanded.

"No," she said, honestly.

"I mean, when we had that – talk———"

"That fight, you mean."

"What were you telling me, exactly? Why were you waiting for me? What do you want?"

She sighed. "I dunno, man. Just…for things to be how they've always been, and for no one else to get in the way, maybe."

"So you don't want to marry me, live with me, have children with me?"

Silence.

"It's not that I *don't* want that," she finally said.

He sighed. "I don't know if I want it either."

Gathering all his courage, he reached for her hand…but she pulled away.

∴

The day they decided to end things, he wept.
    She didn't.
    They were each filled with grief, however, in their own way.

∴

But they both agreed it was for the best.
    And, in their own way, they each got what they wanted.

Chapter Twenty-Seven – Equilibrium

It took Henry a week to come back to the office after breaking up with Toni. When he finally did return, however, he felt rested and reaffirmed in his intention not to pursue any form of romantic relationship, and was so full of gaiety and ardour for the VocaLeague project that he seemed mostly his old self again.

(If Louisa or Joey noticed anything different about him, they held their peace.)

One December morning, he arrived much later than usual (though still well before nine), bearing a tray of freshly baked chocolate muffins, which he offered to Joey and Louisa as they came in the door. "Merry Wednesday," he said gravely, in response to their expressions of astonishment and delight.

"Wow, these look amazing," said Louisa, helping herself to a particularly plump specimen. "What brought this on?"

"Oh, I just woke up and felt a sudden passion on my heart for baking." So saying, he ate three muffins in swift succession.

"I get that sometimes as well," said Joey. "Last time, it was macaroons at 4:00AM. They didn't turn out very good…but ah well, you can't have it all."

"No," Henry said thickly, halfway through his fourth muffin, "you can't."

∴

Having outlined their literature review and introduction on the emergence of VocaLeague and its antecedents in sports and entertainment, they next began surveying groups of VocaLeague and mainstream sports fans across different age demographics, trying to assess how much overlap there was between groups, and whether levels of emotional investment or reasons for enjoyment differed across the various populations. It was very tedious work, and shall not be covered in any great detail here.

∴

"Man, some of these responses are absolutely whack," said Joey.

Henry looked up from his desk. "Such as?"

"'I like VocaLeague because it gives me lucid dreams.'"

"Huh," said Henry.

"Bok choy can also give you lucid dreams if you eat enough of it," said Louisa.

∴

"Henry, my boy," said Uncle Bertram, meeting him at the door after work one evening, "how are you travelling?"

"By foot, Uncle," his nephew said with a slight smirk.

The ghost folded his arms. "There's no need to be facetious."

"No need, perhaps," countered Henry, undaunted as always by any form of reproach from his undead relations, "but the *desire* was there, and that's what really matters."

"How very hedonistic of you," his uncle said sarcastically.

"I'm sorry, Uncle, I'm just not in the mood for a heart-to-heart right now. I didn't mean any offence."

At this, Uncle Bertram looked very sad indeed, even for a ghost. "Well, I wouldn't want to intrude… I just knew that you've had a few bumps on the road lately, and——"

"Uncle," Henry said quietly, "I'd rather not talk about it just now."

The ghost bowed his head and vanished.

∴

Louisa knew, as she always did, that something had happened with Henry. He'd never told her (or anyone, for that matter) about his brief relationship with Toni, but she'd understood a lot without being told, and could, if asked, have made an educated guess that was not all that far off from the truth.

For a short time, this half-guessed, half-imagined reality caused her a great deal of pain, though she had no desire to confront him about it.

However, as the days passed, Louisa found that the intensity of her feelings had faded since she'd spoken to him in her backyard that day. She was a moderate person by nature, and her emotions, if not riled up by external events, tended to balance themselves out without much effort. So it did not surprise her (although it saddened her at first) when the moment finally came in which she could look upon Henry and feel…nothing.

∴

"Here's a response from a fourteen-year-old VocaLeague fan who says, 'I love Miku-san because she fights and kills her enemies with conviction, and that inspires me to lead my own life with conviction,'" said Joey.

"Struth," said Henry. "Is that what fourteen-year-olds are really like these days?"

"You mean they haven't always been like that?" said Joey. "I know I was, at fourteen."

"Same," Louisa chuckled.

"I suppose I have to admire this particular young person for their eagerness to seek conviction," Henry mused.

"What d'you reckon is the difference between conviction and arrogance?" Joey asked. She cherished a great love of abstract conversation, for someone whose field of expertise dealt almost exclusively with concrete specifics.

"Whether you're right or wrong?" suggested Henry.

Joey wrinkled her nose. "Nah."

"Aristotle would probably say they exist on the same spectrum," Louisa said offhandedly.

"Okay, Louisa, we get it, you read *Nicomachean Ethics*," Henry teased.

Louisa poked her tongue out at him.

∴

With each passing day, the sense of
equilibrium amongst them grew.

∴

One morning Joey was late again, and Louisa took the opportunity to ask Henry a question that had nagged at her ever since she'd visited his home.

"Henry?" she said.

"Mmph?" he said, still sipping his second piccolo.

"How do you feel about the fact that you're going to be a ghost one day?"

Henry took a long time to finish his drink.

"I don't really mind," he said eventually. "I'm kind of bummed about the idea of not going to Heaven until the curse on my family is broken, but I don't really know if that's how it works. Anyway," he went on, more cheerfully, "it'll just give me more time to do my research, and I won't have to stop to eat or sleep or any of those pesky embodied soul things, so that part of it should be pretty good."

Louisa nodded, unable to think of a reply.

∴

"You know, as much as lolcow studies has its limitations, I do miss it," Joey said to Louisa that afternoon. (Henry was out at a lunch meeting.)

Louisa smiled. "It *is* fun. I remember when I was doing my undergrad, we used to have a unit called 'Sustainable LOL Farming,' and it was all about the ethics of lolcow discourse, and basically, every tutorial was just an excuse for the lecturer to go on a forty-minute tirade about unconscious metatextual dissonance in *Sonichu.*"

"That sounds rad," Joey said enviously.

"It was," said Louisa, suddenly overcome with a wave of nostalgia for those heady days of scrimping and sleeplessness and thousand-word essays, and the thrill of being in the brief stage of life where autonomy and lack of responsibility collided with each other at the summit.

But it wasn't like life got boring after that, she reminded herself. After all, postgrad had its joys too, and beyond that were other opportunities, like working with Joey on her master's thesis. That had been a lot of fun, too. And then she felt a pang of sorrow, even guilt, as she reflected on what had become of her relationship with Joey since then: how she had spent so many weeks and months nursing this ambient resentment towards her younger colleague for showing feelings and behaviours which were so far from conscious or intentional as to be almost benign.

However, in this moment, there was a grace as well. Louisa looked at Joey (who was still chuckling to herself about the 'ethics of lolcow discourse'), then looked within, and saw that her newfound detachment towards Henry had also brought about a new goodwill towards Joey.

It helped, of course, that Joey had not recently displayed any of the aforementioned feelings or behaviours which Louisa had previously found so aggravating. But even if she had, it wouldn't matter any more. Regardless of what Joey said or did (which, after all, was her own responsibility), Louisa felt convicted that she would never again succumb to that resentment. She was free.

Chapter Twenty-Eight – Friendship

Mathilda was drafting her penultimate scene, and she was stuck.

It wasn't writer's block, exactly. She knew the broad strokes of what she was trying to do: the hero had finally faced his fears, learned about his past, and come to accept himself. All that remained was to have him choose his next course of action and then integrate his new identity and purpose into his existing social group.

But the problem was, Mathilda had no idea *how* to work that kind of personal evolution into her story without it seeming forced. She herself had hardly changed in twenty years (or at least, she *felt* like she hadn't changed), and being a social recluse didn't help. She had no first- or second-hand experience to draw upon, and she didn't believe in trying to fabricate emotions on the page that she had never encountered personally, fearing that they wouldn't ring true.

Previously, she had got around this problem by writing plot-driven sagas about one-dimensional characters who wore their cartoon-like emotions and desires on their shirtsleeves with a kind of garish pride. But she wanted her new book to be *more* than that, to accomplish something which she hadn't previously.

So, she was stuck.

She spent the morning meditating and drinking coffee, neither of which helped. She called her mum and talked for forty-five minutes of unrelated matters, hoping that her subconscious mind would tackle the problem for her. It didn't. She took a nap, woke up, and was still lost for what to do. She walked around the block, listened to writers' podcasts, and succeeded only in becoming more agitated.

Then it occurred to her that she had one final recourse which had always helped her in the past: she could talk to Henry.

She rang him that evening, hoping against hope that he would pick up.

Sure enough: "Mathilda; this is a nice surprise."

"Hi Henry, I hope you're well?"

"Quite well, thanks, and you?"

"Wracked with miserable indecision."

He laughed. "Sounds familiar. So, what can I do for you?"

Mathilda explained to him the problem.

"Hmm," he said. "That's rough."

"Any ideas what I should do?"

(Henry suddenly understood how Toni had felt for the last forty years.)

"Well…" He tried to call to mind those instances when he himself had undergone personal growth and then had to bring his new self and old life into harmony. There didn't seem to be many such instances – certainly none resembling even remotely what Mathilda's hero was supposed to be going through.

"I think," he said, "you should give him a moment where he explicitly acknowledges that he's changed. It doesn't have to be a big speech in front of everyone, but just have him quietly realise it one day, when he's out watering his garden or something. But have him keep the parts of his old self that he still values, so the change feels more organic. Then go through a period of his life, like the next few months or so, where his friends and family gradually notice the changes in him, and show their reactions, but don't make a big deal out of it. That's what I would do, I think."

"Huh," said Mathilda.

"Take my advice with however much salt you want, obviously, I'm a novice when it comes to fiction."

"No," said Mathilda. "No. Thank you. That was very helpful."

"Oh. No worries."

"I'll let you go now," she said, and hung up.

Bemused, Henry went back to his research.

∴

He and Sarah still caught up for coffee every now and again. As much as he adored Corner Shop and would always make it his first port of call, he admired how she had taken the trouble to acquaint herself with every decent café in town, and how she introduced him to a new one each time they met. This time it was a little pop-up coffee stand on one of the main streets in the CBD, and they were seated on wooden milk crates on the footpath next to it, while aimless shoppers and wayward youths ambled by with their tote bags and tiny backpacks and scooters.

"I've been reading this book called *Speaking With Words and Actions*," Sarah told him, "and it's all about how we can tailor our habits to be more affirming of the people around us. For example, if you're in a conversation with someone at a social function, and a third person comes to join in, you can welcome that person and help them feel affirmed through your body language, like making eye contact, and shifting your stance so that you're all standing equidistant, and by verbally acknowledging them before you continue the conversation. It's really cool, I'm enjoying it a lot."

"That does sound good," agreed Henry, who was all for cultivating social generosity.

"But the weird thing is," Sarah went on, beginning to make herself laugh as her thoughts raced ahead of her words and she beat herself to the punchline, "the more I read it, the more I keep thinking about *The Castle*, and how affirming Darryl Kerrigan is."

Henry started laughing too. "Yeah, you're not wrong," he said. "Darryl Kerrigan is perhaps the most affirming man of them all. No matter what his family do, he loves it, and loves them."

"He loves them *so* much," she said, half-laughing, half-crying, "and he loves his neighbours, and his dogs, and his house… Such a good and loving man."

"*Such* a good man," Henry said wistfully. "His balance of strength and gentleness is unparalleled through most of literary history."

Sarah just shook her head and kept on laughing.

They moved on to another topic soon after that; but when Henry replayed the conversation in his head later that night, Darryl Kerrigan was all he could think about.

∴

One evening, after a long stint in the office staring at survey results until he felt like he was developing a brain rupture, he rang Trish.

"How's your project going?" he asked.

"It's great! Phantom currency is the hot new topic now, so I'm trying to get it done as fast as possible so I can beat the rest of the suckers to the punch."

"I expected nothing less," he said.

"How's yours?"

"Oh, trudging along. The surveys are quite complex in the way that they overlap, and we're still trying to up our sample sizes, so I think it'll take us a fair way into the new year."

"Awww, don't say that! It'll be no fun getting front cover of *Forward* if you're not there to compete against me!"

He snorted. "Then hold back your submission until I'm done."

"Nah, that's no fun either," she said. "I'll just do a follow-up study that'll be even *better* than this one, and it'll blow your Vocaloid fluff piece out of the water."

"Bring it on," he chuckled.

"I will," she said, and hung up, eager to get back to work.

She knew, and always had known, that he would never feel for her what she did for him. And yet, somehow, when she stopped to think about it, she found that she didn't really mind. Feelings would come and go as they pleased, but what she loved most was competing with him, and *that* would never change.

Chapter Twenty-Nine – Hard Work

As December wore on, Henry, Louisa and Joey continued working hard on their research.

∴

Mathilda wrote the final line of her manuscript, and so laid fifteen excruciating years' worth of effort to rest.

∴

Trish put the finishing touches on her paper and prepared to send it off for peer review, all the while thinking ahead to what she could write about next.

Chapter Thirty – Victory

It was a Saturday morning, about eleven, and the café smelled of honeycomb and tea leaves and rosehip oil.

"So what are we celebrating?" Henry asked Mathilda, as Barista Frances bustled past and deposited a pair of affogatos on their table.

Mathilda beamed, looking like an entirely different person. "I sent the finished manuscript off to my editor the other day. Just got the email back yesterday morning, and it's getting published next year!"

"Incredible!" cried Henry, shaking her hand. "Why, it seems only yesterday that we met, and you were still stuck in the very middle of it. You've made a valiant effort, Mathilda. I am in awe."

Mathilda received encouragement according to her mood; as she was currently feeling giddy with exhilaration, her receptive capacity was at its zenith. "Thank you very much!" she said. "And thank you for all your help as well. This would have been a much longer time coming if it hadn't been for your insights and moral support."

He bowed his head. "It was my pleasure."

"It still feels so surreal," said Mathilda, stirring her affogato absently. "I've been working around the clock for weeks, trying to get it finished. I've no idea what to do with myself now that I'm free."

"Start writing your next book?" Henry suggested.

She blanched. "I'd sooner die."

"I will never," he laughed, "understand your work ethic."

"There *is* no work ethic," she said, laughing too. "The wretched ideas just *come* to me and they don't give me a minute's peace until they're written. I'm just a little performing monkey who bashes away at the keyboard in hopes of being given a peanut." She couldn't *stop* laughing, she was so carried away by her own rhetoric.

He was crying with laughter. "That's so depressing!"

"Yeah, it is!" she giggled. "Why do you think I'm so sad all the time?!"

They roared and shook with mirth and merriment, howling and clutching at their sides, until Barista Frances came over and politely asked them to lower the volume. They apologised and set to work on their affogatos, unable to look each other in the eye until they'd finished.

"So how's your new paper coming along?" Mathilda asked him. Normally she despised making work the default topic of conversation, because she hated being asked about her writing, and so projected that hatred onto everybody else; but with Henry it was different, since he harboured such love and enthusiasm for his work, and would talk about it animatedly, and at length, whenever given the opportunity.

Now, however, Henry sighed, surprising her almost as much as when she'd first realised his name wasn't George. "It's okay."

She waited, unwilling to prod him but sensing that he had more to say.

"It's just that all it's going to amount to at this rate is a summary of different survey responses, and a general conclusion of 'different people like different things,'" he went on. "I had such a *vision* for it when we first started, but the data we're turning up is just *so* far from making that vision a reality that I almost want to scrap the project entirely."

Mathilda was intimately familiar with the agony he described. "Well, I'm no scientist——" she began.

"Neither'm I," he chortled.

"But if I know anything about what you're talking about, I'd say you're taking too functional a view of your data. You need to let it *breathe*."

He frowned. "Please elaborate."

"Well, let's say I need to write Chapter X of my book," she said. "In order to progress the plot to where it needs to be, Chapter X needs to include elements A, B, and C. Now, *I* just want to hurry up and finish my book, so as I write Chapter X, all I'm thinking about is getting A, B, and C down on the page as quickly and efficiently as I can, with no extraneous twaddle. When I'm finished, I end up with a crisp, concise chapter that fulfils its function perfectly as far as the plot is concerned. But here's the question…" She leaned in. "Is Chapter X fun to read?"

Henry stared at her, utterly lost by the analogy. "I dunno…is it?"

"In my experience," Mathilda said glumly, "usually not. Because it's so functional that there's no room for flavour. I've forgotten to let it *breathe*." She took a sip from her water glass. "Now on the other hand, if I write Chapter X slowly, over the course of a few weeks, and instead of worrying about A, B, and C, I let those things take care of themselves and I simply focus on enjoying each scene as I write it, letting it breathe and come to life and take on all the different qualities which aren't strictly necessary to the plot but are organic to the scene I'm setting, then what happens is I end up with a much more fun and flavourful chapter." She downed the rest of her water with an air of triumph.

"That makes sense," Henry said slowly, "but I don't see how that applies to academic research."

She waved his protests impatiently aside. "What I'm trying to illustrate is the difference between looking at your work *functionally* and looking at it as a *living* thing. You're drowning yourself in all these surveys, to the point where you've forgotten about the *narrative* you were trying to explore. Instead of looking at the responses people send in to you as categorical data – 'yes' or 'no,' 'like' or 'dislike' – why don't you just sit with the responses for a while, and really *immerse* yourself in people's words, and see if any unexpected nuances or side narratives or other surprises start appearing, once you stop focussing on function?"

"Huh," said Henry. "That actually sounds like a pretty good idea."

Mathilda smiled wryly. "I have been known to have those occasionally."

He raised his empty glass and saluted her. "To letting it breathe."

"And to never having another idea for a book *ever* again," said she.

Henry snorted.

∴

Once Henry had changed his perspective on the data coming in from the surveys, it did not take him long to begin turning up some new findings.

"Have you noticed," he said to Louisa one day, "that a disproportionate number of our respondents in the 18-24 demographic refer to a Vocaloid named 'F-sama'? But I've been searching the lists of known Vocaloid characters and there's no mention of one by that name."

"Weird," said Louisa. "Could be a prank… Like maybe a group got together and planned to send in a bunch of phony submissions. Although why anyone would want to interfere with such a niche project as this is beyond me…"

"I don't see how that could be…" said Henry, glued to his screen. "I've run multiple searches for the term 'F-sama' and found nothing, so it can't be an online group that's doing it. And there are too many submissions, from too many different regions, for it to be an in-person group."

Louisa shrugged. "Well, either way, it doesn't affect us much."

"No, no, you're looking at this the wrong way!" he cried. "This is an *opportunity*! This could be our next breakthrough! I'm going to follow this rabbit hole right down to the very end, and you mark my words, Louisa Honeysett, I'll have something interesting to show you when I'm finished. I can feel it in my bones!"

Louisa returned to her work. "Whatever you say, homeslice."

"What'd I miss?" said Joey, coming in with a tray of coffees.

∴

Over the next few days, Henry infiltrated a number of the web-based fight clubs which had given rise to the VocaLeague tournaments. He spent countless hours trawling their chat rooms and forums, asking about F-sama, only to be met with bafflement and derision. But he did not give up, and after wheedling Louisa into teaching him the ways of the deep web, he soon began to uncover the answers he sought…

∴

"It's a *what?*" cried Joey and Louisa.

"A cult," Henry calmly replied.

"You mean a meme cult, like the ones high schoolers come up with ironically, or a *cult* cult?" asked Louisa.

"Well, I think it started off as the former, but gradually became the latter, similar to what happened with Gold Yamre," said he. "Basically, they invented this god-figure, F-sama, strongest VocaLeague fighter of them all. I think she began her life as a character in a fanfic which has since been wiped from the net. Anyway, for whatever reason, numerous people pretended to worship her, and then after a time, some of them began to worship for real. Or so it seems, anyway. The whole thing could just be an even more elaborate ruse-within-a-ruse, it's too early to tell at this stage." He paused, ruminating on the words he had just spoken. "It is said that every now and again, an official VocaLeague cage match is hijacked, and one of the contenders forcibly replaced with an anonymous user's avatar, which acts as the host for F-sama. I have yet to see this for myself, of course."

There was a profound silence.

"But," said Louisa, "what does this…*mean?*"

"It means," said Henry, "that our project just got a whole lot more fun!" He glanced at the clock. "But we'll go over all that tomorrow. For now…who's going to join me at the pub?"

"I will!" said Joey.

Henry looked at Louisa.

She grinned sheepishly. "Sorry…I've got something else on."

Henry shook his head. "Look who's the dog now."

"Yeah, well, it's about *time*," she said with mock severity. "You've monopolised the dog-act market long enough."

(Joey did not understand the subtext of this interaction, and felt mildly uncomfortable at being excluded.)

"Alright then," said Henry, "have fun with whatever it is you're doing. Let's go, Joey."

"See ya, Lou!"

"Bye, guys."

They went their separate ways.

∴

Henry and Joey talked of art and culture over pale ale and pretzels.

"I was thinking about the economy in the movie *Cars*," she said.

"Oh?" he said.

"Yes," she told him, "because obviously the race cars are paid to race, and their crews are paid to do all their maintenance and repairs. But what do all the other cars do for a living? I guess you have the ones who own shops and stuff, but it just got me thinking about what sorts of things their economy is built on. Probably the two biggest industries in their world are racing and broadcast media. Then you'd have all the secondary industries surrounding that, like transport, mechanics, tech support, and so on. And you'd have fuel, of course, and whatever the cars eat…I'm not sure if they eat, but I think they drink, so maybe that's a subcategory of fuel. Wait – I think in *Cars 2*, Mater eats some wasabi or something, so yeah, they must eat food. And then you'd have their equivalent of the beauty industry, like decals and paintjobs and other customisable features they can use to improve their appearance…but really that's a subcategory of mechanics. And *then* there's the question of how the cars are 'born'. Like, are they built? What's their life source? Lightning McQueen and Sally have a romantic subplot, so do the cars have some kind of reproductive instinct? Or is it like in *Transformers*, where they manufacture the bodies and then the AllSpark brings them to life? Don't get me wrong, I'm not a worldbuilding nerd or anything, I just find these questions interesting to think about…"

But Henry, despite his best efforts, wasn't really listening. Eventually, there was a lull in the conversation, and he spoke without fully realising it: "I wonder what Louisa's up to this evening."

Joey smiled mischievously. "She's probably out with *David*."

Henry did not need to ask who David was.

"Oh," he said.

Chapter Thirty-One – Epiphany, Part II

Sarah didn't tend to interview content creators, preferring instead to opt for harder news sources where she could. But XYZ was scraping the bottom of the barrel this week; and besides, she was in one of those moods where the office seemed dreary and suffocating, and Kenneth and Crystal wouldn't shut up about star signs and whatever else they talked about, and so she was damn-well going to get out and interview as many talents as she could, even if it meant writing fluff pieces and trekking halfway across the state for a two-second audio grab. From this perspective, talking with an author about her upcoming work didn't sound too bad.

"So, tell me about your first novel, *Blood Science 2*," she said.

Mathilda winced. "Not a day goes by that I don't wish I could go back in time and change the title of that dumb book."

Sarah fought down the urge to laugh. "Why *did* you put '2' on the end if it was the first in the series?"

"I dunno, I just thought it sounded cool," Mathilda said gloomily.

"I see," said Sarah, bemused.

"We think a lot of things are cool, when we're twenty," Mathilda went on, glaring at Sarah as though accusing *her* of being twenty.

(Sarah had a sudden flashback to the old man with the peg-leg whom she'd interviewed about wind surfing so many months ago. She also didn't know whether to feel insulted by Mathilda's assumption, or depressed that it wasn't true. She reminded herself that she had chosen to be here, and that confronting her deep-seated existential fears through the lens of this sad author was still better than listening to her colleagues' incessant fanatical descriptions of the Pisces' ideal soulmate.)

"I read *Blood Science 2* in preparation for this interview," Sarah said bashfully. "I thought it was pretty good."

"I can't bear to look at it any more," sighed Mathilda.

"It really was quite good."

"I was so young when I wrote it," Mathilda soliloquised. "Mentally young, not just physically. I thought I was *so* clever back then. I really saw my book *going* places. But now that I'm older and wiser, all I see is my own folly laid bare upon its pages. I should have written a blog instead; at least *then* I could have deleted it once I realised the error of my ways."

"Well," said Sarah, desperately wishing to negate Mathilda's misery, "doesn't that just mean your new book, *Blood Scientology 2.2*, will be that much better?"

Mathilda chuckled. "It had *better* fricking-well be, or I just wasted the last fifteen years of my life."

A line crossed Sarah's forehead. "What inspired you to write a sequel, anyway? I thought the end of *Blood Science* was fairly absolute."

Mathilda gestured vaguely. "It just seemed like the thing to do."

Sarah could respect that. "Thank you for your time," she said.

"Don't write a book," said Mathilda. "It's not worth it."

Sarah, who had long dreamt of someday writing a self-help book, titled *How to Choose the Right Self-Help Book*, elected to ignore this sage advice, and headed off to her next interview.

∴

Henry stood outside the Quartermaster's Arms, not knowing whether he hoped Eden would be inside, but determined to enter nonetheless. For one thing, it had always been his favourite pub, and he wasn't about to deprive himself of it just because he and Eden had been through a rough patch. For another thing, he'd been in the doldrums ever since he'd found out Louisa was involved with someone (though he was reluctant to delve too deeply into the reasons why), and he really needed a drink.

As all of these thoughts looped frenetically inside his head, causing him to feel more and more flustered and defensive, he realised that he'd been standing motionless in the street for the last five minutes. He gritted his teeth and pushed open the door, and was greeted by the sound of Nick Drake playing softly over the general merriment within, and the sight of Eden at the bar, wiping down the postmix.

Henry briefly considered seeing if someone was on shift at the upstairs bar, but rejected the notion as cowardly. After all, he told himself for perhaps the fifth time that night, there was little emotional risk in merely asking her to pour him a beer.

Nervously, he approached the bar.

She looked up at him and smiled her old smile. Seeing her now, after so long (how long had it been? Weeks? He didn't remember, but their last encounter seemed a long time ago), he realised again, almost with surprise, how beautiful she was.

"Long time no see," she said.

He forced a laugh. "Well, you said…" (He did not finish the sentence; reminding her what she had last said to him would only bring back memories that were painful to them both.) He cleared his throat. "Anyway, I've been busy. Working on a new project."

She glanced away. "Fair enough." Then back at him. "What can I get you? Wait – no, let me guess. Seven Sheds?"

Henry smiled. It felt good to be known. "That's the one."

∴

Louisa and David walked out of the restaurant in opposite directions.

Before he was out of earshot, she turned and called out to him.

He stopped.

"I'm sorry," she said.

He smiled sadly.

"Don't be," he said.

∴

Several beers later, Henry exited the Arms and went home, feeling considerably worse than before. He hadn't spoken much to Eden beyond the niceties of ordering, though he'd said goodbye as he'd walked out the door. But that wasn't what was bothering him: it was Toni. (Again.)

In the time that had passed, Henry had more or less finished mourning the particulars of his relationship with Toni, and the future that might have been. He had even called her once or twice, and had felt reassured that they were still just as good friends as ever.

But the problem, he thought, wending his sorry way home, was that the entire experience had confirmed the secret fear which he had kept so carefully hidden from everyone, including himself.

All these years he had said – and believed – that he didn't want a relationship, that he was happy by himself. But what if the truth was that he *couldn't* have a relationship, even if he did want one? What if he just didn't have what it took to sustain one? What if he would never, despite his best efforts, live up to the standards which he'd set for himself? And what if, in his desperation to avoid answering these questions, he had simply buried them?

And what if, after being goaded repeatedly beyond his limits by family and friends, these fears had finally been driven to the surface – only to be brutally, *catastrophically* confirmed in the form of his failed relationship with Toni?

Uncle Bertram met him at the door.

"Hullo, Nephew," he said. "What ails you?"

Henry stood there mutely, unable even to walk past and ignore him.

"My dear boy," Uncle Bertram said gently, "you know I only want to help you."

Henry let out a shaky sigh. "Oh, it's just… I've always said – I wouldn't get married. And I was *so* sure of myself…and then everything…everyone…it all just made me doubt myself, so I gave it a try, and it didn't work, and – and what's the *use*, Uncle? I was right all along about not getting married, except *now* it hurts. Because I finally got to the point where maybe I *did* want it, and then I couldn't make it work with Toni, and it just *hurts*, and I wish

I'd never… I wish none of this had happened and I could have just gone on the way I was before, when I was happy."

Uncle Bertram cogitated upon this lament.

"Well," he said slowly, "I'm no guru on matters of the heart, by any means. But just because it didn't work out with Toni, I don't see why it shouldn't work with someone else."

"Yeah, like who?" Henry snapped.

Uncle Bertram shook his head. "That I cannot tell you. I don't know if there is someone out there destined for you, or if it all comes down to your own decisions. But if it is the former, then she'll make herself known to you at the proper moment. And if the latter, then you have the freedom to find her in your own time. So it's a win-win, if you ask me."

"I don't know about that," Henry said, still unwilling to engage with the subject after years of denial.

"Fair enough," said Uncle Bertram. "But keep an open mind, Henry. Do not despair, for despair is the enemy."

Henry slumped his shoulders, partially in gratitude. "Thank you, Uncle."

The ghost inclined his head. "Always, Nephew."

∴

Henry pondered his uncle's words in bed that night. As the inebriation wore off, he began to wonder whether the pain he felt was not, as he had supposed, the pain of deprivation, but perhaps the pain of realising that he hadn't known who he was looking for until it was too late.

Chapter Thirty-Two – Living and Dying

Tuesday, Christmas Day

Dawn broke. Henry got out of bed late, having been to Midnight Mass the night before, and, opening his curtains, felt the heat of the sun through his window, and was merry. He put on his best shirt and tie and trousers, dropped some fish flakes into Martin's tank, gathered his supplies (one homemade pud; two bottles of champagne; three boxes of cherries), hopped into the car, and drove off through the countryside, basking in the glorious lack of traffic.

Henry preferred to avoid spending Christmas with his family. Most years he went on holiday, or joined Mark and Donovan on combined family Christmas picnics. But this year he wasn't in the mood to go away, and both his friends were busy; so instead, he'd invited himself to Toni's house for a barbecue.

It was the first time he'd seen her since they'd broken up, although they had, as previously noted, spoken on the phone during the interim. She was dressed in her usual khaki button-down, work pants and boots, but wore a festive red apron and Santa hat.

"Happy Christmas," she said, kissing him on the cheek.

"You too," he smiled, and pressed a small cloth-wrapped bundle into her hands. "My contribution to lunch," he explained, as she raised an eyebrow at him. "Homemade Christmas pud. My own recipe. Absolutely *no* sultanas or raisins."

Toni rolled her eyes. "You and your weird bloody food vendettas are gonna be the death of me."

"Tough. Now show me what needs doing in the kitchen."

She led him into the dining area, where piles of ham and prawns and sausages lay steaming on platters amidst bowls of salad and Christmas crackers.

Henry's eyes nearly popped out of his head. "It's just us, isn't it?"

"Yeah."

"We're not going to eat all this!"

Toni chuckled. "No, but it never hurts to have variety. Here, have a bevvy." She pulled a Wild Yak from the esky and thrust it at him. "Everything's good to go, so stick the pud on the stove and let's tuck in."

They ate and ate, and grew fat and glad.

Afterwards, they pulled the crackers, which Toni had made herself (with an altered gunpowder recipe so that they would go off with a loud explosion), and which contained fanciful little wood carvings and tiny bottles of bourbon and customised jokes that made them roar with laughter.

Then they sat by the tree, which was decorated with small garden gnomes and empty Cascade tinnies, with Michael Bublé playing on the dusty old stereo, and they opened presents. Toni gave Henry a lavish poker set, and he gave her a box of cigars, and they spent a few hours playing cards, throwing darts, drinking beer (the champagne stood forgotten on the kitchen bench), and discussing the proper method of renovating a hardwood floor.

She took him into the garage and showed him her latest project, an old wooden rowing shell she was repairing, and he helped her work away at it for another hour or so with paint stripper and a couple of shave hooks. Then they went fishing, coming back just as the sun was setting, and smoked cigars on the veranda again until the stars came out.

"You know, I was thinking," said Henry.

"*Here* we go…"

"Someone asked me recently," he went on, ignoring her, "how I felt about being a ghost after I die."

Toni blew a smoke ring. "And what'd you say?"

"Oh, something about doing research forever."

"You would."

He gazed at the sky, an ache rising in his chest as he contemplated the agonising transience of material beauty. "But sometimes… it does depress me. Like, it takes all the *good* part out of dying. The way I see it, either I'm wrong about God, and all that awaits me after death is oblivion, in which case I at least don't have to suffer any more. *Or* I'm right, and there's the beatific vision to look forward to. Either of those possibilities is *way* better than bumming around the family mansion forever and not having any of the fun things about being alive."

"Huh," said Toni.

"'Huh,' what?" he said.

"Well what am I s'posed to say? Not like this is *my* problem."

It could have been, Henry thought.

"Anyway, since when do you *enjoy* living?" she asked. "You're always complaining about it. You get a new outlook on life or something?"

"You could say that."

"I thought that's supposed to happen *when* you find God, not years afterwards."

He shrugged. "Either way, I'm still annoyed about this whole ancestral curse thing. What am I supposed to *do*?"

"You're always asking me that, and I keep telling you, just don't worry about it! The question'll answer itself without you needing to *think* about it all the time."

"Maybe."

"I'm certain." She puffed on her cigar. "Now get out of here, I've gotta get up early tomorrow and get that rowing shell finished."

"Alright." He stood up. "Take care, Toni. Thanks for having me."

"Any time."

He touched her arm, then turned to go. Then stopped.

"Toni?"

She sighed, but said nothing.

He smiled faintly. "I *am* glad that…you know…after…"

The words remained unspoken: *That after everything, we could still go back to how we were before.*

She nodded. "Me too, Hen."

Chapter Thirty-Three – Finish Line

August, 1988

It was lunchtime, and the schoolyard was a hive of activity. Children bolted down their sandwiches and biscuits and small boxed fruit juices, and swarmed over the playground, shrieking and laughing, running and jumping, throwing balls, barking like dogs, and committing various minor acts of violence.

Trish and Henry had wandered away from the chaos and were playing in the bushes at the edge of the school. This had been their usual haunt since the beginning of the term, when a gang war amongst the year fives had driven them away from their old spot by the swings.

"Look out, Henry, this jungle is fearsome and thick!" Trish shouted, swatting at the surrounding branches with a stick. "Stay close to me, or you might get lost!"

"I *am* staying close," grumbled Henry, who, after the third week of playing 'explorers', was beginning to tire of the game.

"Careful of dinosaurs!" she called, racing on ahead.

"There aren't dinosaurs in the jungle!" he protested.

"There are in *this* jungle, stupid. LOOK, THERE'S ONE RIGHT THERE AND IT'S GONNA EAT YOU!"

They ran from the bushes, screaming.

∴

Wednesday 26 December, Present Day

"What've you got on tonight, Trish?" her mum asked.

"Catching up with Henry," Trish said indistinctly through a mouthful of blueberry bagel.

Her mum smiled. "You two and your crazy adventures…"

"Crazy," Trish agreed.

"That night you went out for a picnic and came home concussed was my favourite."

Trish started laughing. "I forgot about that."

∴

November, 2000

It was after dark, and the campus was entirely deserted save for those unlucky few students who still had one or two exams left and were holed up on the top floor of the library, cramming. Trish and Henry had sat their last exam that morning, and had just been kicked out of the uni bar after celebrating a little too raucously.

They raced each other, stumbling and giggling, from the top of the campus all the way down the hill to the bottom.

"What now?" gasped Henry, as they came to a halt by the geology building and stood for a moment, catching their breath.

"Let's have a picnic!" Trish said in a stage whisper.

"With what?"

"I've got VBs and salt-and-vinegar chips in my bag."

"Delightful."

They clambered up the fire escape and emerged onto the roof of the tallest building on campus, which afforded an excellent view of the river, the city spread out over both shores like a great glittering blanket. It was a warm night, with no wind, and the moon was out. It would have taken their breath away if they hadn't been immersed in idle conversation and tepid lager.

"Keen for graduation?" Henry asked.

Trish shrugged. "S'pose so."

He waited.

"I like finishing things," she said, "but I also hate when things finish."

Henry nodded slowly. "I know what you mean."

They sat in silence and watched the moonlight playing on the surface of the water. The city lights winked at them from the distance.

"Not everything has to end," said Henry, after a while.

Trish gave a small smile. "Maybe."

They drank the last of the VBs and resisted the primal urge to throw the empties off the edge of the roof, instead tucking them back into Trish's bag to be disposed of later. Then, the last of their self-control depleted for the day, they raced each other back down the fire escape.

On the very last step, Trish slipped and split her forehead open against a railing.

She laughed all the way to the emergency room.

∴

Wednesday 26 December, Present Day

There was a knock at the door, and Trish answered it.

Sure enough, it was Henry.

"Merry Christmas," he said as they embraced. "I got you something this time."

"Bet it's not as good as what I got you," she teased, handing him a box wrapped in glossy red paper in exchange for the smaller parcel he'd given her.

Henry opened the box and started laughing when he found it contained a six-pack of VB tinnies. "Truly a gift of great cultural significance; I thank you."

"You are most welcome," she said with a slight smirk – which immediately disappeared as she opened her own present: *The Complete Scholastic Works of Dr Henry B., First Edition.* "No *way*!"

"Yes way," Henry said smugly. "Your publisher friend left her imprint on the book you gave me, so I got in contact and asked her for an encore."

Trish shook her head, dazed. "Well…you win this time."

He punched the air. "'God's in His heaven / All's right with the world'."

"Whatever. You used my own strategy against me, so really I just won against myself."

"Still makes you a loser," he said, and laughed when she punched him in the arm.

"So what are we doing tonight?" she asked.

"Looking at Christmas lights. But first I want to say hi to your parents."

"Suit yourself. They're in the lounge, watching *Godzilla*."

"That doesn't sound very Christmassy."

She winked. "Only to the uninitiated."

"Hmm," said Henry, and went inside to the lounge room, where he indeed found Trish's parents sitting on the sofa and enjoying their kaiju festivities. "Hi Jodie, hi Paul. Merry Christmas."

"Henry!" Trish's mother exclaimed. "It's *so* nice to see you again."

"You too," he said warmly. "It's been a while."

"Are you keeping well?" Trish's father asked.

"Quite well, thanks. I've been very busy with work, but I prefer it that way."

"You and Patricia both," Paul said knowingly. "Such a workaholic, that girl! I'm sure she didn't get it from me."

"*Or* me," Jodie added.

Henry smiled indulgently.

"Well, you kids have fun," said Paul.

"But no concussions this time, alright?" said Jodie.

It took Henry a second to catch her meaning, but then he laughed.

Trish was waiting for him outside by the car, a neatly bound sheaf of papers tucked under one arm. "Here, I'll drive," she said, holding out her free hand for his keys. "You're going to read this."

"What is it?" he asked, swapping keys for papers.

"It's the draft of the article I'm gonna submit to *Forward*. I was hoping you could give me some thoughts."

"I thought that's what peer review was for," he chuckled, removing the cover page as they climbed into the car and beginning to read.

"Yeah, but you're the only peer whose opinion actually matters to me."

Henry choked up a little bit, at that.

∴

May, 2007

"This is amazing," he told her, having got her on the phone as soon as he'd read the draft she'd emailed him.

"You really think so?" He could hear the excitement in her voice. Oh, how he missed her, and she hadn't even been gone a year yet…

"Yeah, I do. No one's even *thought* of writing about webinar raves until now. There's no way you won't get published."

"I dunno, man, I'm submitting it to *Forward* this time."

Henry felt his pulse flutter at the mention of the name.

But he just grinned and said, "They'd be mad not to accept it."

∴

July, 2007

His phone buzzed.

It was Trish: *forward didn't want it.*

Not knowing what to type, he rang her. "Hey," she said quietly.

"Hey," he said.

A long pause.

"They're mad," he said.

Another pause.

"They'll be kicking themselves when *TeCH* or whoever publishes it and totally demolishes their impact rating," he said.

It might have been his imagination, but he thought he heard her chuckle. "I'm just happy *you* thought it was good."

"I think *all* your work is good. You see things and write about them like I never could."

Far away, on the other side of the sea, Trish smiled. "Thanks Henry," she said. "That means a lot."

∴

Wednesday 26 December, Present Day

"Where are we going?" Henry asked, looking up from the draft Trish had given him.

"Christmas lights are all well and good," said Trish, making a left turn, "but I have something even better in mind."

"You *never* give me any straight answers," he sighed.

"Well, I'll give you a clue," she said generously. "You'll want to bring those beers with you."

∴

Half an hour later, they stood atop the tallest building on the university campus once again, bathed in moonlight.

"It's beautiful," he said softly, looking out at the river.

"It is," Trish agreed, cracking open a beer and handing it to him. "You can see *all* the lights from up here."

They tapped their tins against each other in a silent toast.

"I can't believe it's been nearly twenty years since we graduated," he said, still staring at the water.

Trish smiled. "Crazy."

"Are you still sad?" he asked. "That our undergrad days are finished?"

"Sometimes," she said. "But not very often."

"That's good." He sipped his beer, then made a face. "I don't miss drinking *these*."

She laughed. "Also good."

They fell back into silence, watching the cars go over the bridge.

"Henry?" said Trish, after what felt like a very long time.

"Yes?"

"Promise you're never gonna stop competing with me."

Henry looked at her, and she could *feel* the fire within him burning.

"Never," he said stoutly. "In this race, there is no finish line."

Trish smiled at him: and her eyes were brighter than the moon and stars and city lights all put together.

Chapter Thirty-Four – Making Time

Thursday

Louisa was away on leave, so it was only Henry and Joey in the office that day. Henry had initially protested when Joey told him she was coming in, saying she deserved a longer break. But Joey had insisted that she had nothing better to do, and it was lonely at home with all her housemates away for Christmas, and anyway, she preferred being productive over getting into strife.

"Morning, Dr B.," she said cheerily, stepping through the door precisely on time for once, and handing him a small foil-wrapped plate. "I baked you some gingerbread rats."

Henry cracked up laughing. "Delicious…" he said, peeping beneath the foil and finding that the biscuits in question were indeed passible rodent simulacra.

"Well, would you rather eat rats, or people?" Joey said reasonably.

Henry, lacking a suitable reply, tried one of the rats and found it very tasty. He nodded his approval, and she returned a gracious bow.

"So, how was your Chrissy?" she asked.

"Oh, fine, thanks. Midnight Mass, barbecue, Christmas lights, all the good kush."

"Noice."

"How was yours?"

"Well," Joey began – then stopped, smiled a little self-consciously, and asked, "how much time do you have?"

Henry chuckled. "For you, Joey, I have ample time."

She beamed at him. "Okay. Well, ages ago, I saw this advertisement on the back of a van when I was stuck in traffic, and it was for a children's party entertainer who does pirate-themed performances and fire-eating and stuff like that, and I had the magnificent idea of hiring him to do a show for my housemates one night – but I wanted to keep it a surprise, so I didn't tell anyone about it, and I booked him for last Sunday night, because that was the only night he was free.

"So it's two nights before Christmas, and my housemates are packing up and getting ready to go and stay with their families, and then this full-costumed *pirate* just *leaps* into our lounge room through the open window, and he's got pirate music playing from a speaker somewhere, and he's got a sword, and he goes up to my housemate Celeste and starts waving this actual sword in her face, and asking about a treasure map she knows nothing about, and Celeste's completely rooted to the spot with shock, and then Anna comes in, crazy woman, and she knows *something's* up, so she decides to play along, and she sneaks up behind this pirate and somehow manages to get his sword off him – and then he pulls a dagger on Anna, and then they're sword-fighting in our kitchen, and me and my other housemate Clare are just sitting at the dining table, watching this all unfold, and Clare's laughing hysterically, and I'm trying to pretend I don't know anything about what's going on – and then eventually Anna and the pirate declare a truce, and at that point the pirate – his name was Sam, by the way – he broke character for a minute and explained to us the rules of the game, and then he got back into character and led us in this sort of interactive pirate adventure all around our neighbourhood, and we were all laughing and making so much noise, I think our neighbours all thought we were on drugs or something, but it was *so* worth it."

She stopped to catch her breath, and it briefly occurred to Henry to ask whether there had been any correlation between the pirate man's performance and the Christmas season – but then Joey started speaking again.

"So the next day was obviously Christmas Eve, and all my housemates went off to stay with their families, but my parents live a couple of blocks away from me, so I didn't bother staying over, but I went there for dinner, and my little brother and I played the most *epic* game of hide-and-seek, and I hid in a drain pipe in the park next to my parents' house, and he gave up trying to find me after forty minutes, and I teased him about it all the rest of the evening. My clothes got absolutely covered in spider webs though, so it was pretty hardcore. Then on Christmas Day, we all went up to my nan's house, and I almost broke my ankle trying to kickflip off her patio, but luckily I didn't; and my uncle gave me a homebrewing kit, so I've started making my own beer; and *then*, best of all, we finally welcomed my cousin Alex back into the family!"

"What?!" said Henry.

Joey laughed. "Okay, so the backstory is, last year my cousin Alex, who's a year older than me and is the favourite cousin, he couldn't make it to Nan's for Christmas because his flight from Brisbane got cancelled, and me and all my other cousins were *so* upset that we decided to write him a 'hate mail,' and in it we told him he was kicked out of the family, and if he wanted to earn his place back, he had to complete a series of challenges which we would give him the following Christmas. So this year he made it down, no worries, and we made him do all these ridiculous things, and he completed them all perfectly and was such a good sport about it, so we accepted him back into the fold."

"What were the challenges?" exclaimed Henry.

"Oh, there were a bunch. One of them was to drink a can of Great Northern which we'd left in the freezer overnight. He had to crack it open with a multi-grip and a knife, and peel the can off the frozen beer and eat it like an ice block. Then we made him Naruto-run up the big steep hill at the end of Nan's street in under one minute. Then he had to film himself replicating Kate Bush's dance moves from her 'Wuthering Heights' music video, and then he had to recite a soliloquy from *Macbeth* in Pig Latin, and last of all, he had to build a big tower out of old furniture we keep in the garage, and then sit upon it and declare himself the Winkly Wizard of Wumble Town and give us all his blessing – but without laughing or falling off the tower."

"Your family sounds *brutal*," Henry gasped, between fits of laughter.

"Aw, we go alright, it's just us cousins who're the rowdy ones. Anyway, Alex enjoyed it. He said being part of the family feels much more special now that he's been formally initiated. Also, this is unrelated to anything, but yesterday I took the bus into town, and the bus driver gave me the biggest smile and asked, 'How are *you* today?' and I said, 'I'm great!' and it made me *so* happy."

"When you get famous one day and write your autobiography," said Henry, "you're going to have to make it a multivolume *series*."

"Aw, stop making fun of me," she laughed.

"No, I'm being serious. What are you even doing in academia? You could make a living just from sharing your life experiences at comedy festivals."

She couldn't stop laughing. "I don't want to turn my life into a joke! I take it very seriously, thank you very much."

"I'm sorry, I'm sorry, I'll stop."

They each took in a breath.

"Oh!" Joey perked up again. "How's Martin going?"

"He's going well. He's at least twice as fat as when you gave him to me, which I assume is a sign of health and prosperity."

"You sound like a fortune cookie."

"He also makes an excellent companion for social processing. I discuss all my life problems with him of an evening." (These words, as he spoke them, felt familiar. Had he heard them somewhere before?)

"Huh," said Joey. "Your friend Eden said something like that when we went camping on your birthday and Donovan bullied her for talking to a lizard."

(Oh.)

Henry decided to change the subject. "Well then…shall we get to work?"

"Let's do it!" she said.

An hour passed in silence. Then two. Then –

"QUICK, LOOK AT THIS!" Joey screamed, even though their desks were a metre apart.

Ears ringing, Henry leapt from his chair and was at her side in seconds. "What is it?"

"*Look*!" She pointed impatiently to her screen, which displayed a fight between two Vocaloids which was in full tilt. "It's a cult match! Like the ones you told us about! This match was slated to be between Miku and Sachiko, but look! Miku's avatar doesn't quite match her character design, and her name's been wiped off the scoreboard!"

Henry looked closer and saw that it was true.

"F-sama!" he murmured.

Mesmerised, they watched as the battle unfolded before them, and F-sama – for this mysterious alien fighter who looked so similar to Hatsune Miku could only be the mass-proclaimed goddess of combat – viciously slew Sachiko's avatar in a matter of moments, tearing her limb from limb and bathing in her pixelated blood. Henry felt sickened when it was over…but also, somehow, enlightened.

"I can see how a cult might develop around this," he said.

"That's crazy, man," said Joey, shaking her head.

"I don't suppose you were recording the match?"

Joey winked at him. "What am I, an amateur?"

Henry sighed with relief. "This might just be the primary text that ties our whole project together. Joey…you're a champion. Thank you so much for all your help. This project and 'Origin Myth' would not be what they are without you."

Joey dropped her gaze. "Aw, shucks." Then, shyly, she looked back up at him. "Actually, I wanted to thank *you* as well. You've always been very kind, and made time for me, and I've always felt like you valued my company. And I've never felt like it was because of anything I did, or like I had to impress you, because that's just how you are with everyone. I don't have a lot of people in my life who treat me like that…and it makes a big difference. So, thank you."

Henry *really* didn't know what to say to that.

"Oh," he stammered, "well…you're welcome, of course, I never… I mean, it wasn't like a calculated move on my part, I just… How could I *not* treat you like that? You're so interesting, and fun to talk to, and you're like no one else I've ever met. I love spending time with you, Joey."

She smiled. "Thanks. I like hanging out with you, too." Then she lit up with excitement. "I'm so keen to have you supervise my thesis next year!"

And as always, he was swept up in that same excitement.

"Me too!"

Chapter Thirty-Five – Good, and Good to Come

Friday, 5:01 AM

It really *was* the extra minute of sleep that made all the difference.

"Dare" by Stan Bush blasted through the tiny bedroom, and Sarah leapt out of bed, eager to take on the new day. The room exploded with early-morning light as she threw open the curtains, and a surge of energy crackled through her veins. Singing along to the music, she dressed and brushed her teeth and made a smoothie, and then hit the gym.

Today was back and biceps. She spent forty minutes on the seated row, and did an extra set of hammer curls with the 12kg dumbbells. Elated and sweaty, she made her way home and had a cold shower, and didn't even flinch.

∴

6:30 AM

This week, she was reading a book called *Why Spend Thousands of Dollars on Therapy When You Can Browse Insta for Free?* – an anthology of self-care tips sourced from numerous lifestyle influencers. So far, it had informed her that she should speak kind words to herself aloud, and eat a vegetable every day. She had already known these things, of course, but it felt good to be affirmed in her beliefs.

∴

8:05 AM

Sarah was in a good mood today, because she had organised an outdoor screening of *The Castle* to be held in the yard behind her apartment block that evening, for the entertainment of the residents and anyone else in the neighbourhood who wanted to come along. She had also invited Henry, and he had said he was looking forward to it.

The weather was perfect, the sky was clear, and she had a six-pack of White Rabbit pale ales waiting for her in the fridge at home, to be imbibed upon the appointed hour. She danced in her car seat as she rocketed down the highway, "Dare" still playing on loop over Bluetooth. She swerved from left to right in her lane in time with the beat, causing the drivers behind her to become concerned and irate.

∴

9:00 AM

She was normally a focussed person, especially when it came to work. But it was difficult to keep her concentration today. She hadn't found a decent story in weeks, and all she could think about was how wonderful it would be to share one of her most beloved cinematic experiences with the few lucky souls who cared to join her.

There was no one else in the office; the others were all working from home today. The newsroom felt lonely without them, even though they wouldn't have talked to her if they had been there.

∴

12:30 PM

She ate lunch alone in the Japanese gardens outside the XYZnews building: chickpea, pumpkin, spinach and fetta salad, with tuna marinated in sweet chilli and lemongrass. Some nights she lay awake wondering whether her healthy, ordered lifestyle was a sham and whether, really, she was pretentious and hypocritical and desperate in her search for ways to feel good about herself. But those nights were few and far between; and anyway, she liked chickpeas.

She thought ahead again to that evening, checked her watch, groaned, and for the first time in her journalistic career, considered taking the rest of the day off. But she didn't have anything else to do, so she finished her lunch and went back to the grind.

∴

4:07 PM

She'd spent hours tweaking and republishing media releases.
Her eyes were burning in their sockets.
She thought of Darryl Kerrigan, and smiled.

∴

5:05 PM

Joyfully, she left the office.
She caught herself nearly speeding once or twice on the drive home, and took a few deep breaths. She switched up her playlist and began listening to Simon & Garfunkel, which soothed her.
Sometimes she was grateful for how her choice of music could affect her thoughts and emotions. Other times, she scorned herself for being so easily manipulated and weak.

∴

6:30 PM

At last, the hour was here!
She sat in a rusty deckchair on the lawn, having set up the projector and screen, and waited as a handful of neighbours began

trickling into the yard, waving greetings and carrying picnic rugs and bowls of popcorn and bottles of wine. She had made herself a stir-fry for dinner and carried it outside in a small Tupperware container, along with the White Rabbits and a jumper in case it got cold.

About this time, Henry appeared, looking more casual than she had ever seen him, in a polo shirt and shorts. She felt slightly unnerved by this, like a small child who hasn't yet developed object permanency and whose parent has just hidden its favourite toy.

"Hi Sarah," Henry said, coming over and setting up a chair of his own. "How was your day?"

"Oh…" For some reason, she was embarrassed to admit that she had spent the whole day looking forward to this event, and that everything prior somehow paled in comparison. But then, she reflected, she *had* spent the otherwise ordinary day in a very good mood, which had coloured her perception and cast said ordinary day in a positive light. "Pretty uneventful, but good. I feel quite refreshed, actually."

He smiled. "That's good to hear."

"Bevvy?" She gestured to the White Rabbits on the ground.

"Well, now you've mentioned it, it'd be *so* rude not to." He helped himself, and together they opened their bottles, clinked, sipped, and sighed in mutual appreciation.

"And how was *your* day?" Sarah asked.

"Really excellent," he said warmly. "We're making splendid progress with the new project on Vocaloid cage matches and the cult of F-sama. If we get it finished as quickly as I think we will, I reckon it'll become the seminal text on net-based religions and intertextual appropriation within hidden sub-communities."

Sarah's eyes lit up: now *this* was the story she'd been waiting for.

"When will you be ready to present your findings?" she asked breathlessly.

He winked at her. "Soon."

She leaned back in her chair, blissful at the thought of good things to come.

"Are we ready to start the movie?" someone asked.

"Yes," Sarah said, and hit play.

Chapter Thirty-Six – More to Life

Saturday

Mathilda woke up eight minutes before her alarm, and felt a sense of deep tranquillity. She was free! No more writing, no more agonising, no more wallowing in self-pity, unless she freely chose to do so! She had no obligations at all today, except to send a couple of emails to her editor and marketing team, which could wait until the afternoon. For the time being, she was free.

She inhaled slowly, then exhaled, peace and joy filtering into her blood amidst the oxygen. Then she rolled out of bed, turned off her alarm before it could rend the silence with its shrill piercing cry, and ambled into the kitchen in her dressing-gown and poured herself a bourbon. She never turned to liquor for self-medication, but, rather, only when she was in a good mood (which was rarely), so it always felt well-earned, regardless of time or place.

She sipped contentedly, and spent some time playing her mandolin, which she hadn't done in a long time, and was not particularly good at (but that didn't matter, because she played music strictly for her own enjoyment and not for the pursuit of excellence, since writing had long ago ceased to resemble any sort of recreational activity). After this, she spent an hour moving furniture around and decluttering her junk room, which she'd been putting off until the book was finished, and it felt *good*. She could sense her mind and self unfolding and expanding, as though she'd been compressed somehow by her writing and was now finally able to breathe.

Just before eleven, she put on her yellow sundress and her favourite cardigan and went to meet Henry at Corner Shop. This morning, the café smelled of pinecones and parsley and butterscotch. Pineapple Pete came out the door as she entered, muttering a greeting as they brushed past each other. He was wearing his usual garb, but with the addition of a belt-buckle shaped like a pumpkin, which Mathilda was sure he'd never worn before now. Mickey the Delinquent was sitting at a different table today, opposite a young man who might have been a friend, date, sibling or cousin, Mathilda couldn't really tell which, but anyway, she didn't recognise him. Everything seemed new today, somehow. Or perhaps it had just been so long since Mathilda had come out of her own thoughts and really *looked* at the world around her. Either way, it was good to see things differently.

(Mathilda thought to herself that it might be nice to strike up a conversation with Mickey sometime, when neither of them were otherwise occupied. Six months ago, she would have balked at the idea, but her recent experiences with Henry had given her a new boldness in approaching strangers.)

Barista Frances greeted her cheerily, as always, and was astounded when Mathilda eschewed her beloved quadruple-shot latte in favour of a chocolate milkshake. "What's all this?" Frances demanded. "Are you quitting caffeine now?"

"Nah," said Mathilda. "I just don't feel like it today."

"You can't drink the amount of coffee you do every day and then just *not feel like it* all of a sudden," Frances protested.

Mathilda gestured expansively about the room. "I don't need chemical stimulants when just *being* here makes me feel so alive!"

"Fair enough," the bemused Frances replied, and got to work preparing the milkshake.

As Mathilda claimed a seat at her favourite table, Henry walked in the door, whistling "The Horses" by Daryl Braithwaite under his breath. He grinned when he saw her. "G'day," he said, approaching and sitting across from her. "How's your morning been?"

"Oh, pretty good," said Mathilda. "I didn't do anything much, just hung about the house and had a bourbon."

"Should I be worried?"

"Not at all: day-drinking is the supreme act of leisure."

Henry laughed. "Please explain."

"Well," said she, "it's like a declaration that you have nothing important to do during the day. You don't have to work, you don't have to drive, you don't have to focus on anything very much, so you can just kick back and relax and have a good time. A *very* good time, if you know what I mean."

He smiled. "I like that. A visible sign of an invisible reality."

"Precisely."

"Nice."

"And how was *your* morning?"

"Cruisy. I went into the office for a bit, sent off some emails, crunched some more data, same as always. I've got to get back to it after this, but it's going well."

"Imagine working on a Saturday."

"You think I do *work* at the university?"

Mathilda chuckled.

They paused to thank Barista Frances as she delivered their drinks.

"How's life post-book, anyway?" Henry asked, sampling his first piccolo.

"*So* good," sighed Mathilda, misty-eyed. "I mean, there's other work to be done, like promotion and whatnot, but for all intents and purposes, I'm free! I feel like I'm finally rediscovering all these different parts of my personality that faded away while I was writing. I played *music* today for the first time in eighteen months! I remembered that I *like* cleaning! It's like I shrank as a person for fifteen years, and now I'm expanding to full size again!"

"That's incredible!" said Henry. "You do seem different now to when I first met you, come to think of it. You're happier, of course, but…it's more than that. Like you're more real – more solid, if that makes any sense."

She nodded. "I think you're right."

"Incredible," he said again.

Mathilda smiled. "What about you? How's your life?"

"Hmm," he said. "There's this idea I came across once, that we grow in spirals. You feel like you're running around in a circle, making a bit of progress and then getting knocked right back to where you started. But you actually *are* progressing – only upwards in a spiral, like a staircase. And I think, over the last few months, I've completed a whole circuit on my spiral, and so I sort of feel like I haven't changed really, but I have. And I'm hoping that means I'm ready to start the next circuit."

"How did you change?" Mathilda asked curiously.

"Oh," he said, slightly embarrassed, "well…for example, I didn't care about anything except my work, for years and years, because I didn't think there was anything else that I wanted out of life. But I've been through a lot this year, and there was a point, maybe a month ago, where I thought I'd changed, and I started…you know, looking at other ways of spending my time. Then I went out with someone for a little bit, but it ended pretty quickly, and so I thought maybe I hadn't changed after all, or at least, I didn't *want* to have changed. But now…I wonder if I *have* changed, but I just don't like admitting it because I don't like facing new challenges, or something like that. But whatever it is, I think…I think there could be more to life than work."

(He did not say 'there could be someone else to love,' but, being perceptive, Mathilda suspected his true meaning. How did this make her feel? She couldn't figure it out at first, and spent the next few minutes subconsciously analysing the question.)

"And I think I've realised," Henry went on, rambling a bit now that he'd been given permission to talk about himself, "that at baseline, I'm a pretty extreme person. Well, maybe 'extreme' isn't the right word, but…all or nothing. Black and white. Structured. Something like that. So if I want to better myself, I have to learn moderation, balance, yin and yang, shades of grey, etcetera."

Mathilda hadn't considered this concept before. "Makes sense," she said, poking idly at the dregs of her milkshake with her straw.

Henry shrugged. "Maybe," he said, and knocked back his second piccolo. "Well, enough about me. What do you think about the Beatles' use of wide stereo separation?"

The conversation wandered along, until eventually Henry had to go back to the office. Mathilda chewed on the end of her straw as she completed her analysis and the data began to trickle into view.

It seemed evident, she thought, that what Henry had really been trying to tell her was that he was in love with someone. But that someone couldn't be *her*, or else, being a fairly direct person, he would surely have said so to her face.

So how did this make her feel?

In fact, Mathilda realised, crumpling up the straw and standing to make her exit, it did not make her feel anything. For since finishing her book, she had grown and changed and expanded so much that the part of her which had loved him had diffused, spread itself thin over too much surface, and dissipated entirely. As her very self became integrated and whole, so with it did her desires. There was more to life than loving Henry Biddlesnoot-Bloomington, and by golly, she was going to go out and make the most of it.

She left the café and sauntered gaily down the road, deciding to take a walk to nowhere in particular.

At the end of the street, she stopped.

The problem with Henry was that even if she didn't love him, she *did* find him jolly interesting. He spoke about humanity in ways she hadn't heard before, and his combination of drive and self-reflection was something she wanted to explore further, and…

And…

The idea snapped into existence.

She had to write about him.

She would never be free until she'd captured his essence and pinned it onto the page.

All was silent for a moment.

Then Mathilda raised her face to the heavens, and *cursed*.

Chapter Thirty-Seven – Truth and Pain

Sunday

Eden sat in her lounge room, crocheting a blanket for Churchill the German Shepherd.

Henry had asked her a couple of days ago if she was free to catch up, and she had suggested a picnic in the Botanical Gardens that afternoon, since the weather would be good, and she hadn't spent much time outside lately. But now she was regretting the idea. What did he want to talk about? How long must they suffer through friendly conversation until he got to the point? For there was surely a point. Every time he asked to see her, it was with some agenda in mind. Their time together had become a means to an end, when it had once been an end in itself.

Eden broke free of these thoughts before they could stray too far into the realm of bitterness. She'd harboured enough bitterness to last her a lifetime, and it had never helped her any.

She glanced at the clock: it was still only ten. They were meeting at twelve. She sighed and continued working.

Churchill padded sleepily into the room and wagged his tail at her.

Eden smiled wryly.

"Ah, boy," she said. "Would that it were as easy now as it used to be."

∴

As It Used To Be

Eden came home from her last class, stepping lightly along the garden path, and smiled as the collie pup bounded out from the backyard, barking a greeting.

"Hi Atreides," she said, crouching and putting her arms around him, "guess what? I made a new friend today. He came over and talked to me at lunch."

The puppy broke free of her embrace and gambolled happily through the flower beds, not listening to a word she said.

Eden smiled. "Yeah, fair enough."

∴

Sunday

Eleven-thirty. Eden put her crocheting away and packed a basket, blanket, umbrella and Scrabble into her car. On the drive to the Botanical Gardens, she listened to Smash Mouth, feeling the bass line permeate her soul. She was less nervous now. It was always like that: she became less nervous as the event approached. She had never understood why.

∴

Understanding Why

The day she realised she loved him, they were studying for their year twelve exams, and the sun was shining outside, and the library felt very dark, and he kept reading aloud from his textbooks in a Slavic accent, and she couldn't stop laughing, and then all at once she realised that, out of everybody she knew, she *saw* him, and in seeing, *understood* him, and in understanding, *loved* him. Not because she had some genius for reading people, but because he chose to show her the truth of himself. He *let* her see and understand and love him. He never hid himself, never tried to impress her. He simply *was*, and she loved him for it.

The discovery was somehow painful, like cutting herself on an unexpected sharp edge.

She didn't tell him until it was too late.

∴

Too Late

"Henry, we have exams *tomorrow*, why are you here?"

"We need to break up."

She stared at him.

"Why?"

He'd never been unable to meet her eye before. "It's just that… I can't think when I'm with you."

"I don't understand."

"Neither do I!" he yelled, and his words were blurring and she couldn't hear him over her own pulse roaring in her ears.

"Fine," she said, forcing the words out before they choked her, "go away and do your thinking, then."

"Eden——"

She slammed the door shut, and didn't move until she'd heard him walk away.

"But I love you," she whispered, too late.

∴

Afterwards, she was shattered. In such a short time, she had built her entire sense of self around him. When he left her house that day, her foundation collapsed, bringing the rest of her down with it.

She learned, however, not to make that same mistake again.

∴

About 5:00 AM on the First Day of the New Millennium

"I can't do this," she said, "any more."

Her words were true, and they hurt.

But beneath the pain lay strength.

∴

Sunday

He was waiting for her by the cactus garden, Dire Straits thrumming over the UE Boom next to his camping chair. He looked oddly gallant, in a loose white linen shirt and dark trousers, sipping a glass of limoncello.

"G'day," he said, spoiling the image at once.

That was what she loved about him: the appearance of elegance, cheerfully belied.

"G'day, how are we?" she asked, offering him a hearty handshake.

"Going alright, thanks," he said.

She smiled. "Glad to hear it."

We will pass over the time they spent together, which was as pleasant as it had always been, but not, of course, the object of their meeting. Because there was always an object, beyond the meeting itself.

The sun dipped lower in the sky, and the gardens were quiet.

Finally, Henry said, "Eden, I have to tell you something."

And in that instant, as he spoke those precise words, with that exact inflection – she knew what he was going to say, and braced herself.

"I've…met someone."

Slowly, she nodded.

"I don't know if it'll come to anything," he added hastily, "I don't know how she feels, but…I felt like I should tell you first, so at least you know."

She nodded again.

He waited, not wanting to ask what was happening in her mind and heart, because he already knew.

"Last time," she said raggedly, "I asked you to reject me, you wouldn't."

He looked down.

"So now," she said, "will you tell me why?"

He met her eye again.

"And don't give me some line about how I'm great but you just don't feel anything for me," she said. "Because I know you, and there's a reason why you don't feel anything. So what is it?"

He sighed.

"The truth is," he said, "I just don't feel like myself when I'm with you."

Her hands clenched. No. Surely that couldn't be it. He had always, always been himself with her. She saw him and understood him. That was why she loved him…

"It's not anything wrong with you," he said. "Please believe me. I could never speak ill of you, Eden, I've always…" (He did not say 'loved you' because he didn't have to. She knew.) "But when we're together I feel…agitated, confused, like there's something wrong with me. I don't know where it comes from, it's nothing you've ever said or done. It's just…not meant to be."

There was a long silence. Everything she had thought she had ever known about him, about *them*, was splintering like glass.

"Alright," she said. "Then that's that."

His words became a plea: "I really don't want to hurt you."

"You hurting me," she said, "and me being hurt are not the same thing."

"I know," he said quietly, "and I'm sorry."

She stood up, and shrugged. "It wasn't meant to be. Maybe I always knew that too, deep down, but I just didn't want to admit it. I've never had that thing for Truth that you have."

He stood as well. "Whatever you need," he said, "it's yours. Talk to me, don't talk to me, see me or don't see me. I don't want to lose our friendship, but I won't ask anything of you that you can't give."

She nodded. "Thanks."

Silence.

"Will you commit to her?" she asked.

"Yes," he said. "If she'll let me."

"Well," she said, "I'm glad, for her sake. If she's really that good…and she must be, to have changed your mind…then she deserves not to be stuffed around."

He bowed his head. "I know."

Eden took in a deep breath, then let it out again. "Well, for what it's worth, you have my blessing. Not that you need it, but you have it anyway."

He smiled. "Thank you."

She took his hand and kissed it, and left.

∴

Her words had been true, but they carried pain.

Yet beneath the pain lay strength.

Chapter Thirty-Eight – Crash

Monday, New Year's Eve

Henry woke early, feeling as though his insides had turned to ice.

He had to tell her. Everything was set, all obstacles removed, and he could deny his feelings no longer. He had to tell her.

He picked up his phone and saw a text from Joey, saying she wouldn't be in today. Fair enough. So he would be alone in the office. Good.

But wouldn't it be better to have the conversation as soon as possible?

No. He didn't know what she would say. And anyway, she was probably busy.

He turned towards the fish tank. "What am I gonna *do*, Martin?"

Martin blew a bubble at him by way of reply.

"You're right," said Henry. "I should just call her now."

So he dialled the number and waited.

Then he cancelled the call and let out a long sigh. This wasn't a conversation he should have over the phone: he needed to see her in person. But he didn't want to do that just now, so he decided to go to work and be productive, and then worry about the conversation later.

He dressed and breakfasted and filled his pockets with cranberry and macadamia muesli bars, and hurried into the entrance hall, where he bumped (figuratively) into Cousin Pippin.

"Hullo, Cousin Henry," she said. "What are you doing today?"

"I have to – work," Henry said, not wanting to reveal his true objective.

"You seem awfully nervous about it," Pippin remarked.

"It's been a strenuous project," he said (which was true).

Pippin shrugged. "Well, don't worry about it. The stakes really aren't that high, you're just writing about dumb stuff on the internet, after all."

"Thanks for the gee-up," he said sarcastically, and left.

He's totally going to ask a girl out, thought Pippin, and crossed her fingers that it would be the right one.

∴

Henry drove to work in silence. He tried listening to the radio, but that only exacerbated his discomfort.

He got to work, and tried working, but that was no help either.

Dr Robert Jones poked his head through the door. "Henry, how's the paper coming along?"

"Slowly," Henry replied through gritted teeth.

Dr Robert sensed that now was not the time for conversation, and left.

After another hour, Henry gave up.

He drove past Corner Shop (Mathilda wasn't there) and ordered two takeaway piccolos.

"You alright, darl?" asked Barista Frances, surprised to see him come in on a Monday.

Henry did not know what powers compelled him to be honest with his barista, but he wasn't inclined to resist. "I have to…tell someone I love her, and I'm not looking forward to it."

"That's rough," Frances said sympathetically. "But you know what I reckon, if you'll pardon my two cents, but you're gonna feel yuck until you tell her, and you might feel yuck afterwards, or you might not. So why would you choose the certainty of feeling yuck when you could choose the possibility of *not* feeling yuck? Best just to get it over with and tell her, and hope for the best."

"Cheers," said Henry, and he paid for his piccolos and departed.

∴

On the way home he dialled her number again – then cancelled again.

He just couldn't do it. His heart was spasming, his hands were sweaty, and his brain had relinquished its tenuous grip on reality, so the odds of anything coherent coming out of his mouth were infinitesimal.

It wasn't that he was afraid of rejection, exactly. He was fairly certain that she'd long since stopped feeling anything for him, and that this conversation could have no outcome save for wiping the slate clean.

But he *was* afraid that, when she confirmed his suspicions and told him she had moved on, he would feel unbearable grief at his own indecision and foolishness, at having waited and waited until it was too late, and at the loss of what could have been. Or worse, that she would say yes, and they would try to make a relationship work, and fail, and then he would know for certain that he wasn't capable of loving anybody. When he looked at it that way, it was a lose-lose scenario, so what was the point? Why bother?

He drank his piccolos sullenly as he drove, still in silence.

∴

He was lying in the dirty old hammock in the backyard, watching badly-dubbed videos of yodelling sewer rats and eating pickled onions straight from the jar, when Uncle Bertram materialised beside him.

"Hullo, Nephew," he said.

"Hullo, Uncle."

"What are you up to?"

"Wallowing."

Uncle Bertram nodded, and Henry took a gloomy sip of pickle juice.

"Have you told her how you feel yet?" the ghost asked.

Henry whirled so quickly to face his uncle that he nearly fell out of his hammock. "How did you know?"

Uncle Bertram smiled gently. "I've lived with you long enough to know."

Henry sighed and returned to his jar of onions. "No, I haven't."

A pause.

"Are you going to?"

Henry chewed pensively. "Do you think I should?"

"It's not for me to say," said Uncle Bertram with a shrug.

"But it *is* for you to ask?"

The ghost chuckled. "Fair cop."

∴

Eventually he ran out of onions, and the day was drawing to a close, and he still hadn't called her.

So instead, he called Trish.

"Hey nerd, what's up?" she said.

"Not much," he said, "how're you?"

"Yeah, pretty good, I went to the ice rink and got in some hockey practice, and tonight I've got a New Year's party at my cousin's, which should be good."

"That's cool."

A pause.

"You seem down," she informed him.

"Maybe I am."

"Why's that?"

He hesitated, not wanting to burden her. But it was *Trish*. He told Trish everything. "I need to have a conversation with someone, but I don't really want to."

"It's someone you like, isn't it?"

"How do you know?"

"You're doing the same voice you did when you used to talk about Eden."

He said nothing.

"It's not Eden, is it?" she asked, suddenly wary.

"No."

"Oh." (She did not say 'Good,' but it was implied.) "Well then, stop stuffing around and just *talk* to her, you absolute mongoose."

"But——" he began.

She hung up.

∴

He went to the family library and read half of *Tender is the Tyrant* by Violet Winspear, before deciding that it contained no suitable wisdom for solving his problems.

"What's the matter, Master Henry?" Great-Great-Grandmother Mildred asked him, popping out of a hole in one of the floorboards.

Henry no longer had the heart to be evasive. "I have to tell a woman I love her, but I don't want to."

"Which one is it?" his grandmother blurted out, anxious to know if she'd won the betting.

"It doesn't matter," he said grumpily, "seeing as I'm never going to get up the courage to *talk* to her. I dunno why it's become so difficult all of a sudden; I've never had this trouble before."

"That's alright, ducky," his grandmother cooed, her familial instincts momentarily overtaking the mercenary, "just tell her how you feel, and she'll respect your honesty. It *is* her, right?" (The familial instincts vanished.) "The journalist?"

Henry frowned. "What journalist?"

"You know, the one you watched the movie with the other night...?"

"Oh," Henry laughed. "Sarah. No, it's not her. Whatever gave you that impression?"

Great-Great-Grandmother Mildred disappeared in a huff, leaving him more confused than ever.

He tried another paragraph of *Tender is the Tyrant*, gave up midsentence, pulled out his phone again, and stared at it.

What was *wrong* with him? What was he so afraid of?

He gritted his teeth.

If he really loved her, he must be ready to suffer for her. And if that meant a slightly awkward conversation, and the possible confirmation of all his deepest, darkest fears, then that could hardly be the worst form of suffering he would undergo for love...

So he dialled the number once more, took a deep breath, and...

She didn't pick up.

He let out a howl of rage and frustration, kicked the wall several times, and charged into the cellar (the rats ran screeching from his presence) and drank an entire bottle of wine, then stomped upstairs and threw himself into bed and went to sleep.

∴

He was woken by his phone ringing. It was 11:32PM.

Dazed and dehydrated, he rasped, "Yes?"

"Henry?" said Louisa.

"Yeah."

"Sorry I missed your call. What's up?"

His eyes snapped open as he remembered. "Oh. Um. Uh. Well. I was wondering if…we could chat. In person. As soon as possible."

On the other end of the line, Louisa felt like a traffic crash was piling up inside her chest.

"Okay," she said. "How long do you need?"

"Only a few minutes. When are you free?"

"Er…now? I'm on the waterfront with some friends, but they won't mind if I dip for a bit. Or I could do tomorrow, around——"

"No, no, now's good," he said, fearing that his resolve would have long since evaporated by tomorrow. "I'll leave right away, see you soon."

∴

By the time he'd freshened up, ubered to town, pushed his way through the drunken masses on the waterfront and reached her, it was nearly midnight.

He hadn't seen her in a week, but it felt like eternity.

She made her way towards him, smiling, but clearly nervous.

"Hi," he said, not moving.

"Hey," she said, and waited expectantly.

Henry looked at his watch. There was no point in dancing around the question. It was almost time for the fireworks, and he was keeping her from her friends.

So he got straight to the point.

"Louisa," he said, "I have given my life to the study of Truth, and the truth is, I have no idea what I'm doing. I have no idea where I'm going, if I'm headed in the right direction, or if I will wake up tomorrow and this will all have been an opium dream. My heart feels like Northeast Queensland in cyclone season, and my head feels like there's a little meth-addicted hamster running around inside it on a wheel, and…well, you get the idea. I've made a lot of stupid choices lately, and done a lot of soul-searching, and I thought I was on the right track, and I was wrong, and I despaired, and…to be honest, I'm not sure I've come to the end of whatever this journey is. But I *am* sure of one thing, and that is that, right now I am – and perhaps for a very long time, I have been – in love with you."

(Louisa felt the motion inside her cease; her insides were clogged with rising smoke.)

"And despite everything," he said, "that I've said to you in the past, about what I did and didn't want, I think…I *know*…that I love you so much that I will throw all of that away to be with you. I am under no illusions about love and relationships. I know that they're messy and imperfect and I probably am not very good at them, and there is every possibility that you'll be disappointed with me, and this whole thing will crash and burn. But I'm willing to risk that, for the chance to learn to love you as you deserve. If you'll let me. But…" He took in a breath. "I understand if you would rather wait for someone a little bit more…consistent."

Eternity passed again as they stared at each other.

"Henry——" Louisa said.

Then the countdown began, and the rest of her sentence was trampled by the screaming crowd: "TEN…NINE…EIGHT…SEVEN…"

"What was that?!" he shouted over the chanting.

"SIX…FIVE…FOUR…"

"I said——!"

"THREE…TWO…ONE…"

"What?!"

"*HAPPY NEW YEAR!*"

The city erupted with fireworks and cheering, and at this point Louisa decided just to let her actions speak for themselves, and she threw her arms about his neck and kissed him.

Epilogue – September

One spring afternoon, Henry went into the garden and met his mother amongst the roses.

"Hello, dear," she said, looking up at him with a gentle smile.

"Hello, Mum," he said. "I have something to tell you."

"What is it?"

"Well…" He shuffled his feet awkwardly. "I, er…asked Louisa to marry me this morning," (he winced as she let out a delighted shriek), "and she said yes."

"*She said yes!*" his mother cried, throwing up her hands and whirling about him in a haze of ambient spiritual manifestation. "Oh, *Henry!!*"

"Yes," he said, looking down at a clod of earth on the ground.

"Oh, this is so *wonderful!*" his mother wept, heedless of his discomfort. "My own darling son, *finally* to be married, and to carry on the family name! I couldn't have asked for anything better…!"

"Er," said Henry, plucking a leaf from one of the rose bushes and shredding it between his fingers, "well, that's actually what I wanted to talk to you about."

His mother looked at him, quizzical.

"You see," he said, "I've had a long time to think about this, and I've decided that I'd much rather take Louisa's name. I think 'Henry Honeysett' has a nice ring to it."

Adelaide Biddlesnoot-Bloomington gazed upon her son in abject horror.

"*WHAT?*" she said.

Henry quailed slightly, but would not be swayed. "Anyway, that's all I came to tell you. I've got to be off now, and sort some things out at the office, but I'll let you know the details of the date and all that as soon as I have them. Ciao." And he marched out of the backyard, into the house, out the front door, into his car, and drove away, leaving chaos and devastation in his wake.

His ancestors were so outraged by his decision that they unanimously disowned him, and shortly thereafter ceased to haunt the family mansion. And so, with the cessation of the Biddlesnoot-Bloomington line, the ancestral curse was finally lifted, and the Honeysetts were left to live out the rest of their days in peace.

References

Walz, J. 2021. That one phone conversation we had on 23 August.

About the Author

Eilidh Direen is a Tasmanian author who lives on servo pies, prayers, and memes. She enjoys movie nights, road trips, and building things – shelves, sandcastles, commercial prawn-feeders, empires, Gundam models, you name it. She has not had a good night's sleep since this one Friday in late August 2022. Her first book (written at age 4) was a five-page illustrated epic called *Tom the Fish*.

www.ingramcontent.com/pod-product-compliance
Lightning Source LLC
Chambersburg PA
CBHW030617120726
47904CB00006B/1937